PRAISE FOR
EMPIRE

"A futuresque zombie saga with enough 'guts' to quench the flesh-eating psycho within you."

—Eve Blaack, *The Hacker's Source*

"David Dunwoody's *Empire* is a macabre masterpiece of post-apocalyptic zombie goodness. If you have waited until the end of the world for a wonderfully told, well written, and exciting as hell novel . . . your world has just ended. *Empire* is *that* novel."

—Dr. Pus, *Library of the Living Dead* Podcast

"*Empire* gives new life to the zombie genre with a unique blend of horror, mysticism, and brutal action in a world of the not-too-distant future. Give it a read—you won't be disappointed!"

—Bret Jordan, author of *Plague*

EMPIRE

A ZOMBIE NOVEL BY
DAVID DUNWOODY

G

GALLERY BOOKS

New York   London   Toronto   Sydney

Gallery Books
A Division of Simon & Schuster, Inc.
1230 Avenue of the Americas
New York, NY 10020

Copyright © 2008 by David Dunwoody and Permuted Press
Originally published in 2008 by Permuted Press

First Gallery Books trade paperback edition March 2010

GALLERY and colophon are registered trademarks of Simon & Schuster, Inc.

For information about special discounts for bulk purchases, please contact
Simon & Schuster Special Sales at 1-866-506-1949
or business@simonandschuster.com.

The Simon & Schuster Speakers Bureau can bring authors to your live event. For more
information or to book an event contact the Simon & Schuster Speakers Bureau
at 1-866-248-3049 or visit our website at www.simonspeakers.com.

Manufactured in the United States of America

10   9   8   7   6   5   4   3   2   1

ISBN 978-1-4391-8072-3
ISBN 978-1-4391-8075-4 (ebook)

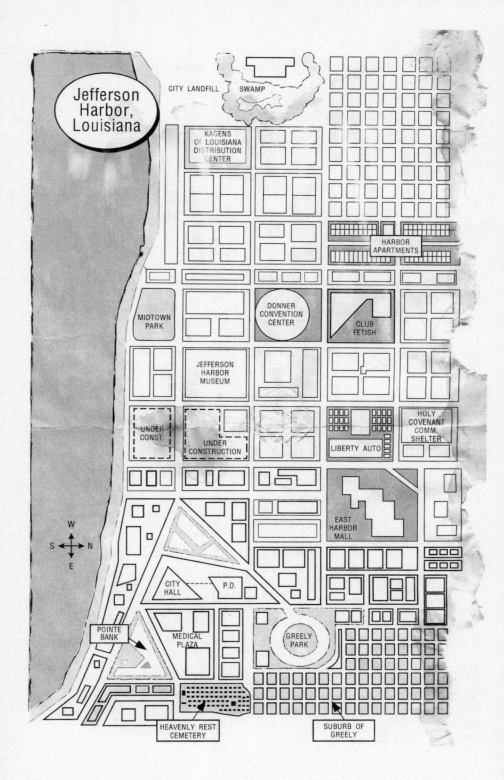

PROLOGUE
Letter Dated September 20, 2007

To whom it may concern,

To anyone: if you're holding this letter, I assume you have broken into one of the auxiliary bunkers at Fort Armstrong in what's left of the state of Louisiana. The electronics down here have a lot of blank panels with no circuitry inside—the boys used to stash girly mags in them, and I figured it's as good a place as any for this letter. The bunkers are pretty secure. You won't find the skeletons of any GIs locked inside either. The base was evacuated when the outbreak began. I've come back into the hot zone to write this and leave it behind.

I considered a safety deposit box in the vault of nearby Jefferson Harbor's Pointe Bank, but looters will probably lay waste to the bank before long. I am curious as to how valuable—if at all—the dollar is in your day. I guess there will always be those who stake their well-being on green pieces of paper, even when society lies in ruins around them.

So what do I need to tell you? You must have already gotten the gist of what's happening. Yes, they're undead. No, they're not your friends or loved ones anymore. The soul has left the building and been replaced with . . . well, something.

Let's go back to the beginning. I mean the beginning of everything.

When the universe erupted into existence, spitting cosmic detritus across infinity, tears were made in the fabric of newborn space. Now, the universe is constantly opening and healing wounds on a quantum level, but these were unintentional rifts. Big ones. And though they were sealed off in a nanosecond, things still managed to pour through.

Tendrils of dark energy stretched out and were snared in the cooling masses that would become planets, moons, asteroids. One of these tendrils was caught by Earth.

There are a handful of places on the surface where the dark energy breaks through. We called them Sources. By "we" I mean the United States government. I assume it's still called the United States? Anyway, these Sources had a singular, horrifying property. Any dead animal—from dogs to humans—lying in the vicinity of a Source would return to life.

Most Sources are located in places Man left long ago. That's why you never heard accounts of the dead getting up and walking around—at least not enough accounts to make anyone believe it—but the government still looked into it. You'd be surprised at the ridiculous bullshit we spent taxpayer money investigating. (There it is again, money—do you know the meaning of the word?)

Now see, those first undead—or "afterdead" as we classified them—weren't contagious. They fed on the flesh of the living, but they couldn't pass the reanimation catalyst into their victims. There was no epidemic, no plague.

Until we made it.

You won't believe me, but it was an accident. We weren't so stupid as to think we should engineer and weaponize a "zombie virus." It just happened. Evolution, perhaps. Judgment, maybe. But no, we only set out to study the afterdead themselves.

Fort Armstrong isn't really an Army base. There were soldiers stationed here, most of them transferred in from elite programs in the military's different branches. The base had warehouses, facilities, housing, even a Burger King (if you know what that is)—but it was all a facade, a facade blanketed in radio and digital interference designed to keep spy satellites and the rest from seeing what really went on here.

The nearby swamp is a small Source. You can feel the energy in the air. You can see it in the thick overgrowth and bogs teeming with microscopic life. Fort Armstrong was established to safeguard the Source and study its power. The first undead seeded by the U.S. Government were seeded here. By "seeded", I mean their corpses were chained up in the swamp to be resurrected by the earth's dark energy. Then they were placed in the housing area of the base, fenced in and left to wander the streets until such time as the scientists were ready to pluck them out of that suburban facade and study them further.

The bodies were those of soldiers killed in combat. They have empty graves in Arlington.

This year, the year of the outbreak, there were hundreds of undead—"afterdead"—roaming the fenced-in portion of the base. Dump trucks filled with medical waste would be driven through the streets, soldiers in the back shoveling "food" out for the dead to swarm upon. We did that to keep them healthy, healthy enough to walk around anyway. You see, the more they feed, the more they regenerate tissue—it's theorized that an undead on a steady enough diet could look as alive as you or me. It's also theorized that they might be able to regain some higher brain functions, learning capabilities—but those experiments were abandoned long ago with the Brownlee project. Too dangerous, at least for the time being. So we just kept them well fed enough to trudge through the roads and yards with those blank stares on their faces.

I don't know what the scientists needed with all those hundreds of afterdead. When on patrol, walking the fenced border between the living and the dead, we'd stare at them and they'd stare at us. Many of them were dressed in different uniforms—

policeman, postal worker, nurse. It was done to identify key subjects, in case they got too rotted or were injured beyond recognition. We'd call them Cop, Garbage man, Trucker. We assigned them personalities based on our own imaginations. It was something to pass the time.

Jesus.

The outbreak—like I said, the contagion was accidental. I don't really know much about it myself, just that we never meant to synthesize a virus. I don't know that we did actually synthesize it in any of the underground labs—I think nature just took its course. With a little help from Hell.

It started with a riot in those labs. It spread above ground. By the time we knew people were being infected with something, the fences had been knocked down by a series of vehicular accidents. The old dead spilled out of the housing area and joined the new dead. People began to flee, people with bites on their arms and necks and faces. They were the carriers who brought the plague out of Fort Armstrong to the rest of the country. Eventually, to the world.

So here we are. At the time of this writing, the infection is spreading at a maddening rate. It's strictly blood-borne but it's already gotten overseas, probably due to base personnel fleeing the country. We're well into the "martial law and religious panic" phase of the apocalypse. The public is learning about the after-dead's abilities. Things you probably already know, things like the dead's ability to regenerate muscle and flesh, to run and jump if they're healthy enough. And remember, the healthiest ones are always at the head of the pack.

If you don't know by now, here's the cardinal rule: head-shots don't kill them. *Headshots don't kill them.* Burn them to ash. Always.

It won't be long before most countries have collapsed beneath the ever-increasing weight of the zombie threat. I believe we're already outnumbered. I can only wonder what sort of world you live in.

Now you know where it came from. I know that, somehow, understanding your end makes it easier to accept. I've accepted it. The bite doesn't even hurt anymore . . . admittedly, I'm a little curious about what happens next.

Sergeant First Class Esteban Cervantes
United States Army

April 30, 2112

Downey set the letter down. He'd read the entire thing aloud to his companions. They all shook their heads in silence, seated in a narrow hallway in the bunker, their gaunt faces lit by an oil lantern Cal had found topside.

"It's cold as hell down here," muttered Reddick, scratching his bearded face.

"At least it's quiet," Downey replied. "Man, you know we're sitting in the birthplace of the fucking plague? Think about that."

"I'd rather not," whispered May, the last of their group and the only female.

Downey stretched his legs across the floor and yawned. He'd rummaged through the blank panels in search of porn, but had only found the letter in its little lockbox. Cal had hoped the box would contain liquor or smokes. No such luck. Their stomachs growled loudly, complaining of hunger, seeking distraction. Downey hadn't had a drink in months. His old mash still, at their previous camp, had been destroyed when a few rotters stumbled upon them in the middle of the night.

"And here we are," he breathed.

"I'm going up for some air," Reddick said, getting to his feet. "I don't want you alerting any rotters to our little hiding spot."

Cal snapped, "There's plenty of air down here."

"Forget that," Reddick shot back, stepping over Cal and stomping down the concrete corridor.

Downey felt a twinge of pain in his thigh and shifted his legs. He hadn't yet told the others about the bite.

It happened when they entered the remains of Fort Armstrong. An ages-old zombie in fatigues had lurched at them from the shadows of an overturned Humvee. He managed to chop its head off with his axe, but not before it tore through the fabric of his jeans and got a couple of teeth through his skin. *You win,* Downey thought bitterly. He didn't know how much time he had, but he wasn't feeling sick yet. People seemed to take anywhere from hours to weeks to turn; no one knew what factors came into play. Some people said it had to do with the strength of one's soul. Downey didn't feel like he had any soul left, so he figured it wouldn't be long. Maybe it was time for him to leave the bunker and his friends. He looked at May, her face thin and pale but still the prettiest thing he'd seen in many miserable years. She smiled a little. "You look tired."

"I'm all right," he said. "Always tired."

"How long do you want to stay here?" Cal asked. "I don't think we're gonna find many provisions around here. I say we ought to move east, to Jefferson Harbor. City's got walls."

"We don't know what it's like in there." Downey shrugged. "Could be a ghost town, or a war zone. Anyhow, I've had about all I can stand of other people thinking they know what to do—or just telling other people that they do."

"I heard what's left of the military is finally pulling out of these coastal cities," Cal said. "Means less quasi-authority."

"Means more rapists and cannibals and all that shit," Downey retorted. "People are better off making it on their own in the badlands."

"You feel better off?"

"I'm never going to feel *good,* if that's what you're saying. I'm never going to feel happy or safe or . . . fuck this." Downey tore at the loose flap in his jeans and turned, so that the lantern's glow caught the bite mark in his thigh.

May let out a quiet little cry. Cal swore. Then they sat in silence.

"When?" Cal finally asked.

"The grunt at the edge of the base."

"Goddammit. Downey. Bill."

"I ought to head out of here. I'll send Reddick back down, and you guys lock yourselves in here. Don't want me trying to come back in."

"Bill," May sobbed. "I love you—"

"I know you do." Smiling, Downey stood up and yawned. "Yeah, I'm tired as hell. Starting to ache a bit. I ought to go."

"You're not going like that." Cal got up. "Give me your axe. Let me go up with you, and we'll take care of this."

May buried her head in her arms and cried. Cal touched Downey's elbow. "Let's go. The axe."

"You really think you can do it?" Downey asked.

Cal nodded grimly. "You're not gonna turn and spend another ten years shambling around up there. Not gonna let that happen to my friend."

"You're . . . thank you, Cal."

Downey touched May, and she pressed her tear-streaked face to his leg, inches from the festering bite. "I'll always love you."

Cal took Downey down the hall, toward the ladder that led to the hatch, to the outside world, to Downey's execution.

The hatch opened, and moonlight poured down on them.

Reddick tumbled down, blood spurting from his throat.

Cal jumped back and brandished the axe. A couple of rotters stuffed their heads and shoulders through the hatch and leered down at them, their faces silhouettes, dark holes raining blood and saliva. Then they came down.

Cal slammed the axe into the first one's head, yelling, "May!" The rotter grabbed his arms and tore into his flesh. Downey shoved the undead back then tackled its companion to the floor, bashing its head against the concrete.

Cal dropped the axe and stared in terror at his wounded arms. May's screams could be heard over his shoulder. "Shit," he whispered.

Reddick sat up and tried to say something. A gout of blood rushed from his throat and over his face, and he fell still.

The first rotter fell on Downey's back and gnawed at his scalp. Downey kept smashing the other's head into the floor, bloody pulp spraying his face. "No!" he bellowed, again and again.

Cal retrieved the axe and split the first undead's head open. He pulled it to the floor, going down with it, shock setting in.

May approached them with the lantern. Downey turned, his face a bloodied horror. "Get out, May. Now."

"Bill—"

"Get out!"

She struggled up the ladder. "Quick, before more show up," Downey rasped. "And I'll—I'll lock it behind you—we'll stay down here—oh, Cal."

Cal stared blankly at the floor, shaking his head.

May turned just before she reached the hatch. She dropped the lantern into Downey's hands.

"The axe," he told her. "I have the axe. We'll . . . go, May . . ."

Gray hands dropped through the moonlight and grabbed handfuls of her hair. A hungry moan cut through the night.

She was gone. The hatch dropped closed with a loud, heavy clang.

Downey sat in the lantern's fading glow, his face contorted with grief, with a growing resignation. He rested his head against the wall and coughed. "Cal. The axe. Please."

Cal didn't say anything.

Reddick began to stir.

The light went out.

CHAPTER ONE
Still Life, Blood on Asphalt

May 1, 2112

Atherton was dying and he knew it. With every weak beat of his heart, he felt his life ebbing out onto the road. He wasn't sure where he was wounded or how. Didn't really matter.

He was lying a few hundred yards from the overturned town car, which rested against a smoldering military Humvee. The road was supposed to be secure, but they'd requested an escort anyway. It was the escort that had flipped and crashed up ahead of them, and Atherton had swerved the town car but not quickly enough to avoid a collision.

He angled his head toward the wreck and looked for signs of life. None. Was he the only one ejected from the vehicles? It figured. Thirty-four, in his prime, handsome swatches of gray just beginning to show in his hair. It figured he would die now, alone. At least he would be prepared for death, could breathe his last words as he felt it coming over him.

A pale horse walked around the wreck and came toward him. Upon it was a rider and Atherton knew his name was Death.

He wondered if Death looked the same to every soul he claimed. For Atherton, at least, it was the traditional black robes, with a hood casting a shadow over the specter's face. As he drew closer and dismounted, Atherton saw his white face and black eyes, like marbles set in clay. "Have I already died?" he asked.

"Not yet," Death answered dispassionately. He stood over Atherton, blocking out the noonday sun, and surveyed the landscape. The silence was unbearable. Would Death just wait there until Atherton bled out? "I work for the senator," he coughed.

"The senator?" Death frowned.

"Moorecourt. He was in the town car," Atherton explained. "I am—was—his aide."

"The senator isn't dead," the specter murmured.

"The others . . . ?"

"They are."

"I don't understand." Atherton could taste blood on his lips and gums. His head was swimming from the heat, and he forced himself to concentrate on speaking. "You just got here. But they're already dead?"

"I don't normally collect souls myself," Death replied. "I merely mark their passing. Only in extraordinary circumstances . . ." His monotone voice trailed off. He was eyeing the wreck. All the while his ghostly steed stood silently.

"Why did we crash?" Atherton croaked. Fate? Was there such a thing? Did Death have a contemporary who wrote the endings of human lives in a great book? Or was it just an accident, a fucking accident? He wasn't sure which possibility offended him more: for some emotionless sentinel to decide that he should be torn open and dumped onto burning asphalt in the middle of nowhere, or for shitty driving to be his undoing.

"There was a body in the road," Death said. "The soldiers drove over it, believing it was dead. It wasn't." Death's gaze was fixed on the wreck, and he reached a chalk-white hand into the folds of his robes.

"It was an undead?"

Ignoring the question, Death pulled his hand out, and with it a massive scythe, far too long to have been concealed on his person, the curved blade catching the sunlight and throwing it into Atherton's eyes. He groaned and rolled his head to the side. That's when he saw it.

The lone undead shambled around the town car and stopped. It could see them both, Atherton realized. Its hands and face were caked with blood, not its own. Must have been in the Hummer, feeding. It had caused the crash, lying prone and then driving some crude spear into the undercarriage of the Humvee, so that it could eat. Atherton felt blood and bile rise in his throat. Wait . . . was that how he'd die? Was Death here to watch as this undead dug out his guts?

Then, the specter took two steps forward and swung the scythe out in a horizontal arc, passing cleanly through the belly of the zombie. He rested the scythe at his side and stood still with the patience of eternity.

The undead didn't move. There was no wound visible across its midsection, as if it had been struck by a phantom blade. Then, like a paper cut, the line bled into view, and the zombie's torso fell to the ground, sputtering brown viscera.

Atherton tried to process what he'd just seen, lying on a deserted road in his own blood with the Grim Reaper leaning against his dreaded scythe. The zombie . . . it wasn't just cut in half, it was dead. Really dead.

"You came to kill it."

Death nodded without looking down at him. "It, and others."

Atherton tried to speak again, but couldn't. His vision was failing. Death turned now, and Atherton trembled at the sight of his blade. Without a word, it was slipped back into the dark robes and out of sight.

Death knelt beside him. "Your life is like a flame." He again reached into his robes, this time pulling out a burning candle. Despite the blinding sunlight, the flame seemed to cast its own luminescence. It didn't hurt Atherton's eyes at all. It was calming, in fact. Familiar.

Death poised his thumb and forefinger around it. "When you die, the flame merely ceases." The tiny, pulsing light grew smaller then faded altogether.

Atherton was dead. Death crushed the candle's wick out and returned it to its place.

The specter gathered his robes and climbed back onto the pale horse. They continued for a while down the road at a lazy gait, down to the gates of Jefferson Harbor.

CHAPTER TWO
AfterBirth

The Jefferson Harbor Landfill was located at the end of town, near the swamp that defined the western perimeter. Concrete slabs had been erected in a crude wall at the edge of the swamp, with wire fencing used to cover any gaps. The whole mess was threaded with equal parts barbed wire and overgrowth. The western wall was a worthless measure if ever there was one, nothing like the well-built barriers on the north and eastern perimeters. To the south was the Gulf of Mexico.

Gene Pastore stood atop a mountain of filth and stared at the dense swamp. What was the point of putting that eyesore inside the perimeter? It wasn't even worth dumping in. The landfill's girth was instead expanding south, onto the beach. He'd have to burn another ton of this shit soon before it hit the water.

There was a police boat just off the shoreline. Gene waved to the two patrol officers standing on it. They stared through him. "Didn't see me, I guess," he muttered. They were local boys, weren't they? No reason not to be polite, unlike the stone-faced Army fellas who had just pulled out of town. The radio said that military support was being withdrawn from all coastal cities. The Senate wanted people to move inland. Why? So the Senators and their families could take all the country's provisions? "Beats me," Gene said to himself. As far as he was concerned, moving everyone up north was like building the rotters a triple cheeseburger.

God, it was hot. Boiling inside his ratty old uniform, Gene mopped his brow with an old handkerchief and dropped it into the garbage. His back was killing him too. At the age of sixty, he had hoped someone else would take his place managing the dump, give the old man a break. But there was no retirement in his future. Just rats.

Rats, rats, rats. Most of them were undead, too. Only Gene could tell the living from the dead. They just had a look about them, a cold, solitary look. And the dead rats were fatter than the other ones. They fed on their own kind, and their kind was plentiful.

He was wearing waders and thick work gloves. The bastards wouldn't try to eat him but they'd probably bite if he wasn't careful. Gene carried a shovel to pin the vermin down and hack them up. Kicking them into a fire was easier, but garbage burns had to be controlled, small. The smoke rising into the sky brought undead. Not only that, but while Gene was used to the stench of the landfill, burns were another story. Maybe it was the charred, half-rotted flesh of the rats, the smell of death after death. Gene spat and wiped his mouth with a gloved hand.

"How does a starving town make this much fucking garbage?" he asked an undead rat. It was perched atop a broken chair, watching him intently. Part of its face had been gnawed off; a tiny red eye still rolled around inside the bony eye socket.

"You and me both," Gene said. He swung the shovel and smashed the rat down through the chair. These little buggers had actually given him a respect for the living rodents that still dared enter the landfill. It wasn't man versus animal anymore—it was the living against the undead. Gene brushed a fly off his cheek and wondered if they were undead too. Gone from eating shit to eating each other.

There was a sharp crack from the ocean, then another. Gene saw one of the police officers pointing a sniper rifle past him, toward the swamp. Must've seen something. What good did shooting at it do? Those boys were too scared to come ashore and properly nail the rotters. Gene hefted his shovel in one hand. He'd take care of any unwelcome visitors himself.

Speaking of which, another rat was lumbering over piles of soggy cardboard, distended belly dragging along. Gene aimed the blade of the shovel at its dark face and thrust downward. The rat skittered aside with surprising speed, just in time to avoid the strike, and the shovel sank into the refuse.

Gene shook the crap off the shovel. There was something bloody underneath the cardboard, too big to be a rat. It was partially wrapped in a moth-eaten blanket decorated with brightly colored smiling dinosaurs. He considered this for a half-second before a terrible thought came to him.

"Oh my God."

He gingerly worked the shovel underneath the blanket and peeled it away. The underside was crimson, yellow dinosaurs obscured by gore. It was difficult to loosen; someone had lovingly bundled the misshapen form, tiny and frail and barely recognizable for what it was.

Gene stumbled back with a cry, dropping the shovel. His foot struck the ruin of the broken chair, and he fell flat on his back. A foul wetness seeped through his uniform and he found himself sliding helplessly down an incline. He pawed at the garbage around him; a glove came off and his bare hand sank into some curdled mess. "Shit! God!" He tried to orient himself so he could see where he was going, but only managed to go elbow-deep into the garbage, all the while still sliding.

He nicked his ungloved hand on something. Yanking it

free, he saw the ragged little bite, and he saw the rat's head as it struggled in the garbage. It was undead.

He plowed headfirst into an array of discarded plumbing. Gene felt the surreal but distinct sensation of metal slicing through his cheek into his mouth before he fell unconscious.

CHAPTER THREE
Off to Market

Fred R. Moorecourt, Senator from the great states of Illinois and Indiana, beat on the gates of Jefferson Harbor and hollered until his already-pounding head threatened to erupt. There was no scaling the gates, with loops of barbed wire welded to each pole. The walls were fifteen feet high and perfectly smooth. He stumbled along the perimeter in desperate search of a hand-hold. Senator Moorecourt cursed the wall and kicked it. That's when he learned that two toes on his right foot were broken. Moorecourt fell to the ground in a ball.

Walls, borders, bullshit. The imaginary lines that defined the United States were eroding every day. Already representing the combined territory of two states, Moorecourt expected more to fall under his jurisdiction as Americans moved inland. Maybe that's why he had risked coming out here: to expand his rule. It was a miserable thought, but it rang truer than any of the noble rhetoric that he and his colleagues broadcast from the north.

Goddamn coastal refugees. Anarchists. Of course, when they ran out of supplies, when troops stopped patrolling their perimeters, then they'd blame the Senate. The Senate told survivors to migrate away from the oceans, to consolidate aid and resources, and men like Moorecourt put their lives on the line on these goodwill missions. Still this stubborn distrust. And now, two broken toes, a concussion and this goddamn wall.

He looked back down the road; the wreck was a blot on the horizon. He should have gone into the Hummer and grabbed a gun. Too tired to go back though. Too risky. The badlands were crawling with hungry undead.

"Oh, Jesus." Turning northeast, he saw two shapes moving through blighted grass. Their stiff movements and emaciated bodies gave them away immediately as undead. God willing, their eyes had shriveled and fallen out of their heads, and they weren't really ambling straight toward him.

Or maybe they were.

Using the wall for support, he limped along as quickly as he could. He thought about Atherton, whom he'd seen gasping for breath in the middle of the road, and whispered a silent prayer that the undead would catch his scent. Maybe they'd even eat the fresh corpses in the vehicles. Moorecourt's sister and her husband remained in the town car. Why Amanda had insisted on coming along, he didn't know. Her husband, Doug, had represented the P.O. Union and was supposed to talk to local law enforcement about withdrawing. But Amanda loathed politics almost as much as she loathed Moorecourt . . .

"It's going to play real well with the Harbor residents when you show up escorted by soldiers," she'd said, sitting directly across from Moorecourt, the sun bringing out deep, cruel lines in her smirking countenance.

Moorecourt massaged his hand and smiled thinly in return. "It'll serve as a reminder of the security they're losing if they stay out here. Believe it or not, I did think this through."

Doug, as usual, was reticent while the siblings sparred. He buried his face in some paperwork, thumbing through the same pages again and again. Moorecourt stared at him until he turned to look out the window. Doug was a strong lobbyist; he fought tirelessly for the rights of others. It seemed, however, that he left in himself no fire to defend his own interests. Over the course of the car trip he'd slowly shrunk into his corner, hunched over like a child begging to wake up somewhere else. Boyishly handsome, his behavior only made him more enticing to the senator.

(Did she know?)

Moorecourt applied skin cream to his hand, frowning at veins visible through papery flesh. Amanda pursed her lips and started to coo something witty. He didn't hear it, because the sun outside seemed suddenly to roll violently across the sky, and Atherton cried out from the front seat, and metal groaned before Moorecourt's head cracked against the bulletproof window.

When he'd awakened, he was lying on the ceiling of the town car. Amanda was still looking at him. Her neck was bent obscenely so that her cheek was crushed against a breast, and her eyes were red with blood. Doug was beside Moorecourt. His chest rose and fell slightly, though the expression on his face was frozen. Moorecourt, without thinking, reached out to touch it. He tried to say something and couldn't. Doug stopped breathing.

The senator was now limping along the north wall of the Harbor, glancing over his shoulder to see the two undead in slow but relentless pursuit. They were starving, desperate, and wouldn't give up until they fell completely apart; just like the survivors inside these walls.

He breathlessly turned a corner and found that the west wall wasn't like the others. There might be an opening! Moorecourt tore at the fencing and felt it giving. His hands were red and raw. He screamed and pulled with his entire body. The fence snapped free, hitting his face and knocking him to the ground. Wetness spread quickly from the cuts in his skin. He didn't care. He went through the fence and into the city.

He was greeted by what appeared to be a cluster of storage units. The size of garages, most of them were wide open and empty. To his right, past a weathered wooden fence, was a foul-smelling swamp. He weaved through the units and ignored the ache in his lungs. At least he still had a good heart. Moorecourt had always kept himself in shape. At first it was for his constituents, but once it became clear that his post was probably a lifelong one he did it for himself. Boys could hardly resist his status; his lean physique more often than not closed the deal. And of course the other senators knew. No one tried anymore to conceal habits that, for previous generations, spelled political suicide. For any Americans who still paid attention to the government, the Senate was their only hope. They were more than politicians now—a woman in Chicago told him that she prayed to the Senate.

There was no President of the United States. After the Secret Service was forced to dismember the last Commander-in-Chief on his desk in the Oval Office, the romantic notion of one man's will leading a people lost its luster.

How long had Moorecourt been running since the accident? An hour? Two? The sun was no help at guessing the time. He couldn't stand to look up at it. Moorecourt paused in the doorway of a storage unit and felt the stiffness in his neck. He couldn't move it at all.

The swamp had ended, giving way to several large buildings. Warehouses? Surely a place to hide, maybe a radio. He pulled himself over the creaking wooden fence and tried not to land on his wounded foot.

BAM! Something struck the other side of the fence. Moorecourt staggered back, seeing the yellowed eyeball of an undead staring through a knothole. His pursuers had caught up with him. They beat their open hands against the wood, gaping mouths never making a sound. The old fence shook precariously. Moorecourt ran.

Faded letters on the largest warehouse read KAGEN'S OF LOUISIANA, a grocery. Moorecourt collided with the nearest entrance and was thrown back onto the sidewalk. Locked? Why? Was there still food kept inside? He couldn't imagine. Moorecourt slammed his fists against the door. "Anyone inside

LET ME IN!" A block behind him, a section of wooden fence collapsed and the two zombies staggered through.

A loud crack tore through the air. The senator looked back to see a chunk of skull and hair flying away from one zombie's head. Thank God! Moorecourt peered around the corner of the warehouse to see where his rescuer was—

Another shot buzzed past his ear. He fell to the pavement again. "I'm not one of them!"

The undead were still coming. Moorecourt searched for another entrance to the warehouse. Another door, slightly ajar, reluctantly gave way under his weight. He fell into the building and kicked the door shut with his good foot.

He was on his back in an enormous room with floor-to-ceiling shelves filled with boxes. Using a shelf for support, he made his way down an aisle, reading the contents of the boxes. Soup, ramen, seasoning, powdered milk, all non-perishables. Just add water. He was shocked to see so much still here. Then he nudged one of the boxes and realized that it was empty.

There was a clatter from across the warehouse.

Moorecourt pushed a box aside and crawled onto the bottom shelf, his foot throbbing now. He eased himself between the boxes as quietly as possible. Damn hands shaking, threatening to give out beneath him; he fought to hold himself steady, knowing that if he lost his balance and fell in either direction, the empty boxes would give way and dump him into the open.

Someone walked past the end of the aisle. Moorecourt saw ratty hair and pale skin, but clean, pressed clothing. The footfalls of several persons echoed through the room. Would they believe who he was? Would they care? Or would revealing himself to them result in a fate worse than being caught by any undead? He cursed himself again for leaving behind the weapons in the Humvee. Then, a young woman entered the aisle, wearing a flowery spring dress, and he saw the dead glaze of her eyes and realized she was a zombie.

She came down the aisle with a man in a suit jacket and

slacks. His hair was combed. *Combed.* Moorecourt looked back at the woman's face, so lifelike—she was wearing makeup. His heart was seized by terror. He had heard that the dead could regenerate tissue if they fed often enough, but had never seen a well-fed rotter. He'd doubted that such a thing could possibly exist out in the badlands. But these . . . had these undead restored their flesh, their muscles, their minds? Were there remnants of memory that compelled them to wear clean clothing and groom themselves? It wasn't possible. Couldn't be. Yet as the lady stood before Moorecourt, the senator cringing, barely concealed behind a box, he noticed the lovely shape of her calves, white as they were.

The dead had a sole purpose: self-preservation. They didn't reproduce, they didn't interact with one another, and they certainly didn't bathe. They only ate and ate and ate in order to keep from rotting into nothing. But these two in the aisle were opening boxes on the upper shelves, searching them—together—for foodstuffs. The male produced a large bag of rice and tucked it under his arm. None of it made sense. They evidently ate enough human flesh to stay healthy, yet they were raiding the warehouse for rice?

Something about it all nearly clicked for Moorecourt as he trembled on the bottom shelf. Makeup, clothes, groceries. But the answer was just beyond his grasp. The answer was something that he could never have imagined, even if he had lived many, many more years, which wasn't going to happen either.

CHAPTER FOUR
The House in the Swamp

It was a three-story manor fashioned from stone, a stately Victorian nestled in the overgrowth of the thick, dark green swamp. Contained within an ivy-thronged iron fence, it barely stood above the heads of the encroaching trees. Some of the manor's outermost extremities had fallen into disarray; the greenhouse adjoining the north wing had lost its roof in a storm years ago. Some of the ground floor's grime-streaked windows were broken. Errant stones loosed from the wall lay in the spongy grass. The south end of the manor had sunk slightly into the mud, and moss crawled skyward over its surface. For all its grandeur, even in such a condition, an air of rot hung over the house. Even the clouds overheard seemed to be stained gray. Things moved in the tall grass, in the remains of a once-beautiful garden and in the swamp beyond the gates.

The gates opened. Four afterdead entered, the first holding a key. He waited to lock up behind the others. They were the ones from the warehouse and they'd brought back several boxes filled to the brim with groceries. The young woman in the spring dress led the procession through the manor's front doors.

It was dim inside. Their vision, poor as it was, failed completely inside the foyer, but they knew the halls and rooms of the house by heart and walked single-file, past the grand stair-case and through the dining room.

"Stop."

The voice came from behind them. The woman in the spring dress halted in the doorway leading into the kitchen.

A man entered the dining room and stared hard at the four undead. They each looked straight ahead, clutching their boxes.

He was in his late twenties, perhaps, younger in appearance than the dead ones; tousled hair fell in front of bright green eyes as he knelt to scrutinize the carpeted floor. He dragged a fingertip along the fibers, pulled up a glob of mud. The man rose to show the mud to the zombies.

"I told you," he said in a calm-before-the-storm tone, "to bring things into the kitchen through the rear entrance. I also told you to remove your shoes when you entered the house. Even in the foyer. It doesn't matter if the floor is stone." As he lectured them, the man seemed to be speaking more to himself, realizing that the dead felt no shame or remorse for disobedience. But there were still consequences, ones that they could understand.

"You won't eat today. Put those things in the kitchen and go outside. Aidan, Harry—trim the grass and maybe you'll eat tomorrow."

The afterdead shuffled out of the room. The man sighed and looked at the filthy carpet. "Prudence!"

A female undead in a maid's uniform loped into the room. One of her legs had been gouged by something, which hindered her movement. The man pointed to the mess. "Clean it. Dust this entire room, in fact." He left her and went into the foyer, up the staircase.

Baron Tetch had lived here for as long as he could remember, but things still weren't to his satisfaction. Maybe they never would be. Not only was he a savage perfectionist, but he was suffering from a growing misanthropy and a bitter contempt for this whole earthly plane. There was little to keep him grounded here. Entering his second-floor study, he locked the door behind him and kicked off his loafers.

A corpse lay on the floor. It had been some intruder from the previous week who'd climbed the fence, probably fleeing from undead. But the feral zombies that occasionally penetrated Jefferson Harbor were nothing compared to Tetch's. They'd made short work of the man. Tetch had rewarded them with his internal organs before having the rest of him brought upstairs.

Swathed in moist rags scented with spices, the body lay spread out in the middle of the room. The face was caved in, gray flesh like paper peeling away from the wound. Tetch spread a blanket over the open cavity of the corpse's torso.

Even those who died under normal circumstances had dormant energy lying in their husks, of that Tetch was certain. Pulling a tattered shroud over his bony shoulders, he straddled the corpse's body and closed his eyes. The wasted energy inside the eviscerated man was drawn through Tetch's flesh, saturating his bones, traveling like a lightning bolt to his head. He plunged his fingers through the blanket and into the corpse. Tetch spread crimson grit across his forehead, throwing open the conduits throughout his self. A throbbing erection grew between his legs.

He heard the study door open. Tetch yanked the shroud around his body and glared.

It was Lilith. Her frail body looked as if it could be torn asunder by the rage from Tetch's eyes; he quickly softened his face, clutching the shroud over his groin, and stood up. "Why didn't you knock?"

In response, she held out her pale arms. She'd cut her wrists. Tetch rushed to her, pushing back the sleeves of her dress and catching droplets of blood in his hands. "Lily, why? Oh, God!" She'd cut across rather than down, and not deeply thanks to her child's strength. Still the sight was horrifying, her perfect ivory flesh marred and her bright blue eyes devoid of reason.

"They don't bleed like I do," she mumbled.

"Of course they don't. You're not like them. You know

David Dunwoody

that!" Tetch grabbed the shoulder of her dress and tore its sleeve free. Lily squealed, but he silenced her with a stern look, tying the fabric over one of the wounds. She didn't say anything when he pulled the other sleeve off. "This is why we can't have nice things," he snapped. She caught herself before rolling her eyes.

There. She was patched up, for now. "Do NOT remove these. Now tell me what you used." He rose over her, arms crossed. She stared at the corpse behind him. He stepped over to block her view. "Lily, look at me."

She complied. Her lip was trembling slightly. In fear? Of him? It was hard to resist the urge to take her into his arms. Her ripening breasts, almost visible through the thin fabric of the dress, reminded Tetch of his erection, and he realized he was idly nudging it with his fist. Turning from her, he went to his desk and fumbled through the drawers until he found his camera.

"Oh no, not like this!" Lily raised her bandaged wrists and frowned at the ruined dress.

"This picture will be a reminder to you," Tetch shot back. He loaded a fresh roll of film. It was a precious commodity, and he only used it to mark the days of Lilith's life. "You're not like your brothers and sisters. You can get hurt, you can bleed, and you can die." A thought struck him: was she bleeding herself to take away the power of his threats? *His* power? He studied her glassy eyes. She could never . . . "You don't want to be like them, Lily. It's not real. Your beauty could never be preserved in death, do you understand? Your soul would be lost." He raised the camera to his face. She forced a smile. "Don't," he ordered. Snap. Snap. Snap.

"Now I want you to stay inside, up here. Don't go downstairs. I don't want to risk anything happening, should they smell your blood." They were animals after all, despite the facade of sophistication he'd crafted. Lilith nodded and left the room.

Of course, she went straight downstairs and out the front doors.

26

Lily saw her brother Aidan pushing an old-style lawn mower through the grass. She wondered how sharp its rusted blades were. "Hello, Aidan!" She waved. He paused, looking blankly at her, then raised his hand as he'd been taught. He then resumed his task and forgot about her.

She walked through the grass he'd already cut and to the fence. Plants grew thick and huge around here. It was like the swamp was wrapping ivy-green arms around her, constricting her, smothering her. Like her brother Baron. But he did love her, she knew that, and he gave her many pretty things. Still, it was natural to be curious about the world beyond the estate. Lily knew she was thirteen or so, and she wondered if there were other children out there. More than that, she wondered if there were women out there—there were books in the house that had helped her make sense of the changes her body was going through, but they were cold, clinical volumes that did little to soothe her ever-increasing feelings of isolation.

Then, there was someone out there. A man in black kneeling in the bog. He had a big stick that he leaned upon and his skin was bone-white. Another dead man like the others? No, his eyes . . . his eyes were alive, and they were fixed on her.

He approached the fence. Lily pressed her face to the bars. "Hi."

"What are you doing in there?" the man in black asked. She saw now that his big stick had a big knife on it. Maybe he was cutting grass too.

"I live here," she answered.

His skin was like clay, wasn't it? So perfectly smooth, even when he frowned. And his eyes were big and black and shiny. Lily thought that maybe that was what beautiful really looked like. "What do you mean, you live here?" He was looking past her at Aidan.

"That's my brother," she explained. "What's your name?"

"I don't have a name," he said matter-of-factly.

"I'm Lily," she told him. "My brothers and sisters all live

here. Daddy doesn't live here anymore. I don't remember him much anyway. I'm not allowed to go outside the gates. What's it like?"

"It's not a nice place." Kneeling to bring himself face-to-face with the girl, the man in black looked at Aidan again. "Do they try to hurt you?"

"No, they're not allowed." She glanced at her wrists and was flushed with shame.

The man followed her eyes. "Why did you do that?"

"I don't know." Lily put her hands behind her back and stepped away. "I have to go." She ran into the manor.

Death studied the architecture of the house. If there was a human quality that he admired, it was imagination. For him, imagination had no purpose; his entire existence was laid out in black and white. But those idling in this life took wood and rock and metals and forged wonders merely from pictures in their minds. It didn't matter that they would one day depart this mortal coil, or that their cathedrals and skyscrapers would one day be razed to the ground. Just to have created, that was enough.

The mowing undead had seen him. Death leapt into the trees with barely a whisper, back into the swamp, back to his white steed.

CHAPTER FIVE
To Have Created

"Did you go outside this morning?" Confusion was a rare feeling for Lee. He usually kept everything in its place with little effort, especially Cheryl. But he remembered awakening from a drunken stupor at six A.M. and hearing the front door before blacking out again. Cheryl's guilty white countenance confirmed his suspicions. "Where were you?"

She only shook her head in response. Her clothes were filthy. Lee could tolerate her plump figure when she at least looked clean; he'd send her to the rooftop today to do laundry. Lee's head ached so he plopped down in his recliner, narrowing his glare. Bitch had better not relax thinking he was just going to sit there and nurse his hangover. "You're lying," he said flatly. "I can't believe it but you are. Where the fuck could you have been that you'd even think of lying to me about it?" Lee tapped his index finger against his cheekbone. "Maybe you were with that guy in the next building. Maybe you went over there to suck his cock."

Cheryl shook her head rapidly. "I wouldn't do that, Lee."

"The fuck you wouldn't. You've always been a whore. Keeping you in this apartment the rest of your life ain't gonna change you, I know that. Hell, I'm family and I've caught you staring at my cock, Cheryl. You don't care where you get it as long as you get it. You'd probably be on the street sucking dead dick if I didn't keep you on a leash. And . . ." He rubbed his neck, grunting, fished through his jeans for a couple of white pills. "And just like that, I pass out for a few hours and you sneak out. Break all the rules. I take care of you, Cheryl. Why do you hate me so much?"

Cheryl didn't have the heart to tell her cousin that he'd been unconscious for a day and a half. Actually, it had less to do with her heart than her nose and the fear of having it shattered again. Even if she was the whore Lee said she was, no man would want her like that. He didn't just make her feel ugly. He slapped her around for good measure. How could he possibly accuse her of being hateful when she stayed for that? She wasn't afraid to fend for herself. She made regular trips to Midtown to get his drugs, didn't she? Lee was the one scared to leave the apartment. He only knew that a man had moved into the next building because he'd seen him from the window. And things had gotten worse since then. Lee wouldn't stop talking about the man—who Cheryl had never even seen—and how she would almost certainly betray her loving cousin for him.

Loving. She shuddered involuntarily as Lee's glare bored into her. He had his hand down his pants. Lee wasn't a hard one to figure out. She knew what he was about. Why he kept calling her a whore. It had nothing to do with his so-called faith or her lack thereof. When Cheryl looked at him (and she *never, ever* stared at his crotch) all she saw was an ugly, possessive addict living in another reality. But when he looked at her, it was with dark desire.

"I don't hate you," she forced herself to say. "I didn't go out. Where would I go? I was here. I was watching TV—"

"Bullshit." Lee turned the recliner to face the television. "My DVD's still in there." One of his pornos. She'd never be caught dead watching that. Cheryl was busted.

Lee smirked at her. His DVDs, those ancient things, were

all he had left, the rest of his things traded away for drugs. As such he spent a few hours of every day jerking off in his chair, usually while high, and Cheryl would get a beating if she happened to walk into the room. He'd probably sooner trade her away than that smut.

Chewing the white pills from his jeans pocket, Lee swallowed them dry. "So, want to tell another lie, or just tell me who you've been fucking?"

"I didn't do anything. I didn't go anywhere. Why don't you believe me?"

Lee stood up. Trying the guilt card with him had been a mistake.

His eyes clouded over and he gave her a familiar, numb look. Then the backhand sent her sprawling.

Cheryl stayed on the floor while Lee yelled. Her ears were ringing but he was probably berating her for making him raise his hand. Tears stinging her eyes, she briefly considered telling him the truth. Fact of the matter was that Lee was all she had, the only one she could ever turn to—but he'd never buy the truth, not when she was a godless whore.

She'd been raped four months prior while on a run to Midtown. Her attacker had worn a moth-eaten ski mask over his face, held her facedown in the refuse of an alley. Had whispered while he was inside her, "Could kill you where you lay bitch, feed you to the rotters. Kill you." He came on the word KILL and repeated it feverishly. Then he melted into shadow and was gone.

Cheryl hadn't known she was pregnant until that morning, until the miscarriage.

Thank God Lee had been passed out, because she had screamed to wake the dead, even with a rolled-up towel clenched between her teeth as she lay on the bathroom floor. She'd screamed even louder and cried and beat the tiled floor when it was over and she saw it. Transferring the towel from her mouth to between her thighs, she used another one to clean the mess and then wrapped it—him, her?—in a dinosaur blanket. Then she'd gone out to the landfill.

What would Lee say if he knew?

"I knew you weren't just getting fat, bitch. Fucking whore. Rape. Rape! Ha." He'd punctuate every word with his fists. Things would be worse than they'd ever been.

"I . . ." she mumbled, though still unable to hear, "I heard a noise. A cat. I was just looking for it."

"You better not have given any of our food to a fucking stray," he snapped.

"I didn't," she replied. "I couldn't find him . . . I wouldn't have fed him anyway."

"Goddamn right. I'd skin and eat the little bastard before taking him in. You better feel the same way, Cheryl, because I'm the provider here. I take care of *you*. You don't have a goddamn thing to be giving away to anyone." He dug his toe into her ribs, making her whimper. "Except that filthy cunt."

He left her on the floor and went into his bedroom. She stayed there another hour, just to be safe.

CHAPTER SIX
Dirt on Dirt

The signage on the Holy Covenant Community Shelter was illegible, every letter of every word punctuated by bullet holes and smeared with crud. It was just as well, seeing how the shelter didn't have much left to offer, just a roof and some blankets. There'd been a time when the Reverend Palmer was able to convince her charges that such meager provisions were a blessing. Nowadays she could rarely say it herself without bitter laughter. Oates, a bearded black man in his late sixties, was helping her put new boards over the windows.

"Just what are we protecting?" Wheeler asked in his usual manner—distrustful of anything the others did, of the Reverend's authority—but less than eager to lend a hand himself. As far as Palmer knew, Wheeler had always been homeless, and it didn't surprise her.

"You," Palmer replied.

Wheeler brushed back his shock of white hair and picked at a scab on his chin. "I ain't worth protecting. None of us are. Truth hurts."

"So why don't you kill yourself instead of bitching all day long?" Isabella barked from a cot across the room. The reverend shot her a look. Wheeler shrugged. "Mother Theresa here says that suicide's a sin. I'll go to Hell if I do that. Apparently Hell's something worse than this putrid shithole."

All things considered the shelter wasn't in awful shape. Palmer knew that Wheeler thrived on misery. He was scared to feel a shred of happiness lest something tear through those boarded-up windows and take it away. Palmer could barely hold her tongue around the man. He never helped to scrounge for supplies, never comforted any of his equally distraught companions. The world owed Wheeler, always would, and that was that.

Something thumped against the board Palmer was hammering. She cried out and Oates pulled her away, turning his hammer to wield its claw as a weapon. "Whoever's out there, speak up!"

"Patrol Officer!" A young male voice.

It was a common ruse among most cities in the badlands, thieves posing as P.O.s. "Let's see some ID!" Oates shot back.

A laminated card slipped between two of the slats and into Palmer's hands. Michael Weisman, it said. Based in Miami, it said. "Long way from Florida," Oates called, reading over her shoulder.

"Florida's gone. I've been here for months. I just want to check up on you."

"No one checks up on anyone," Wheeler spat. Two other men, J.J. and Yeats, trudged into the room. "What's going on?"

"We got ourselves a P.O. outside," Oates muttered. He peered between the boards. "It's Weisman all right."

"The ID's fake," said Wheeler. "Don't even think about letting him in!"

"Come around to the front," Palmer said to Weisman. As she left the room with Oates she glanced at Wheeler. He stuck his tongue out and flipped her off.

She and Oates cleared the crude barricade from the front entrance and unlocked the door. Weisman was wearing his uniform, though it had clearly seen better days. He patted a pistol strapped to his hip. "How many you got in here?"

"Ten." Palmer extended her hand and introduced herself.

"Do you have any food?" Weisman asked. "Medicine? Plumbing?"

"Pipes are fine." Oates slapped Weisman on the shoulder and ushered him in. "You're looking at the Harbor's best plumber. We're getting a nasty soup of ground water and seawater, but I threw together a filtration system."

With sandy brown hair and deep eyes, Weisman was good-looking. Damned good-looking. At fifty-something, swatches of gray among her long blonde locks, Palmer rarely felt attractive nor attracted. But *damn*. She tried to check herself with a reminder that she was clergy, but it had been a long time since she'd held the notion that suppressing her natural feelings was holy before God. She knew she was an unconventional reverend as well as an unconventional woman—tougher than the other females at the shelter, at least, comfortable in her authority.

Smiling sweetly at the P.O., she led him into the building. Oates stayed behind to restore the barricade.

"How long have you all been in here?" Weisman asked next. It sounded to Palmer like he was taking mental notes.

"Most of us have been here a year or so. We took a young woman and her boy in last week, and that's it."

"Has anyone been assaulted recently?"

"No, not at all."

"And how many of the ten are men?"

"Uh, six."

"And there haven't been any problems."

"You sound surprised, Officer Weisman."

"Mike, please." He stood in the doorway of the community room and returned the questioning stares of its inhabitants. "Any of the men ever leave the shelter?"

"Oates—our resident plumber—he leads supply runs every week. Everyone stays together out there." Palmer touched Weisman's arm and lowered her voice. "Why are you asking these questions?"

David Dunwoody

"There—" Weisman was cut off by the appearance of
Oates, followed by a tall balding man in a trench coat. Nodding
to Weisman, the bald man showed his ID to the reverend.

"Senior P.O. Voorhees. We're checking up on Midtown residents now that the military's left us." Voorhees took Weisman's
position in the doorway. He made a not-so-subtle display of the
firearm beneath his coat. "You're Reverend Palmer?"

"Yes. What is this about? Is this about the supplies we've
taken? We only go into abandoned buildings."

"No," Voorhees responded, loud enough for everyone to
hear. "It's about a rapist. He's been roaming Midtown for weeks.
We think he may have come to the Harbor from out West. My
communication with neighboring towns is limited, but there
have been similar reports out there." Locking eyes with the
sneering Wheeler, Voorhees said, "It ends here."

"Shouldn't y'all be playing escort to Senator Moorecourt
right about now?" Wheeler asked. "What does it matter if we're
raping and killing each other? There's an honest-to-God states-
man gracing the Harbor with his presence!"

Weisman interrupted Voorhees' reply. "The Senator never
arrived."

Wheeler groaned. "I knew it. Bastard was never coming.
Just bullshit radio propaganda."

"Officer Weisman and I are going to want to speak with
each of you individually," Voorhees said. "Reverend, would you
get everyone together please?"

She nodded reluctantly and headed down a dark hallway. A
serial rapist in Midtown? None of the women would be going
on supply runs anymore. Oates would have to stay here, he was
the toughest . . . no, no, no. She couldn't let their simple way
of life be turned upside-down by this. If she showed fear or
weakness it would spread to the others. Except Wheeler—if he
saw her limping at the rear of the pack he'd pounce.

She rapped on a restroom door. "Al? Still in there?" Al
had been sick for days since she'd discovered he was still using.

The restroom floor was a terrible place to detox, but there was nowhere else. Palmer pushed open the door.

Al was sitting in the far corner under the window. The window was broken. It had been intact last night. She moved closer and realized he was dead. The needle was still in his arm.

Reverend Palmer sat down beside the cold body, pulling Al's discarded jacket over his chest, over the needle, closing his bleary eyes. She whispered a prayer. It was a little late, but what the hell.

She left the room and shut the door quietly behind her. Death stood beside Al's corpse. It was not infected, and would not rise again. The dying flame of Al's candle would not swell at the last second with a cold blue light. It was as it should be.

CHAPTER SEVEN
Syl Silver's Brains Taste Like Sugar

Two blocks from the homeless shelter, Club Fetish was similarly boarded-up, windows covered with the splintered remains of tabletops and flooring. The main dance floor was all colored lights, no longer aglow. The light and sound riggings hanging from the ceiling were equally useless and their creaking made those in the club nervous. The bar had been cleaned out long ago and the consequences had clogged every toilet in the joint. The air was musty. It was dark. A tiny giggle escaped from behind the bar.

Jenna O'Connell awoke with a start. The tinny laughter increased in volume. She found an empty bottle at her feet and chucked it over the bar. "Fuck you, Syl!"

Lauren poked Jenna's arm. "Don't let him get to you."

"It's past getting. He's already gotten to me. I hate the prick." Jenna ran her fingernails through her golden hair. Lauren had thick red hair that now reached her waist; she actually looked better than she had when they'd first arrived in Jefferson Harbor with their entourage of makeup artists and stagehands. Jenna could feel her hair becoming more brittle by the day. Her eyes ached from straining to see. Her stomach ached from hunger. There was no longer anyone here to wait on her, no one except that gruesome photographer sitting on the dance floor. What was his name, Duncan? Mark Duncan. Even now he was still playing with his digital camera.

Lauren had been the band's drummer, and Jenna the singer. They hadn't known the rest of the band that well; this whole thing had been cobbled together at the last second as a morale-booster for the troops out here. The troops that had pulled out the day Jenna arrived.

And Duncan. What the hell was he following the tour for? The only publications (she could hardly believe they bothered printing *anything* anymore) that got any attention were sensationalist rags about the zombies. They were mostly full of bullshit about religious prophecies and supposed cures, alongside Duncan's daring close-up images of shambling undead. So why document a rock tour? She put the question to him. Duncan's eyes lit up at the attention.

"People are getting tired of zombie stories," he said, dry throat croaking a bit. "They want to see people living. They want to pretend that celebrity tabloid trash still matters in their world."

"Is that what this is?" Jenna gestured around the shadowy room. "Tabloid trash? The life of a celebrity? Hardly. Everything's still a fucking zombie story."

Duncan put the camera down and stretched his legs. Before he could begin opining on his so-called career, club owner Sylvester Silver vaulted over the bar, slipped in something and smacked his head on the floor. "God *Damn*," he muttered.

"Are you high?" Jenna asked. Rhetorical question.

Silver said something unintelligible but surely vulgar in response. He got up and stumbled around a bit. "Z!"

He was whining for Zaharchuk, his dealer. The greasy little sleaze hadn't been here in days. In fact, Jenna had reminded Silver of that fact on several occasions. "Z!" he cried again. A leather vest and pants barely clinging to his emaciated body, he staggered toward one of the windows.

"Oh, shit," Duncan said.

Jenna got up, slapping Lauren's hand away, and chased after Silver. The man grabbed at the boards covering the window. "Fuck this! I'm leaving! Fuck this place!" Jenna grabbed his shoulder and he swatted at her. "Fuck you! You never played one fucking lick! Bitch!"

Duncan joined her behind Silver. "Get away from the window, man."

"I don't want to live here!" Syl bellowed, and he began choking on tears or snot or both.

Jenna rolled her eyes and punched him in the back of the head. He caught her in the mouth with an elbow. She went flying and, just as she'd dreaded, Duncan ran to her. "Stop him!" she snapped.

Silver tore a board from the window. "I'm out-"

A hand came through and took hold of his ear. Syl exploded into hysterics. A second hand grabbed the vest, and blood streamed down his neck as several ear piercings were tugged through cartilage. Syl beat weakly on the two arms, which obviously belonged to the same body, and he howled as his head was pulled out into the open.

Jenna and Duncan ran back and grabbed the waist of his pants. If he wasn't bitten—it wasn't too late—

Outside, Syl felt hair being torn from his scalp and threw his head back, banging against the boards. He was stuck. He was looking into the yellow eyes of an undead. Then his head was forced back down and teeth dug into the skin behind his ear.

"Let go!" Jenna yelled. Duncan did, watching silently while Syl Silver's legs kicked and his shrieks became garbled. He fell back into the room. Sans head.

Duncan puked on the ragged stump of Silver's neck. Jenna spun away, Lauren catching her, both screaming. An old man stared through the window, gnawing on the severed head's cheek. Then he sent his fist crashing into the remaining boards.

"Christ!" Duncan spat bile and grabbed a nearby barstool. "We've gotta cover it back up!"

Jenna thought he'd take a shot at the zombie, but instead he shattered the stool over the bar. Good thinking. Attacking the zombie was pointless. Better to fix the window before more showed up. She busted a second stool and told Lauren to find the hammer and nails in Syl's office.

Duncan brought the seat of the first stool down on the undead's prying fingers. Jenna joined him. "Lauren!"

"Coming!" Lauren dropped the box of nails halfway across the room.

"Just grab some! Hurry!" Jenna yelled. She felt her feet dragging through Syl's spreading blood and steeled herself against vomiting. Lauren drove a tenpenny nail through the seat of Duncan's barstool. Through the tiny gap between the two seats, Jenna could see that the zombie was no longer interested in the window. He thrust a hand into Silver's head through the open throat and yanked out a handful of tissue. The undead walked away from the club, chewing.

"We've got to get out of here," Jenna said.

"We're still safe. This building is safe," Duncan argued. "We're right in the middle of town."

"There's no food," Jenna shot back. "I haven't had anything to eat in days except dry noodles and apple schnapps. Do you want to feel safe or live, Duncan?"

He backed away from her, allowing Lauren a better angle to hammer from, and sighed. "There's a Kagen's at the west end of town. Not a store but a distribution center. I guarantee it's already been raided."

"It's worth a shot." Jenna peered outside again. "It's not like the streets are crawling with zombies. We just need to stay sober . . ."

Gene Pastore spat Syl Silver's hair from his mouth and hooked his fingers inside the head's nostrils. Nightfall was fast approaching. He didn't remember how he'd gotten to Midtown from the landfill, but it didn't matter. What mattered was right now, and right now was hunger. Meat fell through the hole in his cheek. He stooped to retrieve it from the ground.

There was more inside the head but he couldn't get to it. Shaking it over his open mouth, Gene grunted. He remembered something—*shovel*—that could have been used to get to the meat. He didn't have the shovel. He hurled the head into the curb and heard bone crack like a gunshot.

Gene sat on the curb and fished the brains from the fractured skull. They tasted sweet.

CHAPTER EIGHT
Food Run

They left at midnight, going through the recently damaged window and crossing the street to the Donner Convention Center. Streetlamps flickered and made clicking noises. There was no other sound.

Duncan was fiddling with his camera. "Why did you bring that?" Jenna whispered harshly.

"It's got a night-vision mode," he replied. "Not much, but it'll allow us to stay in the shadows." He pressed his eye to the viewfinder and searched the Convention Center parking lot. "All clear." The camera was a model from the early 21st century, one of the last produced; it was built to last, though he'd had to replace a few parts himself since acquiring it. Not many people had digital cameras these days. The earlier, simpler models had been taken up by many in his field. Technology and industry had been dealt a crippling blow by the plague—if necessity was indeed the mother of invention, then it had to be that the child was long dead and mother was alone in her dark house.

Lauren pushed her sleeves up to her shoulders. She was clutching the leg of a barstool; the girl was small but those drummer's arms were strong. She'd fended off enough unruly fans (and some had wanted to bite her too), so the rotters were no worry.

"Four blocks west to Kagen's," Duncan said. He crept along the wall, holding his camera like a weapon.

Jenna wondered what it was like to photograph the undead at close quarters. Maybe looking at them through the camera made them seem somewhere far away, made Duncan feel safe. Maybe he was just crazy.

Duncan ran across an intersection to the burned-out shell of an outlet mall. Peering through the viewfinder, he threw his hand out to stop Jenna and Lauren from following him. Zooming in, he waited for the grainy green shapes in the street to resolve themselves. There was something smoldering . . . no, two somethings. Despite the poor quality of the image he was able to identify them as bodies.

A hand fell on his shoulder and he slammed back into the wall. "Fuck!"

Jenna slapped her other hand over his mouth. "Jesus, Duncan!"

He pushed her away and pointed to the bodies. "Rotters. They've been torched."

"How do you know they're rotters?"

"One's still moving a little bit."

Jenna leaned over his shoulder, squinting. He handed her the camera. "Who do you think did it?" Lauren asked.

"P.O.s," Duncan answered. Did this mean there was still order in Jefferson Harbor, despite the military pullout?

"I thought the cops would've left with the troops," Jenna murmured.

"I'll bet most did." Duncan took back the camera. "Few more blocks. Keep quiet." Shooting a you-should-talk glare at him, Jenna stepped back and let him take point.

The last leg of the journey was uneventful, but still seemed to take a lifetime. Duncan kept stopping at every corner to scan the area. Jenna's heart pounded against her ribs with every distant and unidentifiable noise. Finally, Duncan found the Kagen's ware-house entrance and peered inside. "Okay." He went in first. Jenna followed, and Lauren, just before stepping through the door, thought she heard a soft grunt from the darkness outside. She hurried in without glancing back.

Duncan felt along the wall for switches and flipped them. Only one light came on, in the far corner, past rows and rows of shelving. Lauren tugged the door shut and frowned. "I think the lock's broken."

"Wouldn't surprise me." Duncan shook a nearby box. "Empty. I knew it."

In the far, well-lit corner, a door opened with a metallic squeal.

They all dropped into crouches. The door slammed. Duncan instinctively raised the camera, finger on the capture button. Jenna stole a peek between two boxes, and she saw it.

It was a monster. Its head, a skull, pale and elongated. Eyeless. Fanged. It . . . wait, the bone was actually wired to the raw red flesh of a rotter's head, the skull being worn like a mask. God. What had it been, a horse's? The undead turned in her direction and she realized that, no, it was the skull of a large dog.

That wasn't the worst part. The worst part wasn't even the obscenely-long knife in each hand. It was the surgical apron and scrubs. What had been a simple, animal thing, Jenna now saw had intellect—purpose. The rotter set the knives down on some unseen surface and pulled latex gloves over its scabby hands.

"W-w-what is it?" Lauren stammered. She gripped Jenna's arm like a vise.

Duncan's camera hitting the floor sounded like a thunderclap from the heavens.

He stared in horror at the shattered bits lying at his feet then looked up through the shelves at the rotter. It had its knives back and was moving forward.

Jenna dragged Lauren toward the door through which they'd entered. Duncan was trying to pick up the camera parts.

Jesus! He *was* crazy. "Mark!" she shouted, and the rotter grunted loudly. The photographer snapped back to reality.

The rotter shuffled down the first aisle, then the next, weaving back and forth, *grunt-grunt-grunt-grunt*. It planted a knife in one of the many boxes and hurled it to the floor, stomping through the cardboard. *Grunt-grunt-grunt-grunt.* Jenna grabbed the doorknob and pulled. It was stuck fast.

Duncan wrapped his hands around hers and pried at the door. "C'mon, c'mon," he breathed, barely audible, then a hysteric, "FUCKING C'MON!"

The rotter swept boxes from shelves and searched the room with its empty dog's eye sockets. It began loping down the aisles at a frenetic pace. Lauren screamed.

Then, something fell from a shelf and collided with the rotter's legs, sending it to the floor. The door tore open and Jenna, Duncan and Lauren fled into the night.

The rotter sat up, jerking its head back to see what had tripped it.

Fred Moorecourt pawed the floor in a madness, crawling in place as his bloody feet failed to gain traction and drew crimson scribbles on the concrete. The rotter slapped at his heels until he got a hold of one.

"No!" Moorecourt hollered. He saw the inhuman thing towering over him, then he tasted blood thick in his mouth, and he saw light; an audience of fist-pumping constituents at a speech; Doug's face, his smile, turning away in a silken pillow; he saw his life, and saw that none of it had mattered, then the rotter planted a knife just below his chin and opened his throat.

CHAPTER NINE
Sawbones

Throat to sternum. Blood welling inside canyons as they're carved from flesh and bone. Both knives through the ribcage now, spreading it apart. Skin and muscle strain and finally tear. This isn't one of the warmbodies that was seen coming into the warehouse. Doesn't matter. It's meat. Placing one boot inside the garbage bag to hold it open and feeding pulpy organs into it.

The hunger was strong, worrying at every inch of Sawbones' insides. He hurried to finish bagging Moorecourt's innards then started ripping at his flesh. Thick strips dripping blood came away in Sawbones' gloved hands. He longed to pry apart the dog's jaws and feed. He couldn't. Sawbones grunted and shoved the skin into the bag.

When he was finished, Senator Moorecourt was a ruddy skeleton with a few bits of gristle clinging on. Blood covered the floor and spread beyond the solitary light's reach into darkness. Sawbones splashed through it and out the door.

Eyeing the shoreline beyond the landfill warily, Sawbones made his way into the swamp, trudging through knee-deep muck. The trees were all enormous. Roots and branches threaded around the rotter's boots with every step. Bark and leaves teemed with moss. Algae-covered fungi jutted from semisolid patches of earth. The swamp seethed with life. Sawbones felt warm inside as he passed through it. His hunger subsided.

Aidan and Gerald opened the gates for him. They stared through their fellow zombie, at the garbage bag.

He knew to go around to the rear kitchen entrance. There Uriel was waiting, and he ushered Sawbones in, locking the door behind him.

Rather than entering the kitchen, Sawbones went into a narrow hallway, its floor caked with blood, and upended the bag.

Baron Tetch stood in the foyer of the manor. His brothers and sisters gathered around him, glassy eyes pleading.

"Eat," he said. They rushed into the narrow hallway. He shut the door to muffle the nightmarish din of their supper.

Sawbones padded into the foyer, sans boots and apron. He bowed his head before Tetch. "Go downstairs," Tetch ordered. "I'll be down later." The rotter shuffled off.

Sawbones didn't eat with the others. Measures had been taken to ensure that, the dog's skull among them. He only took nourishment intravenously, not only because he was charged with the task of fetching meat for the undead, but because Baron Tetch didn't want his father to heal too much, to regain any scraps of memory. Worse yet, of his personality.

The manor in earlier years had been known as the Addison Estate. Addison himself had been a surgeon and noted member of the Jefferson Harbor elite. As society's decay continued, Addison had retired and sequestered himself in the house. Soon thereafter, he put out a quiet call to the city's other wealthy families: Send me your children. I can take them off your hands, he said, relieve your burden—what's more, I can protect them. I don't mean simply to shelter your young ones from the undead outside the city. I mean, through my research, to cure this plague.

Addison had adopted eleven children in total. Most of their families left the city in that same year.

He'd never cured anything.

Baron Tetch turned three locks on the basement door after Sawbones went down. He stood back, trying to ignore the ravenous crunching and slurping of his siblings.

Lily came down the grand staircase, dressed for dinner. She was a vision. Tetch clapped his hands and met her at the foot of the stairs, offering his arm. Together, they went into the dining room where Prudence had earlier prepared a meal for them.

"I like your jacket," Lily said. Tetch lifted the cover from his plate and inhaled the aroma of fettuccini and herbs in a simple Alfredo sauce. It drove the scent of spilled blood from his nostrils. "Is that one of Daddy's jackets?" Lily asked.

Tetch frowned. "Don't call him that." She didn't know who Sawbones really was, beneath the mask. "And no. It's mine. Everything in this house is mine."

"Like me," the girl said with a pout.

"What?" Tetch lowered his fork.

"I want to go outside the gates," Lily said boldly.

Tetch nodded, stirred his pasta. "I knew this would happen sooner or later. Was bound to. You've always been brave, Lily, too brave for your own good. If you want to know what's out there, I'll tell you. More dead, only they're not like Aidan and Ruth and Simeon and the others. They've not been taught proper behavior. They'd tear you apart. Is that what you want?"

"Are there more people like us?"

"No." He stabbed his fork into the fettuccini for emphasis.

"I saw a man today. He had all-black eyes."

"A dead man."

"No, he talked."

Tetch's grip on the fork tightened. He wound a spool of pasta around it. The sauce was a bit watery. Prudence would be punished. "You're sure he talked?"

"He asked me why I was in here. Inside the gates I mean."

So, some more of the city's survivors had decided to venture into the swamp. He was certain that Sawbones' exploits had kept the living at bay, but all good things came to an end.

They couldn't enter the swamp. They couldn't find the manor. They couldn't discover what Tetch already knew.

"I'm not hungry anymore," he muttered, rising from the table. Lily frowned guiltily. He said nothing to comfort her, just left.

FIRST STRIKE
Hand of God

Sergeant Gregory had dubbed the squad "Hand of God" in its infancy. Handpicking the men for his elite team, he never openly specified that they be believers in Christ, if only to avoid unsettling the brass; but it was understood by each member that this calling was more than a standard military assignment. "What we do is a cleansing," Gregory told each in their entry interview, "a purification. The earth must be baptized in God's fire before Christ can return—it's written in the Holy Book."

The squad called Hand of God was always on the front lines when Charlie Company's second platoon encountered a horde of rotters. The bastards had begun to exhibit more of a pack mentality in recent months. While they didn't move in any sort of coordinated attack patterns, and while each undead only cared about gorging itself, they were certainly learning that blitzing Army patrols in great numbers increased the odds of scoring a meal. Sergeant Gregory observed the rotters' increasing tendency toward animal behavior, rather than simply shambling along like mindless automatons. He watched and he worried.

It was because of Gregory's unique understanding of undead behavior that Major Briggs chose his squad for a special mission. When Charlie Company withdrew their forces from Jefferson Harbor, Briggs requested that Gregory and his men hang back for a few days. The major wanted to see if it was true that feral packs would be noticing—and following—the withdrawal. Civilians and soldiers alike had expressed concern that the massive exodus would only put every zombie in the badlands on their trail. The Senate, safe already in the cities to the north, decried such a notion as ridiculous. They still believed that the undead were mindless. They didn't watch, and know, like Gregory did.

The mission's first day was drawing to a close. Gregory sat beneath a camouflage tarp and eyed the crescent moon. His eyes, steely gray, were unblinking orbs set in a face of weathered, pockmarked flesh with sharp angles. In his lap, his hands stroked the backside of a machine gun. Whispers of prayer, barely audible, fell from his lips as he stared heavenward.

The encampment was a half-mile outside the city's north wall. Before dawn, they'd be moving to the east side, where the city's main gates were. Not only was Gregory concerned that rotters might be coming together in pursuit of the withdrawing troops, he feared that some might storm the abandoned city, now that the Army was gone and its streets were quiet. Indeed, there might be dead-eyed predators out there right at this moment, watching—watching him. He lowered his gaze from the moon and scanned the horizon. There were sparse clutches of trees here and there, not much else offering cover to man or monster. The swampland on the city's west end was mostly contained within its walls. Everything was out in the open—

He saw a figure loping toward the camp and grabbed his gun. The figure waved a hand over its head. He relaxed. It was only Coates, returning from scouting the east wall.

The young private reached Gregory and dropped into a crouch. The squad's four other members materialized from the darkness, drawing close to hear his report. On Gregory's right knelt Barry, Hand of God's only female. Her ebony skin drank in the moonlight, whereas it gleamed on her "battleaxe"—a broad, cleaver-like blade welded onto a housing that attached to the butt of her shotgun. Both the axe and the gun were close-combat weapons, declaring her proficiency in melee combat. Dalton, the resident sniper, had his rifle strapped across his back and binoculars around his neck. He wasn't afraid to get his hands dirty, but he preferred to take targets down from a distance. It bespoke his general detachment from both the battle and social life; the bald-headed man wasn't unpleasant in his demeanor, but he more often looked through his comrades than at them.

Ahmed, the newest member to both Hand of God and a life in Christ, sat at the rear of the group. He seemed uncomfortable with the arm slung over his shoulders by Logan, who wore his usual smirk and rapped his knuckles against the steel toe of his boot. He was the first to speak. "So what's the good word, Coates?"

"Two vehicles on the road leading to the main gates: one of our Hummers and a civilian car, both wrecked. It looks like a recent accident. I saw a couple of casualties out on the road. Definitely dead," he whispered excitedly. Coates clearly hadn't been anticipating any action at all on this mission. Gregory reminded himself to have a talk with the private about his tendency to let his guard down. He'd gotten bored, as they all had, during their stint in Jefferson Harbor, but they were done baby-sitting civvies now. They were back in the field.

"Now's as good a time as any to pull up our stakes and head out there," the sergeant said. "We'll check out this wreck and salvage anything we can, then establish camp a half-click from the gates."

"I was reviewing what little we know about this area's history," said Barry, "and there was an Army base west of the city—think there's a chance of anything salvageable out there?"

"Fort Armstrong, I believe." Gregory shook his head. "It

was razed to the ground during the outbreaks, a damn century ago. Anything that might have been left behind has got to be long gone, even if it was squirreled away below ground. We've got enough firepower to get by." If there was one thing the military-industrial complex was still good for, it was bullets. Ammunition nowadays could be forged using anything from plastics to stone with the simple but clever technology that had been devised, and it was all good enough to blow the limbs off your average rotter. The important thing to keep in mind was that bullets only disabled the undead, didn't kill them. A clean shot through the brain might render a zombie sightless or crippled, but the real tools of the trade were blades; every soldier carried a hatchet or machete of some type, though many traded their military-issue steel for what they found out in the badlands, in the long-abandoned ghost towns that dotted the American landscape. Gregory looked admiringly at Barry's battleaxe.

They brought down the tarps they'd erected as shelters and set out for the east wall. Coates brought out his pocket Bible, leading the group in mumbled prayers as they crept through the dust, eyes peeled for any threatening silhouettes on the horizon. Jefferson Harbor was silent as the grave. Save a few gunshots, it had been quiet all day. Few civilians had been foolish enough to stay behind. Was it foolish, though? If it turned out that the undead were being drawn to the convoys headed north, maybe some of these folks had the right idea. But their staying behind was likely due to a paranoid mistrust of the government more than anything else.

Gregory did trust his leaders, but that trust could only go so far. He put his real stock in the Lord.

The pair of overturned vehicles came into view. Dalton shook a magnet-powered flashlight to charge it up then trained its blue beam on the wreck. The civilian ride was a towncar, a relic; the last vehicles produced in the United States were over fifty years old, and they were all built for power and rugged terrain. The towncar's hundred-year-old frame had probably been gutted and fitted with crude replacement parts a dozen times, and judging by its companion Humvee, it was probably government-owned. It figured. Few could afford to maintain wheels anymore. Gregory had a dream of owning a little Jeep in his twilight years, but then again, he was getting toward retirement age and there was no sign the Army was ever going to let him go.

The vehicles looked as if they'd been headed *toward* the city, not away from it; that puzzled Gregory. He shined his own light through the Hummer's shattered windshield. Two soldiers dead inside. They had bite wounds on their throats and faces, but it looked as if the crash had killed them before they were fed upon. "Look alive," the sergeant whispered.

A civilian male lay dead not far from the towncar. In the vehicle itself were the mangled bodies of another male and a female. Coates checked them for ID and found none, though there were papers with government letterhead lying about.

Dalton's light found another male on the road. He'd been cut in half. As the soldier approached the body, he suddenly froze, bringing his rifle over the shoulder. "Rotter."

The empty, staring eyes of the rotter didn't react to Dalton's light. He aimed into those eyes and took a tentative step forward. "I think it's . . . I think it's dead." But it couldn't be. Even if half its guts were spilled out over the asphalt, it couldn't be.

Barry stepped past Dalton, holding the battleaxe out in front of her. As soon as she was within range, she struck, hacking the head clean off and sweeping it away from the torso.

"It was probably just immobilized," she muttered. "If it was hit by one of those cars, a spinal injury might have paralyzed it."

"I saw nothing in the eyes," Dalton replied.

"Could have been blind," Barry said. "There's no way it was dead, I mean really dead."

Gregory knelt to study the wound that had halved the rotter. It was one clean cut, smooth as silk. Like a sword, or . . . a strange thought occurred to him, and he brushed it aside. "I agree with Barry," he finally said. "Logan, check the Hummer for supplies. Let's get off the road and set up camp. We'll come back to this in the morning."

BEFORE THE EMPIRE
Before the Withdrawal

February 20, 2112

Stacy Bekins was sitting on the steps of the Jefferson Harbor Museum. Rain pattered on her thick brown hair, running over her shoulders and down her back to the cold stone beneath her. She watched dully as her shoes darkened with moisture, feeling the water pooling in the soles.

"What are you doing out here?" P.O. Voorhees threw a plastic raincoat over her shoulders. "Stacy? You with me?" She was unresponsive. Voorhees knelt to bring himself eye-to-eye with the girl. She stared through him. She was in shock.

Stacy was a checkout girl at the PX the troops had established inside the museum. The portraits, fossils and relics once kept there were decades lost; the building had served off and on as an emergency shelter. Major Briggs, the latest man placed in charge of the Harbor's security, had decided the space would be better utilized as a grocery store.

The soldiers were being paid in credit, and they spent it all inside the museum. MREs were often passed up in favor of luxury items like cigarettes, aspirin and underwear. Voorhees had noticed the soldiers getting thinner and thinner inside their fatigues. And they all smoked.

He helped Stacy to her feet—hauled her, really—and took her through the doors to the guard post in the museum entryway. A grunt with glazed eyes watched them from his reclining chair. "She's been out there for an hour," he said.

"You didn't think to say anything? Ask her if she was all right? Get her out of the rain?" Voorhees gave the soldier a dark glare, but the disinterested boy merely looked away.

A woman Voorhees knew as Corporal Elliot strode toward them from the PX. She had a brown paper bag under her arm. The only things they bagged were personal hygiene items. The young guard also noticed the parcel and smiled slyly.

Elliot kicked the chair out from under him. Chair and grunt slammed into the floor with a sharp crack. "You sit up straight. You're not on vacation," the corporal snapped.

Voorhees gave the guard a sly smile of his own, then turned to Elliot. Stacy hadn't made a sound this entire time; hadn't reacted to the guard's fall. "Something's wrong with this girl," Voorhees told Elliot. She nodded with concern and gestured outside. Her Humvee was across the street.

They hustled Stacy through the rain to the vehicle. Soldiers posted on the sidewalk saluted crisply.

"She works in the PX, doesn't she?" Elliot asked. Voorhees nodded as he eased Stacy into the back seat.

"Stacy, did something happen?" The P.O. looked into her eyes for any glimmer of awareness. It wasn't uncommon for people, especially young people, to have a breakdown or two when faced with the reality outside the city walls. The soldiers had been good, working in conjunction with Voorhees' men to keep the perimeter secure and torch anything that managed to worm its way inside. But the threat of the undead wasn't what made these kids crack, Voorhees knew; it was knowing that they'd never live a free life, the life that had existed a century prior. They would grow up always having to look over their shoulders, like early Man did, except that today's humanity wanted more than survival. They wanted their lives to mean something greater.

He forgot all that when he saw the bruising on Stacy's underarms. He reached gently for her arms to get a better look, and she recoiled. Her face became a rictus of terror.

"Stacy," he asked softly, "it's all right now. You're safe.

"Did someone attack you?"

Corporal Elliot's jaw was working as she silently observed. She knew where this was going. A burning apprehension was building in her breast.

There had been two sexual assaults reported in the city since the year began. The victims were women, both grabbed in an isolated area of town, both raped from behind while their assailant whispered vile threats. Neither could identify him. But they both thought it was a soldier.

Of course they did.

Was there any proof? A shred of evidence? No. It could just as well be a longtime resident of Jefferson Harbor . . . but Elliot's pride would only take her so far before her common sense stepped on the brakes.

The soldiers were the ones in control. The soldiers were empowered to protect civilians from the rotters and each other.

Soldiers whose psyches were bent and frayed by the horror of modern combat sometimes took out their frustration in unspeakable ways. There wasn't a counselor or chaplain in sight to speak to; prescription meds were out of the question in the field. It was all blood and rain and the endless, fruitless battle against the undead.

Was it really fruitless? The corporal asked herself. Did she believe that they were at a stalemate against the rotters—or worse, that they were losing?

Who could say, really? She only knew what was going on with this unit. The radio propaganda from the north wasn't informative in the least. She knew there was talk among the ranks, again, of a possible withdrawal. Did that constitute a stalemate? Or was it merely surrendering to the dead and retreating?

(They'll follow us. You know they will.)

Stacy Bekins looked as if she'd already surrendered her sanity. Voorhees noticed that her jeans were zipped but not buttoned. Her shirt, untucked, had a few stains on the front, but they were faded. She'd walked back to the museum from the scene of the rape and sat there in the rain, trying to wash her body and mind clean.

"Was it just one man?" Voorhees asked. Tears formed in the corners of her eyes. She stared past him still, until her lip began to tremble uncontrollably. Then she looked away.

"Stacy," Elliot whispered, "would you feel more comfortable talking alone with me?"

"I need to be here to take her statement," Voorhees muttered.

Elliot frowned. "Come on."

"It's nothing personal, Corporal—"

"It's nothing but personal, Patrol Officer." Elliot nodded toward Stacy, the girl's white-knuckled hands clasped in her lap, eyes glued to the window. Voorhees didn't have any female officers.

"I . . . I'll stand outside." He turned away before Elliot could respond and stepped out of the Hummer.

Back in the rain. Pulling his walkie-talkie from his trench coat, he tuned it to the band reserved exclusively for his officers. Didn't want any of the Army grunts listening in. "Wood, what's your twenty?"

"Sir, heading south through Midtown Park."

"Good. Meet me at the museum entrance. Looks like we've got another two-six-oh. Weisman, you get all that?"

"Yes sir." Mike Weisman was acting as dispatcher back at the PD. He'd have to record the shift's radio traffic by hand. It was a bitch, which was one of the reasons Voorhees often did it himself; that, and he couldn't read the chicken scratch that half of his officers used.

"You want me out there?" Weisman asked through static. He'd interviewed the last two victims. Voorhees responded, "No, you stay put. We'll compare notes later on."

"Copy that."

P.O. Wood slipped and stumbled as he rounded the corner of the museum. Voorhees waved him over to the Humvee. "Corporal Elliot's in there trying to calm her nerves. It's Stacy Bekins from the PX, looks like the attack just happened. I want you to go in there and get her work schedule. Find out if she was there today."

Wood nodded and hustled across the street. Elliot propped open the Hummer's passenger door. "Officer?"

He stepped back into the vehicle, out of the harsh weather and into a young girl's relived nightmare.

It was hours later, with the sun parting the storm clouds, when Voorhees headed to the Greeley district of town to make his rounds. The residential area was right beside the eastern wall, and though soldiers frequently patrolled the streets, people still liked to see a familiar face out there. He knocked on the front door of the Stanton house. Their boy was sick with a cold.

"How's he doing?" Voorhees asked when mother Marie opened up. She smiled. "A couple of soldiers brought us some medicine. They paid for it themselves down at the PX. Wasn't that nice?"

"It sure was." He felt a twinge of shame at being unable to provide the same services himself. The Harbor Medical Plaza's pharmacies had been emptied out, mostly by looters, and the rest was now housed in the police department's basement, but supplies were running low.

"Cody's feeling much better," Marie continued. "Once he's fully recovered from that bug, I think . . . well, we're talking about leaving."

"Where will you go?" Voorhees asked.

"Haven't you heard?" She replied excitedly. "It was on the radio this morning. The Senate passed a new bill—"

"Hey there, Voorhees." Bill Stanton stepped out from behind the door and gestured for the P.O. to come in. "You want a drink? This Army shit almost tastes like water, you should try it."

"Bill," Marie scolded. Her husband grinned and pulled Voorhees in by his shoulder. "Take a load off for a few minutes."

Twelve-year-old Cody was on the couch in the living room, covered by a blanket. There were a couple of chairs for the adults, and on a table across the room, patriotic hymns played softly on the family radio.

Voorhees took a chair and waved to Cody. "What's this I just heard from your wife?" He called over his shoulder. "About a Senate bill?"

"It's the withdrawal," Bill said with a sort of shrug. "Passed unanimously. It starts in a couple of weeks."

"They want to have everyone out of the badlands by July," Marie said, tucking the blanket in around Cody's legs and feet. "By the badlands, they mean here, and everywhere else outside of the 'New Great Lakes area'."

"So they've redrawn our borders again?" Voorhees smirked and shook his head. Invisible lines that the rotters paid no mind to. He hadn't paid much mind to them either; few people had, in fact, in the beginning. When the Senate started designating areas of the country as "uninhabitable," there had been protests from the cities still standing in those areas. Of course, the cities fell without any federal support. Then, the Senate declared over the airwaves that they'd been right, and more people started listening. And so it went: the government continued erasing and redrawing America's lines, abandoning the East and West Coasts, abandoning the U.S.-Mexico border, abandoning those who had seen their nation helplessly eroding and who had decided that they wouldn't give up their "uninhabitable" communities while they were still breathing.

But this withdrawal, this was something much bigger. As

Bill and Marie described it, the government was giving up all but seven states—and even then, to call those complete states was an exaggeration.

(Had Elliot known about any of this when he'd talked to her earlier?)

"They say they have enough room up there for everybody." Bill sipped lukewarm water from a plastic bottle. "They say we're spread out too much right now for their support to do any good."

"How do they even know how many people there are? Did they take a census?" Voorhees accepted a bottle of water and wrenched the cap off.

"Well, they might not have hard numbers, but what they're saying makes real sense." Bill reached over from his seat to pat Cody's head. "Yeah, this town is done for, but the people in it can survive. We're talking about massive military convoys escorting us north, protecting us from any rotters that might think it's a traveling smorgasbord. Cities with huge walls, thousands of troops, and all the resources you'd ever need. It'll be safe, relatively comfortable, like the way we used to live here. Maybe even better."

"So, our senators-for-life are making us an offer we can't refuse." Voorhees' smile was bitter. He spat a mouthful of water back into the bottle.

"I love the Harbor, Voorhees, just like you, but I can't put my family's safety on the line for that."

"I get it." The cop replaced the cap on the water bottle. "I really do. But there are other people who won't feel the same way. There are people who don't give a damn about lines on a map or any carrot the government's dangling in front of them. They're going to stay and I have to stay with them."

Bill laughed incredulously. "No you don't!"

"When do they want everyone out again?" Voorhees asked Marie. "When are they cutting us off?"

"July."

"Independence Day." Voorhees rose from his chair. "I need to get back on my rounds."

"We're going to leave with the first convoy," Bill said. He averted his eyes to look at his son, giving Cody a reassuring squeeze of the hand. "It just makes sense."

"You're right," Voorhees said quietly. "But I can't leave people here. That doesn't make sense. I'm a cop."

Bill stared solemnly at him. The man just didn't understand. Later that evening, he and Marie would discuss all the irrational reasons why Voorhees must have insisted on staying. They'd call him suicidal, lonely, afraid. Bill's reasons for evacuating were plain as day, but Voorhees . . . Voorhees said he was a cop, and that wasn't an answer, not to them. "Yeah," Bill said.

Voorhees left the house and crossed matted dead grass to the sidewalk. He'd probably be hearing from the P.O. Union before long about pulling out. The Union, a lot of spineless bureaucrats who'd forgotten what it felt like to walk a beat. If they called him north, he'd ignore them, he'd lose his job; but he'd still be a P.O. in Jefferson Harbor, just as those who refused to leave their homes were still Americans.

He wondered if any of his officers would stay with him.

CHAPTER TEN
Only the Living Are Evil

Lee rocked silently in his recliner. He was shivering, Cheryl noticed from across the apartment in the kitchenette. She'd soaked a month-old bag of Fritos in water and was mashing them into something resembling tortillas. There was nothing to top them with but a can of refried beans. The gas had gone out a few hours earlier, so no stove. Lee didn't know yet.

"It huuuuurts," he said through gritted teeth. "Cheryl, it hurts so fuckin' bad." As she watched him cradle himself, she was struck by something, or the lack thereof; she didn't pity him at all.

She hated him.

This miserable man locked in the throes of withdrawal, on the verge of tears, was still the man who'd backhanded her earlier that day. And the day before that. And before that.

What was she to do, make another run into Midtown? Put herself at risk of being assaulted or killed (or eaten) so she could find Zaharchuk? And even then how would she pay for the drugs?

She knew how Lee would expect her to pay. She knew that Zaharchuk liked to pull hair and choke a woman on his unwashed manhood. It was probably another of Zaharchuk's "customers" who'd raped her, if not the man himself. But Lee would expect her to pay, to do the only thing he thought she was good for so that she could bring a fistful of meth home to him. So he could level out and "get right." So he'd be able to beat her black and blue.

Lee turned his puppy-dog gaze toward her and wiped sweat from his brow. "Fuck, Cheryl, please go get me some stuff."

"I'm making dinner," she said flatly. Fished through drawers for a can opener.

"Cher-YLLL," Lee whined. "Fuck dinner. I'm not hungry, Jesus I just need some. I *need* it. I'm dying here."

The TV was on in front of him. Nothing was playing. "We need to save power," Cheryl said, pointing to it. Lee snapped out of the chair. "Are you fucking listening to me? Goddamn!" He kicked right through the television screen. There was a loud *POP* and then black smoke belched forth. Lee grabbed his foot and yelped. "CHERYL, GO GET IT!"

"No!" she shouted. Even as a tiny part of her mind screamed at her to shut up, to get the hell out of there and head to Midtown while Lee tore around the apartment—she screamed at him. "I'm not gonna get it! You can lay here and die if you want to! Nothing's going to change if I get you your fix, I don't care what you say! You know it! I know it and now your damn TV's gone"

He staggered, hit the counter separating the two of them, then caught her by the throat with a white hand and squeezed. She grabbed his wrist. Her other hand was caught in the utility drawer. He squeezed and squeezed, staring her straight in the eye with desperation and something much worse. "You die. You die."

Cheryl's other hand came free. She tried to loose Lee's stranglehold, but his grip was unbreakable. He gritted his teeth and leaned forward. "Die, you whore, you fucking bitch, no one will ever know you're gone but me and I'll be happy. So happy!"

(Could kill you where you lay bitch, feed you to the rotters.

Kill you.) "I'm gonna *love* it," Lee hollered, wrapping his other hand around her neck and thrashing her back and forth. "I'M GONNA LOVE YOU DEAD, I'M GOING TO FUCK YOU RAW AND CUM ON YOUR DEAD FACE OH GOD!" He shoved her so hard she careened into the fridge, bounced back into the counter and knocked the wind from her lungs. Cheryl collapsed on the tile. Lee stumbled into the kitchenette, tugging at his belt.

Cheryl looked for a weapon. She couldn't reach anything from her position on the floor. She couldn't breathe, could barely move . . . and that tiny part of her mind that had pleaded with her to obey her cousin now told her to give up. She felt her will being sapped away.

Lee stood above her, mumbling under his breath, pants coming down.

(Kill you. Kill you kill you.)

He fell to his knees and forced her legs apart. He clawed at her pants, then pushed her legs closed again and tried to yank them off. His flaccid penis swung over her, and she knew he'd never get hard enough to rape her but it didn't matter to him anymore. Lee saw what she was looking at. He slapped her hard. A knife of white light tore through her vision. "Fuck you!" he hollered, and began to choke her again.

(killyoukillyoukillyoukillyou)

He groped briefly at her breasts before slapping her again, then again. It was getting him off more than she did. "Stupid, fucking, goddamn."

(killkillkillkillkillkillkill)

This time it was a closed fist that struck her cheek. A sound like a gunshot filled her senses, though she was sure she couldn't hear anything anymore. Her lungs stopped protesting and she felt darkness overcoming her.

"No," a voice said. It sounded unfamiliar. Was it Lee's, distorted—or was it her own?

"No," again. Cheryl, blind, felt herself being dragged across the linoleum to the carpet in the living room. Her mouth was forced open by several fingers. Please God, she wept in her mind, don't let me live through this. Let me die now.

She slipped away into blackness.

Then she was back. There were lips over hers. They pulled away and she opened her eyes.

A young man knelt over her. "Can you hear me?" he asked. It was his voice she'd heard before. Cheryl nodded.

"Stay here. Don't try to get up." He ran out of sight then came back with a glass of water. He propped her head up to pour it down her throat. "Just take it easy. I think you're gonna be okay."

Her head began pounding. She whimpered, the last of the water spilling over her shirt. The man laid her back down and she felt something like a pillow underneath her head. Taking a few shallow breaths, Cheryl smelled acrid smoke.

"Who was—is—this man? The man who attacked you? Do you know him?"

"You shot him, didn't you?"

The young man sat back on the floor and nodded.

"His name's Lee. He's my cousin. He's dead, then?"

"He's dead. He was . . . he was trying to . . ."

"I know." Cheryl attempted to sit up. The man firmly laid her back down.

"Please don't move. It's for your own good." Almost as an afterthought, the man fished an ID card from his pocket. She saw the service pistol in his waistband.

"My name's Mike Weisman. I'm a Patrol Officer," he said. "I live in the next building over."

"Thank you," Cheryl whispered, then fell unconscious.

CHAPTER ELEVEN
Strays

As dawn crept over Jefferson Harbor, Senior P.O. Voorhees was making his way back to the homeless shelter. He was passing the East Harbor Mall when he saw a dog walking across the parking lot. As it came closer, what he thought to be mange turned out to be rot. The dead dog looked at him with milky eyes and turned to go in the other direction.

He almost couldn't bear the thought of harming the creature. Then he thought of the other dogs it would feed upon. Voorhees dropped to one knee and patted his thigh softly. "C'mere, boy."

The dog glanced back but kept walking away. He couldn't bring himself to draw his sidearm. "C'mere, boy! C'mon!"

Voorhees was fifty-nine years old. The outbreak began nearly half a century before he was born, but when his mother learned she was pregnant she resolved to keep the baby. His father had reluctantly agreed. The old man wasn't a bad parent; he fulfilled all his duties, taught his son to be a man in the face of a nightmare world. The old man just wasn't there in his heart, and Voorhees had always known it, as far back as he could remember.

They had a hound, a mutt named George; Voorhees never

knew his father's first name but he suspected it was the same. One morning, before the sun had risen, ten-year-old Voorhees' father had pulled him from bed and taken him behind the house.

George was tied to a post amidst the tall grass. The property was surrounded by a ten-foot fence and the dog acted as a lookout in case rotters came from across the fields. On this morning, George had been lying on his side. His tail wagged feebly when Voorhees and his father appeared.

"He's been bit," the old man said without emotion. He gave the boy a few minutes to let it sink in, then continued. "A couple of days ago I guess, when we were hunting. I never saw the dog—or whatever it was—that did it. Didn't even notice the bite until last night." Voorhees thought he heard his father's voice break and looked up. The old man quickly knelt to raise one of George's forelegs, exposing the wound.

"We're all scared to die," he whispered, "even George here. He knew what was gonna happen and he hid it from me. But what's best for George—son, you know what's best."

Voorhees tasted tears on his lips and nodded.

"There's a reason why I'm making you do this," the old man said. He pulled a revolver from his jeans pocket. "You love George, don't you?"

The boy nodded.

"So do I," his father replied. He pushed the gun into Voorhees' trembling hands. "But this is what's best, what's right."

"Dad—" the child began.

"One of these days," the old man stammered, and tears formed in his eyes, the first and last time Voorhees would ever see such a thing, "one of these days, son, I'm gonna get bit. It just happens when you go out there as much as I do. And I'm gonna hide it . . ." He choked, cleared his throat loudly, continued in a croak. "And I'm gonna beg you not to kill me, son, but it's what's best. I need to know you'll do it and then burn what's left."

The old man stood back, away from Voorhees and George. He did one more thing that he had never before done and would never do again.

"I love you, son."

"I love you too, Dad."

Voorhees knelt and scratched George's head. Through a blurry sea of grief he aimed. The mutt sniffed the barrel of the gun and rested his head on the ground, as if to say it was all right, that he understood, even if every animal instinct in his body was telling him to run.

Thirty years later, Voorhees had seen the same look of pained acceptance in his father's eyes. He'd raised his service pistol through a blurry sea of grief, blinked the tears away to ensure his aim was true, and pulled the trigger.

"C'mon then, George," Voorhees said to the dead dog in the parking lot. He held his hands out. Something in the vestiges of the canine's brain stirred. It sat and stared at him. Then it came.

The gun was meant for the living. It could only slow an undead down, and that was a crapshoot in itself. Even a bullet to the head only did so much. No, fire was the only way to end them, and the best way to incapacitate a rotter prior to setting it ablaze was decapitation. A "widowmaker" was a sort of cleaver designed for that purpose, capable of parting bone as easily as flesh, in the right hands; Voorhees loosed his from its sheath on his back and waited for the dog.

When it was done, he drenched the body in lighter fluid and struck a match on the asphalt. Its soiled fur went up in seconds. Voorhees sat on the curb and watched it burn away.

His P.O. training had been co-sponsored by the U.S. Army, and when he qualified for the Senior Leadership course, they'd brought the select group into a basement room and set up a digital projector. It played a low-quality video dated September 11, 2007—the last President's last State of the Union address. He'd delivered the address to Congress via closed-circuit television from the Oval Office. At the time, it had been thought to be an extra security measure, as the plague had just gone global; but as the address played out, another reason for the Commander-in-Chief's isolation was revealed. This speech, available now on bootlegged discs, was the death knell of the executive branch and the United States' form of government as it was known at that point.

Due to the video's choppy quality, the lead trainer (Voorhees recalled his name was Trejo) handed out typewritten transcripts of the address, and the young Voorhees read along as he watched:

President: Madam Speaker, Mister Vice President, members of Congress, fellow citizens.

This evening, our union faces a new and grave threat, not in the form of a terror attack or an enemy regime, but a silent, invisible enemy in the form of a virus previously unknown to the global medical community. Intelligence, at home and abroad, indicates that the virus is a naturally-occurring organism, and was not created in a lab, by man, for any purpose.

At this time, major cities in the states of Louisiana, Texas, New Mexico, Arizona, Missouri, Alabama, and Tennessee are under quarantine. Their borders have been closed to civilians and flights to and from these areas have been suspended. International flights to and from the U.S. are on temporary hold. We have news of minor outbreaks in Britain, France and Mexico. It is our duty to contain this threat so that our allies are not affected as we are.

Our allies in the U.N. have pledged to aid us in understanding and combating the pandemic in our homeland. The National Guard has been activated in quarantine areas to maintain order as Homeland Security brings additional aid and relief to those residing in these areas. The federal government is working closely, around the clock, with governors' offices to promote security, to prevent the spread of infection, and to provide care to sick Americans.

Soon, states declared disaster areas will be under full federal supervision with all the support we can provide. To those of you in these affected areas, know that the prayers of this nation are with you. Know that every available resource is on its way to help you in this time of consequence.

Six years ago, on this . . . today, September the 11th, was another day of great consequence. Our nation was struck by a network of evil. We soon had a name for this enemy. Tonight we are up against a faceless, nameless threat, without ideals or conscience. We can only respond with force, in the form of medical technology, strict government oversight, and, where necessary, military order. As before, we must face this enemy head-on, with our allies at our side.

(long pause)

An unyielding commitment to purify our homeland, so that future generations will not . . . not have to fear this unseen enemy.

We must not only for us, or . . . not only face this task with a firm conviction of mind, but of spirit. The god who has blessed all of humanity with . . .

(long pause)

God has, will give those of us—

(coughing)

(President collapses)

(Secret Service agents attend to President; unintelligible murmuring)

Secret Service Agent: Cut the feed. <Expletive> cut it!

(President sits upright)

Secret Service Agent: <Expletive>

Secret Service Agent: Sir.

(Secret Service agents restrain President.)

Secret Service Agent: Don't make me use force, sir. Don't make me hurt you.

Secret Service Agent: <Expletive> bit me!

Secret Service Agent: Do it!

David Dunwoody

(Secret Service agents push President onto desk and respond to his aggression with widowmakers. President's arms and head are severed.)

Secret Service Agent: God. I'm bit, Peter.

Secret Service Agent: The feed, is it still on? Cut it!

Off-Camera Voice: Don't let her in!

Secret Service Agent: No one gets in! Code Green! Get the VP out of there!

Secret Service Agent: He's not the VP.

(feed stops)

At the conclusion of the viewing, the Senior P.O.s were issued widowmakers. The St. John model (some, for reasons unknown, called it "Jessica") was a Chinese cleaver with an extended handle, a titanium blade 225 millimeters long with a thickness of 2 millimeters. Though the government would claim up and down to not have purposely engineered the plague, they had these perfect weapons made to order. Efficient decapitators, like their progenitors the machete and katana, these were meant to disable a rotter at close-combat with a single stroke.

There were boys, the born heroes, who took on two widowmakers and made a new fighting style of it, fusing it with Capoeira, but Voorhees always thought there was little use for the dance against the undead hordes. It looked beautiful, though. Beautiful—an odd sentiment.

At the Holy Covenant Shelter, a new arrival was being checked over by Yeats, the resident doctor. He'd been a paramedic at some point in his youth; without the proper medicine and equipment, his knowledge wasn't really worth much, but it brought peace of mind to the group.

"What's your name again?" he asked the grizzled, muscular man sitting on the cot before him.

"Shipley," came the answer.

"And where are you from?" Reverend Palmer followed up.

"Nebraska."

"What brought you here?"

"I was . . . I was with an Army platoon, you know? They gave the order to start pulling back and, I dunno, I just didn't want to go back."

"Why not?"

"Prison tats." Voorhees' voice startled all three of them. He stood with Oates, who'd just let him in. Lifting the sleeve of Shipley's t-shirt, the P.O. studied the numbers there. "When did you get out?"

"I was drafted while I was still inside, man. Couple years ago." Shipley eyed Voorhees suspiciously. The look was returned tenfold. Yeats and Palmer excused themselves.

"So you deserted, rather than head north with your platoon?" Voorhees scratched the stubble on his chin. "They probably wouldn't have locked you back up. They need soldiers more than inmates." Shipley shrugged, and Voorhees finished, "Maybe you just didn't want to be someplace where it'd be so easy to get caught committing another offense."

Shipley grimaced. "Man, I ain't gonna do anything else wrong. It's just, I still had another seven years on my sentence."

"They didn't commute it when you were drafted?"

"I don't know what that means."

"Right. What were you in for?"

Shipley looked down at his grimy sneakers. Voorhees waited. "Assault. Of a minor."

"You mean sexual assault."

Shipley nodded, almost imperceptibly.

"Just one minor?"

"Just one."

Voorhees sat on the cot and clamped a hand on Shipley's knee. "So, what does it for you? Boys or girls?"

"I haven't even thought of doing it again. I swear."

"Boys or girls?"

". . . She was a girl. She was fourteen. And it was fucking consensual, I don't give a fuck what the court or anyone else says. They weren't there. Okay? I'm not a repeat offender, it wasn't like that. I *loved* her. It wasn't like I just saw some random piece of ass at a bus stop—"

"It's never 'like that,' is it?" Voorhees put on a pitying frown. "It's not like you're a filthy pedophile. Not like you deserted so you could come down here and pick up where you left off. Are you always the victim, Shipley?"

Shipley didn't answer. Inside he was fuming, but he didn't dare lose it with this guy. He'd hacked his way across the badlands of five states to get here and it sure as hell wasn't for any girl.

Across town, in the landfill, Gene wiped a syrupy film from his pale skin. He was secreting fluids, attracting flies and ants; there were ants in his pants, something that briefly struck him with an odd feeling before he forgot all about it. The insects were feasting on his flesh, and though he didn't register any pain he did need to stop them. Gene went into the shack where he'd once lived. Card table, bed, radio, shelf of foodstuffs and chemicals. He fumbled through the shelf's contents while hiking up his pants leg. There were a couple dozen ants teeming on his calf. Ants. Ants. He repeated the sound in his head and studied the cans on the shelf. Ants. Ants. The letters on the cans were all gibberish, lines and loops forming a language he no longer understood.

One of the cans had a cartoonish drawing that resembled the insects eating his leg. He pried the lid from the can, exposing a spray nozzle. The cartoon ant grinned happily at him and he wondered if the stuff inside the can was good or bad for the bugs.

Kneeling stiffly, Gene sprayed his leg up and down. A faint burning sensation accompanied the writhing and falling away of the ants. He followed them along the floor with the spray to make sure they didn't come back. Maybe there were some on his other leg. He sprayed down the front and back of his uniform until the can sputtered and gave out.

Bluebottle flies swarmed around his head. He searched the shelf for a can with flies on it. There wasn't any, but one can had other winged bugs on it. He sprayed it up and down his body. His eyes watered, but he could still see.

Gene walked out of the shack. He thought of something. *Shovel.* He could get at more meat inside a body with the shovel. Where was it? It was supposed to be here. He tried to

(remember)

picture it. In his mind it was laying atop of mountain of garbage. There were lots of those here. Gene clambered up the nearest one.

Reaching the top, he didn't see a shovel. From here, though, he could see the next hill, and there it was.

A sharp crack drew his attention to the boat chugging along the shoreline. A half-second later the bullet tore through his shoulder and he fell.

CHAPTER TWELVE
Duel

Death sat on his steed outside the walls of the city. He sensed with every passing moment the birth of new afterdead; were he able to deal with them in his true element, all their flames would already be long extinguished. But he had to be here, in the living world, and bound by unnatural laws.

Throughout existence the Reaper had silently walked along an endless tunnel, its walls lined with candles, each tiny pinprick of light a soul. When a light died—sometimes when the candle was melted completely, other times when it had barely sprung to life—he marked another passing. Without question or emotion he walked the tunnel. He watched each flame dance and struggle and eventually join the shadows like all the others. There was no warmth from the fire, no texture to the cave floor—there was neither a sensation nor detail without purpose.

That was a long time ago. Time had held no meaning for Death there, but here in the living world every second was like an eternity. The insignificance of days, years and millennia had become startlingly relevant to the specter.

He'd visited this world many times before—mostly in earlier times, when Man still communed with the other side. Though he had no name, he had been given many by those who would presume to know him—Thanatos, Azrael, Yama. He was assigned genders. "He" only thought of himself as a male because that was the most popular conception. It seemed to hold more authority with the living, though females clearly held the key to life. They'd also dreamed up manners of appearance, clothing, and equipment—and when appropriate he did indeed present himself as a winged angel, or a skeleton in a tattered shroud. In many ways, Death realized, he had given himself over to the whims of Man's imagination, perhaps because their ability to imagine fascinated him so.

When the outbreak occurred—when orange flames blinking out were suddenly replaced by undying blue ones—he had assumed a look that was an amalgamation of several mythologies for his journey to this world. Still, he didn't often allow the living to see him. The undead were another story. They saw him always. He had no influence over them—hadn't, at least, until he'd forged a scythe from their bones.

There was one crossing the badlands toward him now, a female with rail-thin legs and a lipless grin. He drew the blade of bone from his cloak.

She knew he was not meat; there was something intrinsic about his offensiveness, about the way her insides burned when she saw him. Patches of scalp dangling over her eyes transformed her face into a glaring, toothless jack-o'-lantern, and she quickened her staggering pace.

He dismounted and walked toward her.

As he raised the scythe, she lurched forward and tore a bloodless gash in his chest.

Death stumbled back, the blade missing its mark, and he barely warded off her second attack. He brought the scythe's handle up against her knee. Bone blistered and fell apart; she clawed at his robes, the slightest touch opening fissures in his being. He swatted her to the ground.

The horse stamped its hooves in the dirt. Glancing back, the Reaper saw wounds like stripes opening along its flank to mirror his own. Sitting up suddenly, the she-zombie buried her fingers in his thigh, pulling out a handful of crumbling clay. Death retreated. She followed.

He feigned a stumble and threw the blade back, under his arm and through the cloak, into her sternum.

She stood impaled on the scythe, watching streams of black ichor wind down her shriveled breasts. Death smoothed the blemishes on his chalk-white body and jerked the blade free.

The she-zombie crumpled without a sound.

She had marred him; nothing that couldn't be restored now, but it was troubling nonetheless whenever he allowed one to get that close. "I still have much to learn," he told the horse, patting its wounds together. They passed through the gates back into the city.

Death rode along a residential street, its houses abandoned and looted, some of them burned-out shells. The steed took him from there into a cemetery. The uneven earth was dotted with burial vaults. For whatever reason—maybe none at all—they'd been looted too.

There were two men standing in the open door of a family vault with GREELEY chiseled into the stone over their heads. He walked the horse around the vault, listening as they spoke.

"I like this guy Shipley for the Midtown Rapist," the balding one said.

The other one, standing in the bald man's shadow, picked lichen from the vault wall and replied, "I met a woman last night. Well, met . . . she was being attacked by her housemate. I shot him."

"I never saw a report," the bald man scolded.

"What's the point?" the young one shot back.

The bald man was ready with a retort. "If it weren't for reports still being filed in other cities, I wouldn't know that we had a serial rapist on our hands."

"I just don't see—"

"We continue doing things by the book. Mike, if there's no

book, what is there? What authority do we have? Might as well throw out our shields too."

"All right, all right."

"Anyhow, what about this woman?"

"She was raped a few months back. Never reported it."

"Jesus, another one . . ."

Death's thoughts drifted. He could see both men's candles in his mind's eye; both were perilously small.

CHAPTER THIRTEEN
Among the Dead

They were howling, reaching for her, clambering up the sides of the stage. Her song turned to a hellish scream and yet Jenna couldn't drop the microphone, couldn't fend off her audience as they tore first at her clothes, then her skin.

She woke up in the backseat of a car. The sun shone directly through the windshield, but she was wracked with shivers.

Lauren and Duncan lay in the front seats. His seat reclined, Duncan's head lolled to the side and his eyes settled on Jenna. "You okay?"

"Fine." She didn't remember screaming herself awake. Maybe it was just the look on her face. Sitting up, she eyed herself in the rearview mirror. She was a picture of misery.

They were in the Liberty Auto lot, in one of the few un-stripped vehicles still sitting out. This one had windows intact and locking doors. That was all that mattered. Lauren idly turned the stereo knobs. "Maybe the keys are still in the office?" She wondered aloud.

"Isn't going to run without wheels, hon," Duncan said.

Lauren narrowed her eyes. "I mean for the radio."

"Does it matter?" Duncan stretched his arms, yawned and studied the streets. They hadn't been followed by the rotter with the dog's-skull, he was pretty sure of that. He'd sat erect through the night, waiting to see it, until finally passing out.

"There could be food inside," Jenna said.

"Doubt it."

"It's still worth a look, isn't it? God, Duncan, if you want we'll go look and you can stay here and play-drive."

He scoffed and threw open his door. "Way to lead, O'Connell."

"Who said I was the leader?"

"You haven't listened to a damn thing I've said. I did the math."

Lauren and Jenna walked together behind Duncan on their way to the sales office. "I know what it means when you talk to a guy like that," Lauren said softly.

Jenna elbowed her in the breast. "Don't start."

Duncan checked for zombies and gave the all-clear. The first thing Jenna saw upon entering was a toppled vending machine, its contents gone. Duncan yanked open a few desk drawers. "Nope, no food here. Anyone need a pen?"

Jenna stared at a banner sagging from the ceiling across the room. WELCOME TO THE LIBERTY FAMILY. She imagined that the Liberty Family wasn't looking well these days.

"I found it!" Lauren cried. "A radio!" She held up a small boombox, then placed it on the nearest desk and pulled on the antenna. The radio signal was faint, like the batteries were on their last legs, but there was a signal. A voice.

"The withdrawal is proceeding on-schedule, even as thousands of civilians join the troops in their move inland. Measures are already in place to provide medical aid and nourishment to everyone who's answered the Senate's call. Seven states with powered and fortified cities are ready to house the American population."

The voice was Senator Gillies of New England. Most of his territory had been wiped out. "Most important of all," Gillies went on, "to answer a question that I'm sure is on every

American's lips—the dead are *not* following us inland. Rather, they are descending upon each coastal city as the living vacate. So it is more prudent than ever that we come together as a people. Your Senate and military have spent months planning this operation, and we assure you that, together, we will succeed."

"Bullshit," Duncan said. He punched the radio's off button. "The zombies aren't following them? What a load of buuuuullsheet."

"So? The zombies are after *everyone*. Might as well hedge our bets with a military convoy," Lauren snapped.

"They're *lying*. Get it? If they're lying about that, they might be lying about everything else." Duncan shook his head at the girl. Her face reddened. "Lauren, ever read about when New York fell? After evacuations failed, they told everyone to gather in hospitals, stadiums. They said everyone would be protected. It's all bullshit. All it takes is for one barricade to slip, for one survivor to get bit and hide it beneath his sleeve. People forget it's a fucking virus that's spreading this. You concentrate the population, all you do is speed infection. Get it?"

"Yeah, I get it. Fuck the establishment, every man for himself. I get it. You're too scared and stupid to put your trust in other people." Lauren turned and stalked into a manager's office.

Jenna said nothing. Sighing, Duncan turned the radio back on.

"Hi," Zaharchuk murmured behind Jenna's ear. She felt the barrel of a gun nudge her neck.

The dealer's face was gaunt and translucent, his hair missing in spots where it had been pulled out. An unlit cigarette dangled between his lips; baggies filled with white rocks were tied around the belt loops of his jeans.

Duncan sat up. Zaharchuk put the gun on him, staying behind Jenna. "So," he said in his lilting voice, "I was just at Fetish. Went to see my friend Syl, ya know?" He sniffed, laughed. "You cut his fucking head off? Why'd you have to do that?"

"No," Duncan said, "It was a rotter—"

Lauren exited the manager's office. Zaharchuk turned the gun on her with a scream. "STAY THERE! EVERYONE STOP MOVING!"

"Okay. No one's moving," Duncan stammered.

"Turn that fucking radio off!" Zaharchuk ordered. Duncan got a good look at the gun; it was a .50 Desert Eagle. Seven in the magazine at best, maybe one in the chamber. Overkill for a dealer in a ghost town, even with the occasional zombie. He was itching to use it, too.

"Z," Duncan said slowly, "Listen. A rotter killed Syl. He was trying to climb outside. Why would we murder him?"

"Why would you leave?" Zaharchuk spat. "I came back and . . . and . . ."

"We didn't know you'd come back," Jenna said. She could see the pistol shaking in the corner of her eye. "We're here now, all right?"

"I don't want to stay with you people," Zaharchuk whispered. He backed toward the door, alternating his aim between Duncan and Lauren. "You killed him, you fed Syl to the zombies. You'll do it to me. No. NO!" He bolted out of the building.

No one moved. They waited, waited for him to reappear and start shooting, for it all to end. He didn't come back.

"We should get going," Jenna said. Duncan nodded in agreement.

Lauren pointed to the manager's office and said, "There's a hall that goes to the rear exit."

"Good idea." Duncan looked at Jenna. "You okay?"

"It wasn't pointed at me," she replied and went into the manager's office.

CHAPTER FOURTEEN
Surf and Turf

"Was that the garbage man I shot?" Patrol Officer Douglas asked, propping his rifle on the bucket seat beside him.

P.O. Hamman shrugged and kicked an empty cooler across the floor. Every flat beer he'd drunk had made him more seasick as they patrolled the Harbor coast, but it was better than being sick and sober. Steadying himself on the boat's railing, Hamman stepped into the pilot cabin and slapped the radio. "Damn thing. I know I heard something about a storm earlier."

"So let's go to shore," Douglas rummaged through their dwindling supply of ammunition. "We can camp on the beach for a few nights."

"I'd rather drop anchor and stay out here," Hamman replied. Every rotter they'd picked off was probably on its feet and walking through the city. In better days, they'd been able to radio the positions of downed zombies to burn teams on the shore; now they were alone. Even Voorhees, it seemed, had forgotten about them. "What if we're the only cops left in town?" Hamman mused.

"Then we can run ashore and steal some more beer," Douglas quipped. He stared down the barrel of his sniper rifle, finger brushing the trigger. Another ounce of pressure and he could send his brains out across the water like chum for fish, the living ones anyway.

Hamman eased his partner's head out of harm's way. "I need to eat something, man."

"We could cast a couple of lines and see if anything's still biting."

"Fuck fish. Dammit." Hamman really didn't want to go ashore, even for an hour. He'd fired two dozen rounds into the city in recent weeks. There were rotters waiting for him, his bullets swimming in their soft guts. When he managed to catch a few hours' sleep he always saw their gray faces crowding around him. He was always helpless to defend himself, or even to run away.

Douglas scanned the city through his rifle scope. "You know, us being stuck out here, with only these guns, we can't kill the rotters."

"I know."

"We could stop there from being more of 'em."

Hamman frowned at Douglas. "Whaddaya mean?"

"I mean, anybody still in the city's gotta be infected. Or will be. Right?"

"I still don't follow."

"Buddy, if *we* got rid of 'em, like now, we could go home."

Hamman was chilled to his core.

Douglas smiled as if he'd just crapped a kitten out on the deck. "We'd be done. We could call off the patrol and get the hell outta here! Think about it!"

"I ain't shooting civilians," Hamman said slowly. "You need to listen to what's coming out of your mouth. Been drinking seawater again?"

"Irrelevant." Douglas scooted another empty cooler out from under his seat and beckoned to Hamman. "Look what I found." He pried open the lid.

Inside lay a severed fish head, ragged pink tissue trailing from its gaping mouth, a mouth that opened and closed as its eye darted back and forth.

"Douglas . . ."

"I think it's funny." Looking up at Hamman, Douglas scowled as if offended. "It's a joke! C'mon! Holy Christ, we're not at a funeral here. You need to loosen up."

"Loosen up?! You were talking about murdering people!"

"They're already dead, they just don't know it." Douglas picked up the fish head. "They're like this guy here. See? And so are we, except we don't want to stay in this town! It's them that's keeping us here!"

"No." Hamman stepped back into the cabin. "If you want to leave, just leave now. Go. I won't tell anybody. I'll take you in to shore and you can just go. You'll leave that goddamn gun here, but you can go."

"We're partners." Douglas tossed the fish head overboard and wiped his hands on his pants. "I'm not gonna leave you behind."

"It's either that or stay with me and shoot rotters."

Douglas seemed to consider the ultimatum. He sat back and gazed over the ocean, watching clouds gather on the horizon. He saw a dorsal fin skimming the surface of the water and grasped his rifle. "Shark? No, dolphin." He pointed and stood up. "You see it, Hamman?"

"Yeah, great." He'd seen enough sea life to last the rest of his own life; the natural beauty of the dolphin's form, knifing through the water, was lost on him. Even before he came to the Harbor to serve as a P.O., he'd been intimately involved with the ocean's denizens. In 2105 he'd been part of an effort in Galveston, Texas to salvage healthy fish and create a hatchery for sustenance. They'd gone out on rickety old fishing boats and dragged their nets through the depths, pulling up huge bounties of fish—most of them undead, rotting horrors. The fish deemed healthy would be plucked from the mess and isolated for observation. If their condition remained unchanged, they'd be tagged as clean specimens and taken to the seawater hatchery a mile down the coastline.

Hamman went out one blustery morning with a skeleton crew of men who dared brave the dark clouds gathering overhead, a promise of storms. The captain, Skinner, sat on the deck with his mangy old cat and barked orders. "Drop the net! Hold 'er steady now! We'll be lucky to meet half our quota today."

Skinner stroked the nappy fur of his constant companion, a red-orange tabby with diseased eyes that raised its nose to the wind, searching for the smell of fish. Skinner spent most of the day restraining the cat from eating scraps of undead fish that littered the deck. The old man knew where his priorities were, didn't he? Hamman couldn't really blame him, though—to have a reliable friend like the cat close by at all times was a rare thing.

The net was brought up by the crewmen—and they staggered back as a thrashing great white tore at the net's seams, eyes rolling over madly, black blood issuing from its slack jaw.

It was undead. Twelve feet long, a series of scarred-over gashes behind its gills, rows of jagged teeth gummed up with the flesh of its prey. The net fell on the deck and the shark flailed violently, freeing itself and sliding toward the men.

Skinner rose, his cat gripped tightly, and turned to run—but his boots slipped on the wet deck and he fell on his ass. The cat sprang from his hands with surprising agility. It landed before the shark, and leapt back. Too late. The shark snapped it out of the air.

The captain let out a yelp. He pulled himself to his feet, screaming incoherently. The cat's lower half fell from the shark's mouth, followed by the rest, as the zombie rejected the meat of another species.

Hamman snatched up a ten-foot boathook and slammed it into the shark's head, trying to split it open, to spill the brain out and disable the thrashing body. Skinner grabbed the handle from him and buried the hook in the animal's eye. "BASTARD!"

Another crewman grabbed the shark's tail, for what reason Hamman didn't know. The tail lashed him against the railing. He bellowed in pain, slumping to the floor.

Skinner shoved the boathook as deep as he could into the shark's head, then fumbled through his rain slicker. He produced an antique revolver. "Step back!"

He fired into the nose and mouth of the half-blinded beast, causing it to roll and thrash even more, gnashing its teeth madly. Skinner ran out of bullets and fell upon the shark, beating it with the gun. Hamman grabbed at his arm, but the captain threw him off and continued his relentless assault, tears of grief and rage streaming down his face.

The boat rocked with the growing waves. A gale had kicked up while the crewmen were busy with the shark. "We've gotta head back to shore!" Hamman yelled. The first mate nodded and ran for the forward cabin.

The shark caught Skinner's forearm and tore it off.

He fell back, staring in shock at the stump gushing blood, painting the shark's head crimson. Hamman dragged Skinner back, not knowing what else to do or how to help the captain, who began waving what was left of his arm and sending gouts of blood over the side of the boat. "I'm dead!" he cried. "I'm dead—oh God—"

The boat lurched as the first mate reversed their course. Skinner fell unconscious in Hamman's arms. The other crewmen deserted them there, leaving Hamman with the dying captain and the undying shark, leaving him to clutch the railing with his bloodied charge under one arm and stare at the fish, which rolled over to stare back at him. Rain started to fall on its back. In its gaze, Hamman saw a quiet calm, an unfeeling regard for the two men, one of whom it had killed. Hamman saw something in that which was almost desirable—*come be dead with us,* the gaze said, *be dead and feel no more. No longer will you crave happiness or companionship or a greater purpose. You will have only one purpose. To eat.*

Join the dead.

Hamman shut his eyes tight, forcing the memory away, and returned to the present. Douglas took aim at the dolphin's dorsal fin. Hamman almost made a move to stop him. Almost. But he saw his partner's eyes glazed over with madness and stayed put.

The rifle bucked in Douglas' hands. A chunk of the fin sailed into the air. "Ha! Nailed the fucker." The fin stayed visible, and he followed it with the scope. "Five will get you twenty that it's undead. I'll bet its head is right . . . about . . . there . . ."

Something knocked against the boat, spilling Douglas onto the floor. He swung around and spotted more fins at his back. "It's a school or pod or whatnot of the fuckers! Get your rifle, Hamman!"

Hamman stayed in the cabin, fiddling with the radio. No signal.

Douglas righted himself and aimed for one of the other dolphins. The boat rocked again. "Dammit!"

Standing straight up, he fired through the floor.

"Douglas!" Hamman left the cabin now, grabbing his partner's wrists, but Douglas fired again and again into the floor. Water spurted over their feet. "What've you done?" Hamman cried.

"I dunno," Douglas stared blankly at the holes he'd made. "Well, why were they bothering us anyhow?"

Hamman spun Douglas to face him and shook him by the shoulders. "They *weren't!* "

Douglas pulled himself away from Hamman and sat back in his bucket seat. "Huh."

He put the barrel in his mouth and pulled the trigger.

Hamman stood and watched Douglas' brain matter spray into the air and then pepper the waters above the heads of the dolphins. One of them poked its head out to look at Hamman, and he saw that most of its snout and the skin around its eyes were gone. A pinkish stream shot out its blowhole, and it sank below the surface.

David Dunwoody

Hamman started the motor and headed to shore. He never saw the wet hands clambering over the boat's rear, never heard the squishing of footsteps entering the cabin, felt nothing at all until teeth sank into his neck.

Gene stumbled back as the boat ran aground. Hamman's corpse fell atop him, still gushing blood, and Gene opened his mouth to catch it.

He sat on the deck for hours, watching the sun crawl across the sky as he chewed. The weakness in his arm, where he'd been shot, went away earlier.

Then he remembered something. Eating until his stomach could hold no more, he climbed off the boat and headed back to the landfill. He would return once he had his shovel.

CHAPTER FIFTEEN
Tea in Hell

Harry, at twenty-four, had been the eldest of Addison's adopted children. Two years his junior, Baron Tetch never wasted an opportunity to remind Harry and his other siblings who the man of the house was. He arranged for tea in the early afternoon, and they all gathered in the sitting room, which looked into a lovely wooded atrium, sun streaming down through its skylight. Harry served them.

Tetch looked around the room to see that they were all holding their cups properly, dressed and groomed neatly for the occasion. Bailey had a spot of dried blood on his cheek. Tetch grimaced. Lily, of course, looked and behaved perfectly. So much easier to train a person than an animal.

And they were animals at best, weren't they? But he'd domesticated them, and easily understood their most primal need, which made for the rule that gave him absolute authority in their cloistered little world: *obey me and you eat.*

Aidan looked questioningly at Tetch. The latter nodded his permission, and Aidan spoke in a garbled, broken voice, as if he did not truly understand the words he was saying.

"Lurvley day."

"Love-ly, Aidan."

"Lo . . . lurvely."

Tetch took a slow sip of chamomile. "Harry, another sugar." The afterdead in his butler's uniform hastened across the room.

"I saw a bird on the fence today," Lily said brightly.

"You didn't touch it, did you?" Tetch replied.

Lily's smile faded slightly but she pressed on. "Of course not. I just looked at it. It was three colors—brown, red and white."

Tetch raised a hand to silence her and leaned forward in his chair. "Ruth, your dress." A brackish stain was spreading across the material covering her legs. The undead looked down and lifted the dress. Tetch gasped, not at the fact she was naked beneath, but at the gaping flayed wounds extended from toe to thigh. "What did you do?" Ruth gave him a vacant stare. Must have been some rudimentary attempt at shaving. But shaving what? She didn't eat near enough to be growing new hair. Sakes alive, she was wearing a wig! "Get out," he growled. "Disgraceful."

As Ruth shuffled past the others, Lily patted her hand. Tetch's glare burned into the little girl's head, but she would not meet his eyes.

"Man," Aidan said, tea dribbling down his chin.

"What, Aidan?"

"Man, at outside. Yurst-day."

"Yes-ter-day, Aidan. It's not worth teaching you to speak if you're going to sound like a mongrel."

"Yes."

"Anyway, what man?" Was it the man Lily had told him about last night? "Outside the fence?"

"Yes."

"He was meat?"

"No," came the answer. But Lily had said the stranger was alive . . . no matter, the child was probably mistaken. "So he was like you, then."

"No."

Tetch sighed. Aidan, the most able of his servants, had seemed worthy of speaking privileges, but he didn't know what he was saying. Just making nonsense sounds to placate the hand that fed him.

"So the man wasn't alive, and he wasn't dead either. Very good."

Lily realized what Aidan was talking about and picked up his end of the conversation. "His eyes were all black. They were pretty."

"I don't want to hear any more talk about this man," Tetch said. "Aidan, you and Uriel walk the grounds tonight, watch the swamp until sunrise. Lily, forget about it. Understood?"

"Yes, I guess."

"Don't give me any crap, young lady."

There was a thud beneath them. Sawbones in the cellar. Tetch took another drink and tried to force the thought of strange dark men from his mind, but it brought memories to the surface.

He was thirteen, Lily's age, when he first came to the house. Dr. Addison was a large, steely-eyed man who always wore his lab coat, and was usually flanked by an equally imposing Great Dane. He usually took dinner by himself in the cellar. None of the children were allowed down there; it was said to house his research on the zombie plague. Whether or not that meant there were rotters in the basement, Tetch had never dared ask.

One morning he'd gone upstairs and into Addison's study. The doctor was there, turned away from the door, a box on his desk. As Tetch silently watched Addison had poured a cup of dead flies into the box. A moment later, they filled the air around the doctor's head.

He saw Tetch, saw accusatory eyes. "Baron!" He thundered across the floor. The boy scarcely made it out the door before a hand clapped down on the back of his head, then all was dark.

His eyes opened to a sea of garish crimson light. Head throbbing, limbs paralyzed, he tried to orient himself. Was he lying on his back? The room had no definition, no depth. It was all red. It was hot. He opened his mouth and a tiny croak escaped.

A huge, angular head with colorless eyes lurched into view. Tetch wet himself at the sight.

At the time he was certain that it was the Devil, and at that point he believed he understood what had happened and where he was. Yet he had no strength, no breath, to scream. He could only shake his head from side to side until he lost consciousness.

The next time his eyes opened, he was lying in his own bed, Addison holding his wrist and glancing at a pocket watch in his other hand. He felt thick gauze around his crown. "What happened?"

"You fell down the stairs. Don't you remember?" Addison's tone was dispassionate. "Before I had a chance to explain what you saw in my study—which you wouldn't have seen at all, had you observed the house rules—you practically threw yourself down the staircase. You were actually dead for a time before I managed to revive you."

The mind of thirteen-year-old Tetch was gripped by terror: it *had* been Hell, after all. But why would he be so condemned? Because he was disobedient? Addison stayed at his bedside for a time and lectured him about interrupting important work in forbidden rooms. Tetch resolved to stay out of the doctor's way from that day forward.

Two years later, after he'd murdered Addison, Tetch would discover that the garishly lit "Hell" was the cellar, and the head he'd seen looming over him but a crude mask carved from wood. He suspected he hadn't been the only child put through that nightmarish routine. The only one, in fact, who probably never saw Addison's "Hell" was young Lily. And now she was a naughty girl.

Nightfall found Lily slipping down dark corridors in her nightgown, whisper-quiet, bounding down the stairs and out the front door.

Uriel was at the gates with an axe. Keeping to the shadows, Lily stole around the corner of the house. She darted through the grass to the ivy-wrapped fence and peered into the swamp's inky blackness.

There he was, as she'd known he would be; the man in black came forward with a beautiful white horse. He stood silent as the horse bowed its head, and Lily reached through the fence to stroke its muzzle.

"Why aren't you afraid of the dead?" the man finally asked.

"Baron makes them be nice," she answered. The horse had black eyes just like its owner. "He won't let them eat if they do bad things. Like one time Bailey bit me, and Baron put a rope around him and tied him to the fence and he had to stay there all week."

"You were bit . . . ?" The man in black knelt and she held out her hand. There was a faint white scar below the thumb. "Didn't you get sick?"

"No. They aren't like the other dead people."

"How?"

Lily shrugged. The man in black studied her hand and her face. He touched her fingers with his, briefly; though his skin was icy cold, Lily felt warm in her chest and she couldn't help smiling at him.

"Do you like it here?" he asked. She nodded quickly. "Then tell me why you cut your wrists," he said. She stared at the ground.

"I'll come back later." The man climbed onto his steed. Lily wanted to ask him if she could ride the horse, just around the house a little, but she knew he'd say no. Despite that, she looked forward to his next visit.

CHAPTER SIXTEEN
Safer?

"Yeah. You'll be safer with me, at my place."

"I appreciate it Mike, really. But—"

"Cheryl, I understand why it's hard for you to trust me—or anyone for that matter. I really do. And my saying that probably isn't going to ease any tension either, but the simple fact is that if you stay alone in this apartment, you run the risk of being cornered by rotters, looters—maybe friends of your cousin."

"Lee didn't have friends. He didn't even go outside."

"But he had a dealer . . ."

"Yes."

"Look, I've been sleeping on the floor in my living room. You can have the bedroom, I'll help you move your things in there. And I've installed new locks on all the doors. Nabbed 'em from the hardware store. No one can get into the apartment if I don't want them to. No one will be able to get into your room if you don't want them to."

"It's not so much about trust, Mike. It's just . . . I don't know. Lee's dead. I've been staying with him since I lost my brother, and I don't even remember how long ago that was. My brother controlled me too—he wasn't mean though, he had the best of intentions—but still I couldn't make a move without him. Then Lee. Nothing I did was right in his eyes, even if it was his own damn idea. I just want to run my own life for a change."

"Makes sense."

"But?"

"But safety in numbers still applies. And I broke your lock when I kicked the door in."

"Nice."

"You're right though. It's your choice. I'm just putting the offer out there. Okay?"

Mike pulled a pistol out and handed it to her. "I assume you know how to use this."

"I do." Cheryl was still reluctant to take it.

"The least I can do," he said.

"I'll think about it, okay?" She smiled. Mike doubted that, but he smiled back and left.

Meanwhile, the guests staying at the Holy Covenant Community shelter had already worn out their welcome. Oates threw open every cupboard in the kitchen and swore. "When did we run out of everything??"

"There are too many of us here," Reverend Palmer said, leaning against the sink as she filled a pitcher with water. "But I'm not going to ask anyone to leave. I've got no right to decide that one life is worth more or less than another."

"Then let me do it." Wheeler stood in the doorway. "That ex-con can go first."

"Shut up, Wheeler."

"You heard him talking to the cop. He's a pervert! None of us know him anyway."

"I barely know your ass," Oates barked, "and I hate you more."

"I'm not leaving," Wheeler said firmly. "I was here 'fore the troops cut and run off. But like the Rev said there's too many damn people here now. You know more are on the way, Oates—and I'm not giving this place up just because she can't say no!"

"This is my shelter," Palmer said, her voice barely above a growl. "If you don't like the way I run it, too bad."

"You're running it into the fuckin' ground."

"Then save yourself, Wheeler."

"I ain't the one leaving!" He stamped his feet like an obstinate child. "You leave, Palmer! Go somewhere where there are still resources to be wasted on goddamn charity! These are the fuckin' badlands, sister! Those soldiers left us high and dry!"

"Then. Save. Yourself."

Oates stepped between the two of them. Though neither had made a move toward the other, threats burned in both their eyes. Oates had never seen Palmer like this. She was fed up with Wheeler's bullshit, and so was he. "Take a walk," he told Wheeler. The other man snorted in his direction. Oates stood his ground. Wheeler finally groaned and left the doorway.

"Thanks." Palmer set the full pitcher on the counter. Her hands trembled. "What do you think, Oates? Should we leave the Harbor?"

"Hell no."

"He may be a bastard, but he's right about one thing. No matter how many people we have in the shelter, be it ten or two—it won't be long until the city's got no resources left. We're fighting a losing battle."

"Well, Reverend," Oates replied, his voice shaking as much as her hands, "I don't think nothing's gonna change that."

He picked at a splinter on one of the boards covering the kitchen window. "This is the end after all, ain't it?"

Funny, the reverend didn't think about it too much. When Palmer was born there had already been zombies walking the earth. If this plague was the end, *the* end, then it was taking its sweet time.

A young woman named London poked her head into the room. "Can I grab that water from you?"

"Of course. Sorry." Palmer handed over the pitcher. Oates rapped his knuckles on the boards.

"No, I don't imagine I'm gonna find a better place to die than this."

"So you say stay put?"

"That's what I say."

"All right then."

On the other side of the boards, standing outside the broken window, Aidan listened. The words that he recognized wormed into his brain, the rest quickly faded from memory.

He straightened his necktie and walked off down the street at a measured, almost-human pace.

CHAPTER SEVENTEEN
Clown

It pulled itself through an opening in the west wall, jagged bits of fencing flaying open its back, and staggered onto an empty street. Most of its colorful costume still clung to the body, pasted there by grime and by fluids seeping through bloated skin.

The clown stood in the street and looked from side to side. Its red rubber nose was distracting; the clown pulled the nose off and felt most of what was underneath come away with it.

Painted lips were turning gray and falling off as the clown idly chewed through them. The white grease paint covering its face was hardly whiter than the skin beneath; an orange wig crawling with maggots was stuck to its bald head. Kid gloves stained brown with old blood. Oversized shoes filled now with pus and rot that squeezed out over the laces with each heavy step.

It was a good eighty years dead, and still wearing its old getup. The clown's odd appearance seemed to give it a peculiar advantage with the meat. The young meat. The clown stood in the street and looked for food.

Someone was coming now, but he wasn't alive. The clean man in his nice suit gave nary a look to the other zombie as he passed. The clown thought of following him, but a few seconds passed and he couldn't recall what he would be following, and where.

The clown walked down the street. Innards sloshed within its distended belly. A maggot squirming in the rotter's navel dropped past urine-soaked trousers to the ground and was pulverized by a red size 15.

Time passed; the zombie felt what might be a fracture grinding inside one of its legs. Then it heard a voice and stopped. The voice was coming from a nearby building.

Inside that building, inside the homeless shelter, a young woman sat with her son. Kipp had been Wendy's foster child for a decade, and any boundaries created by their legally-defined relationship had been forgotten in short order. Kipp was desperate, not for someone to love him, but for someone he could love. Every day his eyes were alight with what seemed an endless affection. He was sixteen now, probably half that age in an emotional sense—Wendy wasn't qualified to make a diagnosis but she'd known from the beginning he was handicapped.

He was peering through the paper-thin space between slats in a boarded-up window. Wendy sat on a nearby cot fixing one of his worn sneakers.

"The circus!" he said softly, breathlessly. Wendy looked up and he smiled at her. Climbing down from his perch atop a broken radiator, he padded across the community room in his socks.

"Kipp!" Wendy called. "Don't go anywhere we haven't talked about. Especially without your shoes."

He nodded and continued out of the room. London followed Wendy's loving gaze. "He's a sweet boy."

"Yes, he is."

"What did you do before you ended up here?" London asked.

"I was—am—a social worker. I work with a lot of children like Kipp. He's actually helped me a lot with that—he always sees the brighter side."

"I think they've got it better than we do," London said, then blushed. "Sorry, that must've sounded awful."

"No, no, I think you're right," Wendy replied, "and we could probably stand to learn a thing or two."

At the shelter's front entrance, Kipp quietly moved the barricade back.

The clown stood out front now, listening intently. Its gloved hands tightened into hungry fists. A young boy's laugh floated through the door.

The door cracked ever so slightly and the boy peered out. The clown stood still, waiting to see what would happen.

Opening the door just enough to get his skinny body through, the boy came out, stood and smiled broadly. He was waiting too.

The clown opened its mouth. Its painted smile split like a wound to reveal the remnants of decayed teeth. It reached for him.

The boy screamed. He threw himself at the door, not thinking to try and squeeze through the space he'd made, his frail body useless against the barricade. The clown fumbled at his shoulders. Its hands were broken and numb. Carefully, it stooped so that it could reach the boy with its open mouth.

A woman's hand thrust out and slapped at him. "Kipp!" the woman shrieked. The boy grabbed her arm, sobbing, and buried his face against the door. Other voices now. The clown was desperate. It grabbed a mouthful of the child's hair between its teeth and pulled back.

A man thrust a metal spike out, some length of pipe, spearing the clown's eye and sending the rotter stumbling back. The same man tore the door all the way open and grabbed the boy. The clown struggled with the pipe. It couldn't see straight, couldn't steady itself. Feeling was leaving its legs. It twisted the pipe around inside its brain and moaned.

Wendy seized Kipp from Shipley's arms, backing away from

the door. The others crowded in to restore the barricade. Shipley stood silent, watching the child and his mother.

"Wait!" came a cry from outside.

"What the fuck?" Wheeler snapped.

Oates shoved him aside and pried the door back. "Hey!"

There were three people—two women and a man—running across the street from Liberty Auto. The clown spun around and lunged at them. The blonde caved the rotter's face in with a brick.

Against Wheeler's mad protests, Oates opened the door wide and waved them over. The clown lay on its back, fists clenched. Watery discharge pooled around its shattered skull, the pipe sputtered dark chunks—still the thing lived.

Oates slammed the door behind the newcomers.

Far from the writhing clown, far from Jefferson Harbor's last pocket of humanity, Baron Tetch listened to Aidan's slurred words and nodded. "All right, I understand. Go downstairs."

Uriel was at the study door. Tetch pointed at him. "Do you remember how to use the rifle?"

The afterdead responded with a blank stare. Sighing, Tetch rose from his desk. "Let me show you again."

It was time to take the city.

CHAPTER EIGHTEEN
Mouths to Feed

Mike's radio, strapped to his belt, squawked as he was helping Cheryl carry a few boxes up to his apartment. He'd scarcely returned home and locked his door when he heard her knock. Setting the box in his arms on the living room floor, Mike spoke into the radio. "Come back?"

"Weisman. What's your twenty?"

"I'm home."

"Good. Grab something flammable. I've got a—wait for it—a damn clown thrashing around outside Holy Covenant. Need some help torching him."

Mike acknowledged the request and went to peer beneath his sink. "I've got to leave you here for just a few minutes, Cheryl. You gonna be okay?"

"I should be." She eyed the eight locks installed in the door and smiled wryly.

Laughing, Mike grabbed a bottle from under the sink. "Go ahead and get settled in the bedroom. I've got the only set of keys so don't go and get yourself locked out. I'll make you some copies at the hardware store in a little bit."

"Mike?"

"Yeah."

106

"Thanks."

She touched his hand timidly, a sign of gratitude, reaching outside a claustrophobic, barely-existent comfort zone to make contact. He nodded and headed out the door.

When Mike arrived at the shelter, the front doors were open and Reverend Palmer was arguing with one of the bums, Wheeler. Voorhees stood nearby, gun in hand, watching the streets.

Mike ignored the confrontation and emptied his bottle's contents onto the ridiculous zombie lying there. It swiped blindly at his feet, to which he responded by coolly crushing its fingers under his boot.

"You got a light?" he asked Voorhees. The bald man nodded and fished through his trench coat for his matches.

"Three more?" Wheeler bellowed. "You just let them walk right on in here after what happened?!"

"They stopped the damn rotter, Wheeler!"

"That retarded kid is the reason the rotter was a problem in the first place! Too many strangers running around this god-damn place!"

"All right, Mister Wheeler," Voorhees said. "We've heard enough."

"You can't tell me what to say or do! You can't push me around because I'm homeless! We're *all* homeless! I don't care where you're squatting or how long you've been there, it's not your place! Never will be! This isn't even a city anymore!"

"You want to bring more of them?" Mike snapped, pointing to the clown. Voorhees struck a match and held it over the moving corpse. "If that's what you want to do, Wheeler, just keep throwing your tantrum."

It was like he didn't even hear them. "Don't burn that here!" Wheeler cried. "Not right in front of the fuckin' building!"

Voorhees dropped the flame. The clown was instantly bathed in fire, still kicking, still trying to grab something warm and alive.

Voorhees pushed Wheeler into the shelter. Mike followed and helped Oates restore the barricade. "What's this about three more?"

"Survivors." Oates pointed into the community room where the trio was sitting.

Mike squinted at the blonde. "Is that . . ."

"Jenna O'Connell, in the flesh." Oates grinned. "She is something, isn't she? Even all roughed up like that."

Mike murmured something and surveyed the rest of the community room. "Where's our friend Shipley?"

"Dunno. He saved that slow kid, though," Oates replied.

"I want to talk to him."

Voorhees already had Shipley cornered in the restroom. He'd found the ex-con zipping up at the urinal. "That thing even work?" the P.O. asked.

Shipley shrugged. "Who cares?"

"You know, Shipley, the police station's in decent shape. Rotters can't get in. No one can. I've even got some food down there, if you care for coffee beans."

"Not interested. I'm not gonna let you lock me in a cell."

"I'm not giving you a choice." Voorhees produced a pair of handcuffs. His other hand was on his gun. His grim smile was dark from eating coffee.

"I don't have enough room at the station for all these people," he continued, "but I do have a room just for you. It'll be better for everyone. No harm will come to you."

Under any other circumstance, Shipley would have given up. But now he didn't. "I can't leave here."

"Why, pray tell, is that?"

"That kid . . ."

In the community room, Wendy stroked Kipp's hair and kissed his forehead. "I'm so sorry. It's my fault." He shook his head in the crook of her neck. "It was my fault, Mom."

"No. It's never your fault. You don't . . ." Her voice trailed off. She sat up slightly and brushed back the hair on Kipp's scalp. She saw the bite.

Not far away, Isabella was staring out the window. "Hey," she said, "I think I see another one out there. Hey, Voorhees!"

The boards over the window exploded, throwing splinters into Isabella's eyes, and before the pain could even set in, before she could make sense of what was happening, a gray claw tore through the opening and gripped her by the jaw.

Fingers stabbed down her throat and she bit into them. Her jaw was torn away with a wet crunch. Wendy screamed; Oates uttered something that was both profanity and prayer, and Mike Weisman yanked out his pistol and chased it as it clattered across the floor.

Hands, several of them, grabbed Isabella's tongue and hair and shoulders and dragged her out the window.

Oates ran to the front door and threw himself against the barricade. A half-second later, a rifle blast tore through the door and threw him into the opposite wall.

Mike gaped at the smoking hole in the door. A rotter crouched to stare back at him.

"Christ," Mike breathed, and around him, every covered window in the community room warped and groaned under the weight of a single, unified assault.

SECOND STRIKE
Hand of God

Dalton lay prone on the ground, supported only by his elbows, peering through the scope of his sniper rifle at the city gates. He'd glued a mess of leaves and dirt onto his blanket and used it now for cover. It hung over his head and stretched all the way to his heels; it smelled like years-old body odor, almost like decay, but he'd become used to the scent and put it out of his mind. He was just another hump in the badlands. Stock-still, he peered through that scope, which he cleaned and calibrated twice every day. He stared at the gates. At the corpse of a female.

He'd seen a rider, on a white horse, approaching the female. She'd been undead. Dalton hadn't seen a horse in decades and was fascinated by the creature's gait as it came upon the lone rotter, a skeletal figure on her last legs. The horse's rider had dismounted and produced, from out of nowhere, a scythe. The female fell upon him; he threw her back, drove the blade through her body and . . .

. . . And she died.

Returned to the dust, just like that.

He'd seen one of the Horsemen. He knew it. Dalton moved his eye away from the scope and thumbed through his pocket Bible in the dirt. King James, Book of Revelation. Had it been a white horse, or a *pale* horse? He chewed his fingernails and exhaled, scattering fragments of leaves. No, it hadn't been a proud, shining white steed, but a chalky, ghoulish thing, and its rider had been clothed in dark rags. It had been a pale horse, and its rider was Death.

"And Hell followed with him," declared the Holy Book.

Dalton shifted slightly. He'd been at this post since dawn. Hadn't had a drink of water or a piss. Needed neither. Logic told him to question himself: *seeing things, Neville? A horse, for Christ's sake? Out here? When was the last time you saw a horse?* There'd been wild horses in the Northwest, when he was doing sniper training. They were infected and Dalton's instructor had used them as targets. "See that one, Neville, the paint running up the slope? Take its head off just when it crests the hill. They'd only shoot the poor sick bastards if they were back at the stable, so you may as well shoot them out here." And he did.

In the back corner of his mind Dalton registered someone shuffling toward him. Logan. It was a good thing the horizon was clear right now, or he'd fire a warning shot at the soldier for disturbing his cover.

"Why don't we run out to the coast and get a tan as long as we're here?" Logan whined, playing with his sidearm. "Not like we'll ever be back again. We're a half-day from the ocean and we have to sit here and stare at walls. I see you've got your book out, Dalton—God wants us to enjoy the world He's made, not eat dirt."

"We have a duty," Dalton replied. He rose from his post, shaking excess dirt from the blanket. He needed to clean his rifle again. Recalibrate the scope. "You think this world's made to be enjoyed? We're working, Brother Logan. We're toiling in the shit that Man's made of creation, and we're gonna wipe it clean. That's when you can enjoy it. After the baptism."

"You mean the 'baptism of fire'?"

"We're bringing the fire, Logan."

"You sound like the Sarge, all parables and prayers," Logan

said. "I believe in the Lord as much as the next guy but I don't believe in suffering day and night. I know eternal peace is still out there waiting for us, but that doesn't mean we can't kick back here once in a while. What's wrong with a little pleasure? Say Dalton, you're a dog guy, right?"

Dalton smiled, a rarity. He was already digging through his back pockets for photos of his boys—Rottweiler puppies he'd left in Gaylen, a city just southeast of Chicago. Once the withdrawal was complete and he was stationed permanently in Gaylen, he wanted to train the dogs to run local patrols. Between the inner and outer gates of America's safe zone, there would be quarantine areas that would need to be policed. That's where Dalton wanted to be: somewhere between the living and the dead.

"I hear gunshots," Logan said. He looked toward Jefferson Harbor.

Dalton heard them too. "I think it's just civvies fighting over scraps. What do they stay for?"

"Some notion of freedom, I guess," Logan spat and propped his rifle against his leg. "I wouldn't tell most people this, but . . . well, you know I came down from Canada before they closed the border, issued the shoot-to-kill edict and all that. I had dual citizenship. I wanted to fight and in the end I decided to go along with the American military. Seemed like they had a handle on things. Anyway, I was set to leave Toronto, and I was in a filthy old hotel in a semi-secure zone with a bunch of guys who had applied for American citizenship by way of joining the Army, you know, when we were really hard up for troops. So this hotel, with no electricity or water, was a steamy hell-hole. If a window couldn't be opened it was busted out. The mattresses were all soiled and the carpets were growing mushrooms, swear to the Lord. It was damp and disgusting and hot as hell but we had to stay there so we could be registered and get across the border. So picture nineteen-year-old Logan pacing around this nightmare tower, stewing with a thousand other men who hadn't seen a shower in weeks. God, we'd go to the roof and pray for rain. We'd stomp and kick and scream. If the wind even picked up a little bit, guys would get excited. They'd start tearing off their clothes, the only clothes they had, praying for thunderclouds. I was there for a week and we did get one good thunderstorm—you should have seen them naked in the streets. It was insane. But that's not the story. The story is, one day, a couple of days after that long-awaited shower, I was sitting in my t-shirt and pants in a hall and this ratty-haired guy next to me asks, 'You a Christian?'

"'Yeah, I guess.'

"'You're a young kid. What? Eighteen, nineteen, twenty? Jesus boy, you've probably never played a game of ball or touched a girl in your life, have ya? You've had to run from town to town with this fuckin' plague hangin' over your head, sayin' your prayers every morning and night and wallowin' in this piss-filled ass of a world.'

"That's exactly what the guy said, and all the while he was clutching a crucifix to his chest. It was on a chain around his neck and with every sentence he'd close his fist around that crucifix and pound his chest. *Hard.* This ratty-haired guy sitting in the hall of a steamy, nasty hotel pounding on his chest, with guys stepping over him hollering about a thousand other things, had me mesmerized because of the way he was preaching. I know the words he said don't sound like preaching, but it was in the way he said it. He had fire in his eyes. He said, 'Kids like you are the ones who have to get out there and fight this war for Christ, and you ain't never been able to live a regular day in your life! You ain't been made a man! See, that's what I'm getting at, Christian—if you're gonna go out there and do God's good work you have to be a man. You have to have known a woman. You see?'

"So this guy took my hand and tugged me down the hall, past all the other would-be Americans, into a dark stairwell where it was still raining a bit. We went down, down, down, into the basement of this hotel, where the rainwater was draining into the sewer and electric torches hung from the walls. 'Down here,' said the guy, 'there's a girl who'll make you a man. Get it? No questions asked, you just walk outta here a man with a real fire in ya. It's the true way.' And he was pounding his fist against his chest and that crucifix was biting into his palm.

"There was a room down there, with a couple of guys who were smoking some kind of hash guarding it, and they let the ratty-haired guy through with me. So picture me, little Logan standing there, trying not to puke because the sewers are looooooong backed-up and the air's thick with the smell of men and shit and hash, and I'm led into a room where there's a single candle on a stool and the most beautiful woman I have ever seen is lying on a mattress.

"And she was. She was painted up like a model, reclining on that mattress with a full head of blonde hair and taut legs splayed. She looked right at me with baby blue eyes, and she smiled wide—and there really was a second there, a picture-perfect second when I hadn't realized she was undead, that I thought I was about to lose my virginity to an angel.

"There really was a second when I didn't notice the mismatched dentures or the wig or the layers upon layers of makeup, when I didn't notice that they had taken out the real, lifeless eyes and replaced them with glass ones that sat cold in the socket. She had full, beautiful breasts and hands grasping in the air. They drew me to her. I almost let her pull me in . . . until I realized she was just hungry.

"'Go ahead!' encouraged the ratty-haired man, pounding with his crucifix. 'She's chained up! She's not a woman anymore. She's not human! That's a dead, soulless thing—it's not rape, young Christian. Now you make yourself a man and sow the Lord's seed! As an affront to the Devil himself—'"

Dalton interjected in a slow, calm tone. "Why," he asked, "did you choose me for this?"

Logan rapped his knuckles against the steel toe of his boot. "I figured you wouldn't tell anybody else."

"What's the point of telling me?"

"I had to tell somebody. You *know* people do it. You know once the withdrawal's done and over with, when we're all in the safe zone, there'll be people there who will still want it."

"You fucked a zombie, Logan."

"Fuck you, Dalton, I didn't! I never said that. I got the hell out of there."

"Did you?"

Logan didn't say anything. Dalton peered through his scope at the city gates. Did his comrade really believe for a second that he'd found God in the basement of that madhouse in Toronto? Was he seeking some sort of affirmation from a man who'd looked upon one of the horsemen of the apocalypse?

When Dalton glanced back up, Logan was gone.

BEFORE THE EMPIRE
Tour Diary

March 17, 2112

Jenna here. Caylen says it's St. Patrick's Day. Never heard of it.

Caylen's cool. She was brought on as lead guitar, but put any instrument in her hands and she's a prodigy. I wouldn't be able to stand it if she wasn't so modest. She said she's a fan and playing with us is a "blessing." I told her playing at all is a blessing. I don't know if I meant it.

I haven't been able to write shit the past few months. Scratch that, the past year. The more I think about the last album (and cringe), the more I'm glad that it was only released on a few thousand cassettes or whatever Ben said it was. I don't want to write about zombies, but I don't want to *not* write about zombies, you know? I don't want the effort to be so conspicuous as to seem disingenuous.

I guess anything that isn't about zombies is disingenuous. That's all we are anymore.

We're in Denver right now. Ben says for us to watch ourselves around the soldiers, like he always does, but the fact of the matter is not a single one has made a move. I honestly wouldn't mind getting laid and "supporting the troops" a little, but either these guys have been threatened by their sergeants

116

or they're all just too numb, even for something as meaningless as getting off.

(In case anybody ever finds this, I'm not usually such a cold bitch. Can you blame me though? I also haven't had sex in two years.)

I've thought of maybe coming on to a soldier after a set, but I don't know. It'd be nice. It would. I just don't want what may be my last time to be . . . like that.

Two years ago it was Ben's brother. Derek, gorgeous. He understood what I needed and he needed the same thing. It hasn't been the same without him. It's never the same, day to day, is it, because we're always losing somebody.

Lyric:

We're always losing somebody
We're always needing some body

No, doesn't work, I don't want to write about sex, I need to get sex off my mind. It wouldn't change anything, would it? Not really.

Mark Duncan, this freelance writer-photographer, is following the tour. Maybe he's hoping some rotters will descend on the stage some night and tear us apart (God, that nightmare again) so he can write it up. He's a smug prick. I hate seeing him snapping photos when we perform. Who the hell is he snapping them for, anyway? Who gives a damn, other than the people who are here, with us, hearing the music?

Maybe it's not even about hearing the music, it's just about seeing us. I don't mean seeing US like we're goddesses, I mean seeing a band playing on a stage with the lights and the hands reaching toward the singer while she belts out a tune. There's something dreamlike about it, something unreal. For the troops, the scene is a nice departure from reality. I guess that might work for someone staring at a picture. I don't know how it could. It barely does anything for me to be the singer belting out tunes.

We go on in a couple of hours. I've got to get my hair and shit done. Later.

March 20, 2112

Ben's dead. It all happened so fast . . . I woke up to the sound of gunfire. It was already over before I got there.

The door of Ben's trailer was hanging open, and soldiers were blasting away at a rotter on the ground. They didn't stop until it was nothing but smoldering bits. I could only stand there while they shot it. There was blood all over the inside of the trailer door and I wanted to run in there, but something told me that if any of the troops sensed me running at them in their peripheral vision, they'd turn the guns on me. So I just stood there and stared at the blood.

The soldiers kicked the rotter's remains, scattering them. A sergeant started yelling about they needed to gather it back up so they could burn it all. Ben's door just swayed in the wind. No one was looking inside. I knew he was gone. I just had to see. I'll regret that for the rest of my life.

The way he was splayed out over his bed, eyes wide open in surprise. There were drops of blood on his eyes. I wanted to wipe them away, telling him to hold still, not to blink, I'd get it, he'd be okay but some grunt screaming, "Don't touch it!" dragged me back outside.

It.

I'm in my trailer now. Lauren's crying. She wants to comfort me, I don't know why. I'm not holding back any tears. I don't feel anything. I guess that's how I protect myself. You'd think that being so self-aware like that would enable me to break down and cry like a little girl, but no, and it's not that I won't . . . I can't. I think I've just smothered that part of myself.

Caylen's here. I'm not looking up at her. I'm just writing. Writing, writing, writing writing finally she went over to Lauren.

She just said Mark Duncan's taking pictures.

Fuck him. FUCK YOU.

March 21, 2112

Caylen thinks we should continue the tour. I guess we'll just leave Ben's memory in Denver and keep on truckin'. You know, for the troops. And of course for ourselves. Yeah, let the healing begin. We'll sing the songs that Ben co-wrote, and wave at the soldiers who let him die, and Duncan can snap pics with a camera that has photos of Ben's corpse in it. Here's Ben lying on the bed with his throat ripped out, here's Ben being carted out of the trailer by soldiers in hazmat suits, and here's his funeral pyre where he burns along with the remains of his murderer.

They burned the trailer too, after they looted it.

I want to write a song about it, about their callousness. I want to perform it in the next city and watch the troops applaud and holler while I tell them what pieces of shit they are.

We're always losing somebody
Why should we mourn for anybody

(Use something about fire, fire as a cleansing force but in this case the stain or ashes or something remains)

When I woke up this morning, Lauren was in my bed. She was shivering like she'd just come in from the cold. It was pathetic, not in a mean way. Just sad. It was like she wanted that sadness to rub off on me. Sorry, but why would I *want* to feel right now?

Derek had died a lot like Ben did. It was in Vegas. He left my place while he was drunk, stumbled downstairs as I slept. They found his feet (still in their shoes) and hands (still in their gloves) just outside the city walls. The P.O.s who retrieved his extremities told me that, based on the blood spray, he'd probably been unconscious when the rotters attacked, his heart still pumping. Just never woke up. Yanked apart.

I don't know why he went out there, but I know it was on purpose.

We're always losing somebody
Why should we mourn for anybody
Why should we finally feel
And open wounds that never heal

I'll tell Caylen later that, yes, we should continue the tour. Not for the troops, nor ourselves, but for Ben. I guess it's the least we can do.

March 28, 2112

We passed right through Oklahoma City. Most of the troops had already pulled out. Signed a few autographs at the checkpoints.

I'm completely numb right now, and maybe I have been this entire time; it seems like I only really feel when I'm angry or depressed, and who wants to feel then? I guess I'll just keep getting up on stage and going through the (e)motions, if only for the others. I don't think I'll be continuing this journal, though. Jen out.

CHAPTER NINETEEN
Kipp

"How are there so many?" Miss Palmer was asking the bald cop, but before he could answer Miss Palmer ran over to Kipp and his mom and took each by the hand.

It felt and sounded like they were caught up in a river's raging current, dragged helplessly along.. Kipp briefly felt weightless as he was pulled across the community room and he imagined being sucked down beneath the water's roiling surface. Perhaps into the waiting arms of a hundred, a thousand dead men, all with blood-red painted smiles.

Wendy glanced back at him as the two of them were pulled along. She saw him looking at the wet stains near his crotch, saw him fighting to speak, but interrupted him. "It's okay it's okay it's okay," she said breathlessly. Her grip was tight on his shoulder. Miss Palmer's fingers were interlaced with his. Miss Palmer opened a small door and pushed Kipp and his mom inside.

"The chapel," Miss Palmer said. She stepped back and shut the door behind them and darkness flooded the room. Kipp screamed.

Hands slapped the walls; his mom's hands. She found a

switch and soft lights powered by a generator flickered on overhead.

Kipp turned to look around the room while Wendy ran to the door to see if it had a lock. It didn't.

The chapel had four rows of long wooden seats. The walls were wood-paneled, floors swept clean; Kipp felt oddly detached from the rest of the shelter. He thought it might be a secret room. Then, as his eyes adjusted, he saw the effigy: the dead man nailed to a crossbeam, his face sallow and streaked with blood.

Kipp threw himself gibbering into Wendy's arms. She pulled him down behind a pew and tried to calm him, but he wasn't hearing her words anymore as she assured him that the dead man in the chapel wasn't supposed to be like the things outside, that He wasn't really there.

And He wasn't, was He?

She had taught Kipp prayer, but Wendy herself didn't keep the habit up enough to set any kind of example. She didn't think much about God anymore. It wasn't that she questioned how God could let bad things happen to good people; she accepted that He did so and hated Him for it.

Wendy crossed the aisle and pushed one of the pews in front of the door. The reverend had whispered as she pushed them into the chapel, "Don't open it for anyone." Through the wall she could hear the others arguing and pounding, trying to drive back the attack.

Kipp drew himself into a ball. Kneeling beside him, Wendy gently pried his hands from over his eyes. "Honey, we're safe in here, I promise. But I need you to get up, okay?" She motioned to the front, to the crucifix. "We need to move up there so we can push these seats against the door."

He shook his head with a whimper. She took his hands and pulled. He resisted, his body—and fear—stronger than hers.

Something thudded against the chapel door. Kipp jerked away and buried his head in his arms.

"Open up! C'mon!!" It was the ex-con. The door rattled in its frame but held; Wendy grabbed another pew and dragged it across the floor. "Please help me, Kipp!"

Staring into the dark shelter he'd created with his legs and arms, Kipp ignored her and tried to wish himself away from this place, back to happier times, back, back . . . he barely remembered life before Wendy, whom he'd come to know as his mother. He had a few snatches of memory, of sitting in a dark room with a man and an older girl, of a big city. Those didn't seem like happier times. He only wanted to be with Wendy and no one else.

In the community room, Shipley hammered frantically. Most of the windows had been cleared of boards, but thankfully were too high and narrow for the undead to climb through. The living fought off the rotters' grasping hands using the fallen planks.

Voorhees had followed Shipley back into the room. He aimed his pistol at a thin female face peering through a window. She met his gaze and opened her mouth, as if to protest; a second later she went reeling backwards, leaving a red mist in her wake.

Yeats dragged Oates in, crying, "One of them's got a gun!" Checking Oates' pulse, he groaned. "He's dead!"

Palmer saw the gaping hole in the front door and grabbed Mike's shoulder. "We've got to put more shit on that barricade!"

The P.O. shook her off and aimed out one window, then another, as if he couldn't decide where to waste his bullets first.

She spun him around to face her. "They can't get in that way! They *can* through the door!"

Mike stared dumbly for a moment, then nodded and followed her from the room.

Voorhees fired a second shot and turned to see Shipley

wrestling with the chapel door. "Back off!" he shouted. Amidst the chaos, Shipley probably didn't hear him, or even know who was being yelled at. Voorhees crossed the room and shoved him away from the door. "Forget it! Help us out here!"

Shipley turned and threw a fist into Voorhees' gut. The cop doubled over, nearly dropping his gun. Shipley went for the door again and Voorhees grabbed his leg. He yanked the ex-con to the floor, pressing the gun hard into Shipley's back. "I said *forget it.*"

"Okay," Shipley said to the floor, relaxing his body. Voorhees rose slightly, keeping the pistol against Shipley's flesh. "Help us secure the building or everyone dies. You, me, the people in the chapel. Everybody."

"You don't understand," Shipley argued, still lying prone. "The kid—"

"I don't wanna hear about it!"

Across the room, a board cracked over a leering zombie's head. Voorhees looked up. Shipley rolled over beneath him and drove a work boot into his groin. Voorhees buckled again as the ex-con scrambled to his feet and grabbed at the chapel door. "You gotta let me in! Listen to me!"

Voorhees drew the widowmaker from beneath his coat and sliced cleanly through the meat of Shipley's right calf. The man howled and staggered back. Voorhees tackled him to the floor, snapping a handcuff around one of his wrists.

He yanked Shipley across the room and slapped the other cuff onto the broken radiator, just below an open window. A gray hand lurched inside and groped blindly. Shipley flattened himself against the floor. "Lemme go!"

"You're staying right there." Voorhees fired out the window and the hand retreated. With a sneer, he muttered, "Worthless," and left Shipley to his protests.

Inside the chapel, the soft lights flickered and dimmed. Wendy collapsed onto a pew while pushing it. Then Kipp was beside her, trembling, but fighting to keep his head up. "I'll help."

Though she barely had any strength left in her body, Wendy got back up and braced herself against the pew. "Okay, honey. Let's go."

He brushed his hair from his eyes. She saw the dark outline of the bite again, just above his hairline, then the lights went out completely.

CHAPTER TWENTY
Wheeler

"J.J.!" Wheeler shouted from the men's room. He pulled a screwdriver from his coat and worked furiously at the hinges of the stall door. J.J., the last of the shelter's residents—who had been a silent fixture in the corner of the community room all week, face hidden beneath a rotting straw hat as he played idly with his Confederate flag belt buckle—ran in to see the boards dropping from the window. The rotters would be able to get through this one.

"What do I do?" J.J. cried. Screws clattered at Wheeler's feet.

"Just keep 'em away til I get this fuckin' door off!"

J.J. edged toward the window. A dead man thrust his hands through. J.J. staggered back into the doorway.

"C'mon!" Wheeler bellowed. He dropped to his knees and worked at the last hinge.

J.J. slammed both fists down on the sink faucet, knocking the rusted drain pipe loose underneath. "Okay!" Taking the pipe up in his hands, he turned to face the window.

Another rotter had taken the first's place. He pointed a rifle at J.J. A *rifle*.

The stall door slammed against the rifle just as it discharged, and huge chunks of plaster exploded from the wall, spitting dust and debris into the air. J.J. felt tiny, hot daggers lashing his cheek and fell to the floor.

Wheeler pushed the rifle outside and held the metal door against the window. "Get up, J!"

The door rattled in Wheeler's grip. He put all his weight against it, but then there was a gunshot and the door rocketed into his face.

J.J. watched Wheeler drop. Getting to his feet, he caught the warped, smoking door and thrust it upward again. A dead hand snaked around it and grabbed him by the hair. "Aaaah!" J.J. let go of the door and grabbed the rotter's wrist, snapping it. As the door fell aside, J.J. saw something pushing past the other rotters, some kind of animal skull wearing the clothes of a doctor, holding an axe.

The strange monster planted the axe between J.J.'s eyes with a solid thud. The man's body was pulled outside.

Right before Wheeler feebly pulled himself from the room and kicked the door shut he saw their faces crowding the window; a cry escaped him.

The young cop hauled him to his feet. "Are they in?" the cop shouted. "ARE THEY IN?"

Wheeler nodded. "Addison. They're the Addison children, I know them. He sent them."

"What? Who?"

"Addison," Wheeler answered, then passed out.

Several years prior to taking up permanent residence at the shelter, Wheeler had moved from building to building, squatting a few days at a time, stealing what he could. Sometimes it was an abandoned construction site or an alley, and without fail it would rain on those nights. It had been raining when he'd entered the cemetery, and though he first huddled beneath a stone angel in his stinking wet rags, Wheeler was forced to give in and enter one of the burial vaults.

It would be safer in the vault, he told himself. All he carried for protection were a switchblade and a bat. The vault with its shadows and its coffins at least offered a place to hide. Maybe he'd spare himself pneumonia. Settling on the floor, Wheeler gripped the bat tightly and fought sleep until there was no fighting it.

A scraping sound woke him. He sat perfectly still, eyes wide open in pitch blackness.

"Mrm," came the voice from overhead. The coffin that Wheeler was crouched behind trembled, then the lid fell on his head. He didn't move. Jesus, the body in the coffin wasn't *alive*, was it? It didn't work like that!

"You'll do," said the voice. Wheeler shut his eyes and waited for death.

"Who are you?" the voice snapped. Wheeler opened his eyes to see Dr. Addison standing there. He'd seen Addison a few times before, back when he'd earned a few meals working as security

(decoy)

at one of the west end's wealthy estates. Addison was the one that adopted all the kids, claiming he could cure the plague. And here he was, pulling a papery brown corpse from its coffin and piling it into a garbage bag. The doctor shot another look at Wheeler. "Do you live here?"

Wheeler shook his head. "Just getting out of the rain."

"You could probably use a shower and a shave."

Wheeler couldn't give a fuck about the shave, but a hot shower sounded like Heaven. He nodded.

"Help me here, then."

So Addison and Wheeler loaded a second corpse into a second bag, then carried both out to a pickup with some land-scaper's faded logo on the side. "This yours?" Wheeler asked. He knew the rich guys still had cars but he thought they'd be a little nicer.

"Don't ask questions," was all Addison said in reply.

They drove across town—it took a couple of hours, Addison silently cursing at the manual transmission—to the edge of the swamp where Addison's house lay. Addison turned on a powerful electric lantern. They got the bags out of the back. Then they set off into the swamp.

"Does anything strike you as unusual about this place?" the doctor asked. He was short of breath, as was Wheeler; the soft earth was threatening to swallow the damn bags.

Wheeler shrugged. "It's creepy. People don't come out here much."

"Why is it 'creepy'? What's so unsettling about it?" Addison pressed. Wheeler looked at the gnarled trees, their clusters of branches covered in moss, with great leaves dragging them toward the boggy ground. The night sky was completely obscured. He opened his mouth to speak but Addison spoke first.

"You don't see plant life like this anywhere else, do you? So green, so full, devouring everything around it—it won't stop growing. We have to cut it back every day to keep it from overtaking the manor. What's your name?"

"Wheeler."

"Mister Wheeler, this swamp is a sort of Source—a wellspring, if you will, of some energy. It feeds the swamp, engorges the swamp, infuses every cell of this place. Hold tight to that bag! This place . . . well, rather than try to explain it I'll just show you."

Stopping, Addison opened his garbage bag and let a pair of bony arms fall out. Barren of life, wrapped in shriveled skin and tissue, the arms lay like little fallen branches among the trees.

Then they moved.

The skin tore and stringy tendons produced only subtle, jerky movements, but Jesus Lord they were moving. That's when Wheeler felt something shuffling inside his own bag and dropped it with a cry.

"It brings the dead to life," Addison said, his smile horrific in the lantern light. "This is the Source of the plague. Here it isn't contagious, caught up in the simple trappings of a virus—I suspect we're responsible for that particular development—but it still infuses dead tissue." Addison watched the two corpses shaking themselves free of the bags, teeth in hollow skulls click-clacking and the bodies themselves crumbling under the strain of new life.

"How does something like this exist? Why? Did God put it here?" Wheeler realized that what Addison was talking about had nothing to do with science or medicine.

The doctor knelt and rapped his knuckles on the forehead of his corpse. "This isn't of God. He and the life He's slapped together are impermanent. Look at our bodies. He did make us in His image, after all, didn't He? Do you know why, Wheeler? We're just a shallow attempt by God to leave His mark after He's long gone.

"This energy came before God."

Wheeler was backing off, in the direction from which they'd come, but he wasn't sure he'd be able to find his way out of the swamp before—before—

"We can rise above the flaws of our 'Father' and His finite purpose. We need only appeal to the Old Ones that have given us this gift." Addison saw Wheeler backpedaling through the mud and laughed. "Run if you want. Where are you running to? Man has already set the wheels in motion, whether or not he knows it! God is dead, Wheeler, and He's not coming back!"

So Wheeler ran. He ran and ran and ran until his legs burned and his lungs screamed. He fell into a ditch and covered himself with dirt and prayed that he'd never wake up.

Now, in the shelter, he did wake up.

To the realization that Addison had been right.

CHAPTER TWENTY-ONE
Mike

After getting Wheeler on his feet, Mike returned to the front entrance where Palmer was throwing anything not nailed to the floor onto the barricade. Undead hands came through the hole in the door to sweep the obstructions away. Now would be a good time to use his gun.

He emptied the clip through the hole and went into his jeans for his backup. This was the last of his ammo. He shouted for Voorhees.

Outside, Aidan pointed to the smoldering clown; it had stopped moving. Harry lifted the mass into his arms.

The corpse crashed through the upper half of the door and clipped the light overhead, throwing the room into a tumult of shadows. Flames from the clown's ruptured gut lapped at the surrounding debris and cast an eerie new glow.

Voorhees grabbed Mike's arm. "Kitchen! The fridge!"

Palmer stomped the clown, choking on smoke; Mike pulled her off and gave her his gun. The others came running from the community room with boards in their hands. "Keep the rotters back!" Mike said, and followed Voorhees.

They wrenched the refrigerator away from the kitchen wall and lugged it across the floor with an earsplitting screech.

Gunshots were heard, and the pounding of Mike's heart drove the other sounds away.

As they passed through the community room, he saw Shipley cuffed to the radiator.

"Voorhees—"

"Forget him! Move!"

Palmer tried to keep her hands steady as she held Mike's gun through a thickening haze of smoke. The evening sun backlit the undead as they tried to get in; they were a mass of writhing silhouettes, heads barely distinguishable. She whispered a prayer and pulled the trigger.

One of the dead flew back into the street. A second later Palmer was jostled aside by the moving fridge. Slamming it into place over the doorway, Mike grabbed the gun from Palmer's hands and gasped a quick "thank you" before turning away.

Jenna and London pulled the clown into the community room and smothered it with blankets. The stench was nauseating. Blackened fingers on one hand curled into a fist; Jenna nearly fainted, but London shook her roughly. "Stay with it now!"

In the street, Harry raised his arms and studied them. His sleeves had caught fire when he picked up the clown.

Aidan nudged him toward the broken door even as the living blocked it off. Harry, his flesh being rapidly devoured by the heat, threw himself at the door. The refrigerator, with the survivors behind it, held fast.

Sawbones appeared with the axe; he pushed the other undead back and attacked the fridge.

Harry shuffled around the corner of the building by himself.

Mike looked from the entryway to Shipley. "We need him," he told Voorhees.

The bald man shook his head. "He's the last damn thing we need."

"Give me the handcuff key."

"Weisman . . ."

"I won't ask again!" There was the slightest tremor in Mike's voice as he realized he had no idea what to do, if not ask.

Voorhees leaned against the fridge and once again shook his head. "No."

Harry's flaming arms plunged through the window over the radiator. Shipley screamed.

Harry fought to get his shoulders through the window before the living reached him; bones snapped and flames swept up over his face. He could no longer see. There was no feeling in his upper body. Still he thrashed and thrashed and then felt himself hitting the floor, inside the shelter, bathed in fire.

Shipley kicked madly at the zombie. Mike ran up and beat at it with a board. The blanket on the nearby cot went up in flames in seconds. "Voorhees," he hollered, "the key!"

Voorhees entered the room. He pulled the widowmaker from his trench coat. Shipley cowered at the sight.

But the P.O. lopped the zombie's burning head off and kicked the body across the floor. He tossed the key to Mike. "Cut him loose if you want." Voorhees upended the flaming cot.

Mike knelt by Shipley. The handcuffed man kicked his legs and cried "Look . . . !"

The decapitated body had rolled underneath another cot and set it ablaze. "Fuck, Voorhees, fire over there!" Mike turned back and unlocked the cuffs.

Another cot was burning—dirty clothing piled beneath it sent a foul-smelling smoke into the air to join the clown's putrid odor. The whole place was going to go up. Palmer entered the room. "We've got to get out of here!"

"That's what they want!" yelled Mike. "They're smoking us out! They're all around us, waiting!!"

"But we can't—" Then, realizing their means of escape, throwing her arms into the air, Palmer screamed "Shit!" and ran to the chapel door. "Wendy? Kipp? You've got to open up!"

"Didn't you hear what I said?" Mike snapped.

"Yes, I fucking heard it!" Palmer shot back. "We can get onto the roof from inside the chapel!"

"Then what?" Voorhees coughed violently, swatted at the smoke around him.

"The auto shop next door," Palmer said, trying to calm herself, to think. "Its roof's lower. We can make it over there, I'm sure of it."

Voorhees looked at Mike, who returned his hapless expression. "We're surrounded. They've got weapons. They've got a *plan.*"

"Then we've got the roof," Voorhees muttered. "All right, everyone c'mon!"

Through all this Shipley was silent, rubbing his tender wrists, watching the cops through the smoke.

CHAPTER TWENTY-TWO
Tetch

Lily knocked on the study door and Tetch bade her enter. "Where is everyone?" she asked.

"Come over here, and I'll tell you." He motioned to a chair on the other side of the desk. Atop the desk, where stacks of books had been pushed aside, sat a shoebox filled with dirt. Lily eyed it with interest.

"I know how you've been wanting to go outside the gates," Tetch said, "and the truth of the matter is, I've been laying plans to make that possible. I'm tiring of the house myself, large as it is, and I don't want you to grow up and live your entire life inside these walls."

He emptied something into his palm from a paper bag. It was a dead frog, hard and black. Lily grimaced at the sight.

Tetch dropped it into the shoebox.

"You know your brothers and sisters aren't like the other rotters," he said. She nodded. "Here's why." He gestured to the box of dirt, and she craned her neck to peer inside. The frog's frail little legs were kicking.

"It's earth from around the estate," Tetch explained. He loved the way her eyes shone as they followed the tiny movements of the born-again amphibian, the way she looked up at

David Dunwoody

him, he who had performed the miracle. "Harry and Prudence and all the others were brought back this same way."

"How did they die?" Lily asked boldly.

Clearing his throat, Tetch placed the frog on the back of his hand. "It was Doctor Addison—Father." He was lying, of course, but she was still too young to fully understand. They had died peacefully, slowly poisoned by the exotic toxins Tetch had used to flavor their meals. None of them had ever suspected him of foul play; after all, he was the one who'd saved them from Addison.

The memory was clear as day, one he often replayed. Addison strapping the fifteen-year-old boy to a chair and presenting an instrument tray. A mallet and steel spike rested upon it. "You're stubborn," Addison said while jotting notes. "Your soul simply isn't pliant enough—yet—to accept the Old Ones." These Old Ones, Addison was always rambling about them but refused to explain who they were. He refused to explain how feeding the children dirt and pricking their arms a hundred times a day did anything to find a cure for the plague.

Addison raised the spike; Tetch's arms tensed, but found resistance in the leather straps binding him. "This will be painless. Soon you'll be a more agreeable subject—they'll be pleased with you, I think."

"Th-they who?" Tetch demanded, trying to sound strong. "The Old Ones?"

"The Old Ones." Addison set the tip of the spike just below Tetch's eye and reached with his other hand for the mallet. Tetch, unable to look directly at the spike, glanced down at Addison's notebook. He saw FRONTAL LOBOTOMY scrawled haphazardly.

"Living tissue, living bodies for them. Much better than the rotting animals out there, so much better." Addison leaned forward and moved the spike slightly. It was huge and cold in Tetch's tear duct. He was terrified. His arms strained and he felt the buckle give on one of the straps.

136

"Oh, no." Addison lowered the mallet and grabbed Tetch's arm. "I told you this won't hurt, Baron. I need you to relax. I've brought you out of Hell, son, in more ways than one, and I need you to trust me."

Son.

Something about that, at that moment, in that precise tone of voice, caused Tetch to snap.

He yanked his arm free and snatched the spike from Addison's hand. Tetch said something then, though he could never recall what it had been; nor could he recall planting the spike in Addison's throat. He only remembered the doctor flailing across the room with gouts of crimson erupting from him. Then suddenly it was over.

Under cover of darkness, Tetch had taken Addison into the swamp to dispose of him. There, as he saw the body resurrect in the bog, saw it stagger about and then look questioningly at him . . . he began to understand.

Killing the doctor's Great Dane was done out of necessity more than anything else. Tetch did take exquisite pleasure, however, in wiring the skull to Addison's head.

"Father" had been going about it all wrong: groveling to the Old Ones, thinking that they wanted these fragile human bodies, living or dead—it was all utterly beneath them. Tetch had completed Addison's research and realized his own gifts. Now, it was he who had pliant, undying servants. It was he who had mastered necrophagy, feeding his body on dormant energies— but unlike his siblings, he retained his soul.

Lily was captivated by the frog. Tetch extended his arm and allowed her to scoop it up.

"Gifts such as these weren't meant to be squandered in some rotten old house hidden from the rest of the world. I want to go outside the gates as much as you do."

"When?"

"When we've secured the city. When everyone within its walls—living or dead—belongs to me. It's about trust, Lily."

Later, she took the frog outside and let it go. The man in black was standing at the fence.

"Why do you keep coming here?" she asked.

"I wanted to see if you were still all right."

"Yeah. Soon I can go out there too, but Baron says everybody has to belong to him." Casting a downward glance, Lily continued, "I think you'll probably have to leave."

"I won't be doing that." The man crouched, his smooth black eyes drawing her in. "Baron is wrong. These things he wants, they won't happen. I think you know that."

"H-he's always right."

The man pointed to the fence. "In there. Not out here."

She didn't respond. She was mulling it over, but as a child she couldn't avoid some truths, even those that made no sense, like the frog in the shoebox coming back to life. It was just . . . just so . . .

"It's sad," the man said. He said it like he didn't know what sad was. "I have to go back into the city. Be safe." Then he was gone.

Lily turned and froze. Her blood ran cold at the sight of Tetch in the yard. He'd seen the man.

CHAPTER TWENTY-THREE
Palmer

The reverend was the first onto the roof. She turned to help Voorhees, but he was already hauling himself through the open vent cover, then reaching down through the chapel ceiling for Kipp.

Mark Duncan and Mike Weisman lifted the teen up to Voorhees. They had decided they would go up after all the others; a ladder leaned against the wall for whomever was last.

When Kipp stepped onto the roof, he started shouting for his mother. Palmer took him in her arms and assured him with an urgent whisper, "She's coming right up! She's next!" The rotters on the ground must have heard him . . .

Down below, Wheeler elbowed his way forward after Wendy. "Ladies first," Duncan said. Wheeler opened his mouth to start a tirade, but Mike shoved him back into one of the pews blocking the door.

Dead hands exploded through and grabbed Wheeler's coat.

Mike whipped out his pistol and pushed the hands aside. They clawed at him; he dropped the gun. Wheeler fell to the floor in hysterics.

"Help me out!" Mike yelled, sweeping the floor. He couldn't

see shit. The gun might be under one of the pews. "Fuck fuck fuck—"

The head of an axe split the top of the door, and the rotters' hands began prying, trying to tear the whole thing apart.

Palmer watched from over Voorhees' shoulder. How could the damn things be so smart . . . how could they be working together like that?

"Found it!" London cried. She reached between two of the barricade's pews to grab the gun. A rotter snatched her long hair and yanked her into the door with a crash. Mike leapt atop her and struggled with the hand. "Get the gun!" Wheeler hollered.

London's head smashed into the door a second time, leaving behind a bloody stamp matted with hair. Her body sagged in Mike's arms.

"The *gun,* man!" Wheeler wouldn't dare approach the barricade but he didn't hesitate to scream orders. Yeats got on the floor to reach underneath the pews. Brushing the pistol with his fingertips, he wedged his shoulder deeper.

Suddenly he screamed. As the door was ripped away, piece by piece, he felt his arm seized and wrenched from its socket. Flesh tore and muscle snapped and he was soaked in blood.

Mike rolled him away from the pews. The arm was gone. Yeats, already half-dead, stared dumbly at the spurting stump. Jenna O'Connell mashed her fist into her mouth with a cry.

Shipley waved at Duncan. Together, they lifted a pew off the floor and turned it toward the crumbling door like a battering ram. "Everyone out of the way!"

The axe burst through again, and behind it moved a skull-faced monster that surveyed the chapel's inhabitants with empty eyes.

The pew plowed straight into the rotter, sending it careening into the fiery community room.

Yeats was gone. Mike and Duncan immediately returned to the spot below the vent. "Let's get outta here!" Duncan grabbed Jenna and lifted her foot into his hands, boosting her into Voorhees' grasp.

Lauren was next, then Wheeler got his turn. After Shipley went up, Duncan and Mike found themselves alone with undead clambering through the doorway. Mike knelt and cupped his hands. "No, you first!" The other man argued but Mike shook his head grimly. Duncan stepped up and was thrust skyward.

Voorhees dumped Duncan roughly on the tarpaper and dropped his arms again through the ceiling. "Weisman!"

Mike started toward the ladder, then stepped back; he'd never get around the rotters if he went for it. Standing atop the nearby pews couldn't help him reach his escape route either. The dead lurched into the room, one after the next, and fixed their eyes on him; the gun was still under the barricade, it was hopeless . . .

He remembered Cheryl, sitting alone in his apartment. And no one knew. Voorhees didn't even know which unit he lived in.

The zombie with the rifle lifted it to its shoulder. Lunging forth, Mike grabbed the barrel, twisting the weapon from the undead's hands. He smashed the butt into the zombie's teeth and spun the rifle around to point it at the others. Smoke poured into the chapel, hungry flames close behind.

He fired and fired and fired until his hands were numb and the rifle was empty and all the dead were flailing on the floor with chunks of flesh and bone scattered around them.

Mike hurled the rifle through the door and grabbed the ladder. A female swiped at his ankle, once-full lips now ragged and host to gnashing teeth. He stomped her face into a pulpy ruin. Staggering up the rungs, Mike linked his arms with Voorhees' and felt himself rising into the fresh evening air.

Palmer pointed to the auto shop at their rear. "It's an easy jump." The last syllable had scarcely left her lips when Shipley leapt across the gap, dropping into a roll as he hit the steel roof on the other side.

David Dunwoody

"The kid!" he called, opening his arms.

Voorhees placed a firm hand on Kipp's shoulder and held him still. "Weisman, you go next."

Palmer knew that Voorhees had Shipley pegged as the Midtown Rapist, but what did that have to do with the boy? Maybe he thought Shipley wanted Kipp as a hostage, to secure his freedom? Hell, he could just run right now if he wanted to. The fact was, there was as much "freedom" out here as there was law.

The reverend watched Mike jump across, and he motioned for Kipp to come over. "You can make it!"

Shipley stepped aside with a look of resentment.

"Can you do it?" Duncan was asking Jenna and Lauren. They both answered in the affirmative and approached the edge of the roof. The entire shelter shuddered. "We've got no time! Move, move!" Voorhees barked. The two women jumped.

Palmer steeled herself for the leap. She bent her legs slightly, took a deep breath, and ran forward. As her feet left the tarpaper, she said a silent goodbye to her home. She collided with the edge of the other roof, knocking the wind from her lungs with an impact that wracked her entire body. Everyone watched in horror as the reverend tumbled unconscious to the ground below.

CHAPTER TWENTY-FOUR
Jack-O'-Lantern

Voorhees slung his legs over the edge of the roof and dropped into the alleyway between the two buildings. Lifting Palmer off the ground with one arm, he yelled, "Just get across!" to the others above him.

He hefted his pistol in his free hand; a few bullets left, something to slow the undead horde for a few scant seconds before they overran him. He ran onto the street and saw the chained doors of the auto shop. Now there was a better use for the bullets. Voorhees held Palmer tight and took aim.

Atop the garage, Wheeler stomped on a cracked skylight. It fell in with a shriek, the glass landing on the roof of a rusted-out van. He jumped down without hesitation.

Voorhees emptied his gun into the padlock securing the door. A kick finished the job, and he lugged Palmer's dead weight inside. The others were climbing down from the van. Mike, already down, shut the door behind Voorhees and slid a metal shelf in front of it, some of the tools on it clattering to the floor.

"She smacked her head pretty good," Voorhees observed, laying Palmer out on the floor. Concussion, maybe, but she'd come around before too long.

As soon as Mike stepped back from the door, Wheeler went to it and started moving the shelf out of the way.

"The fuck are you doing?" Jenna snapped.

"We've gotta keep moving," Wheeler snapped back. "Grab what you can and let's go." As he spoke, he snatched a wrench off the shelf.

Before he could nudge the shelf another inch, Mike braced himself against the other end. "Have you lost it?"

"They'll be here any minute!" Wheeler protested.

"They're still in the shelter. Probably feeding . . ."

"Not with that fire raging! Look, you don't know who they are. Those are the kids from the Addison estate!"

"Addison?" Palmer sat up, looking at Wheeler through half-closed slits. Voorhees pressed an oily rag, the only fabric he could find other than his own grungy clothes, to the gash on her head. "You mean from the house in the swamp?"

"Yes! I'm tellin' you, Addison sent them out here! He wants bodies for his fuckin' research! I know what I'm talking about!"

"You want to talk about it without screaming?" Jenna said.

Wheeler was ready with a smug retort. "The nice officer here says all the rotters are having dinner next door. What're you worried about?"

"Shut up, Wheeler." Palmer got to her feet and took the rag from Voorhees with an appreciative glance. "We just need to keep quiet until they're either dead or gone."

"I won't shut up!" Wheeler hurled the wrench across the room with an ungodly clatter. Mike wrestled the bum's arms behind his back and produced his handcuffs. "Oh no you don't!" Wheeler hollered. "You've got no right! No right!"

Palmer picked up the wrench. Wheeler's eyes met hers and he yelped as she came at him.

The window in the door exploded inward, peppering Mike and Wheeler with glass. The axe head swept through, only to get caught on the edge of the shelf; holding the weapon was the skull-faced rotter.

"We know him!" Lauren cried as Jenna pulled on her. "We saw him, remember?"

"Get into the pit!" Voorhees gestured to the dark workspace beneath the van. Breaking away from Mike, Wheeler pushed past the others to crawl under the vehicle.

Sawbones freed his axe and attacked the door with renewed vigor.

"I'm out of ammo," Voorhees told his fellow P.O.

"No gun," Mike replied.

Palmer tapped his shoulder and handed him the wrench. "Just split his damn head open so he can't see straight."

"Easier said than done," Mike murmured. The reverend slipped down into the pit, leaving them alone. Then the shelf fell over.

The door swung inward, and the rotter entered to face the two policemen.

Voorhees grabbed a length of pipe by his feet. In the pit, Kipp screamed. It didn't matter, the rotter already knew where they were.

Sawbones ran at Mike and swung the axe. The cop ducked aside and the axe buried itself in the side door of the van. As Sawbones tugged frantically to free it, Voorhees smashed the pipe against the exposed backside of the zombie's head.

Sawbones lurched, turned and snorted. He jerked the axe free and delivered it to Voorhees' gut.

"No." Mike could only stare in disbelief as his mentor doubled over.

But it was the blunt side of the axe head that had struck Voorhees; he rose and hit Sawbones square in the chest with a hollow-sounding THUNK!

It made no difference to the rotter, despite bones cracking. He lifted the axe again, this time for the kill.

Mike shook himself from his frozen stare and bashed the zombie in the side of his head. The dog's-skull cracked. The wrench struck again across his face and Sawbones careened into the far wall.

Voorhees was on it. No sooner had Sawbones bounced off the wall than the pipe came down to blow out the thing's knee. The rotter slumped against the axe handle for support; Voorhees kicked it away and delivered another blow to Sawbones' head. The fractures already present in the skull webbed out, and bits of bone fell to the floor. The cop followed up with his bare fist.

Seizing Sawbones from behind, Mike hurled him face first into the wall. The snout of the dog's-skull ruptured like cheap plaster. Dust filled the undead's eyes; he thrashed blindly, but his clawing hands found no purchase.

In Mike's hand, bright red fire spewed from a road flare found among the spilled tools, and he crammed it into Sawbones' eye socket. The skull lit up like a hellish jack-o'-lantern. Sawbones mewled and dug his rotten hands into his mask to get the fire out.

With a roar, Voorhees lifted the toppled shelf and threw it onto the monster.

Mike leapt atop the shelf before Sawbones could buck it off. Taking up the axe, Voorhees held it over the thing's kicking feet. "Hold still, Mike. I don't want to get you."

"I'm doing my goddamndest."

Voorhees slammed the axe through Sawbones' left heel, then his right, tangling the axe blade into the shelving unit and getting it stuck. Ichor pooled around the severed extremities, now attached only by a few stringy bits, as he fought to get the axe free again. He wanted to behead the thing (and burn it; always burn what's left Dad had said, *burn every infected thing to ash),* but there wasn't time to try and maneuver the axe through the shelf.

"Everybody out here quick!" he yelled. The others obeyed, each gazing in horror at the squirming zombie as they passed it.

Mike wriggled off of the shelf and left Sawbones to paw at the floor.

Running to the door, Voorhees peered outside. "It's clear—"

"Wait."

Mike narrowed his eyes. "Is that a bite?"

Wendy clutched Kipp to her breast, heart pounding. But he wasn't looking at the boy.

Wheeler followed Mike's gaze to his hand and snatched it into the sleeve of his coat, looking at the others. "What? What?"

Barring the doorway, Voorhees' cold stare bored holes into the back of Wheeler's head.

The others stepped away.

"It—what, this?" Wheeler held his hand out now, shaking it at them as if offended. "The kid did it, down in the pit! He was scared!"

No one spoke. The pit had been dark and horrifying; with the fight going on overhead, everyone was in a stark panic. Reverend Palmer looked at Kipp. Maybe the child really had bitten him. "Kipp?" she asked. Wendy shook her head quickly. "No, no, we weren't anywhere near him—"

"Then who the fuck did it!" Wheeler snapped. "Because it happened down there, and if it wasn't that retard I don't know who it was!"

The wrench smashed into his brainpan with a solid THUNK; strands of bloody hair came away on the tool, then it struck Wheeler again, this time with a wet sound, and he fell, gibbering.

Voorhees knelt over him and brought the wrench down one last time. One last time, he told himself, because he *had* to, because he'd been given no other choice under the terrible circumstances.

Wendy smothered Kipp against her. The others just stared. Blood pooled rapidly around the bum's dashed skull, nudging them further back.

Mike stooped on the other side of the body, opposite

Voorhees, and took the wrench away. He turned Wheeler's hand over and examined the bite. It had broken the skin, barely, and if it was a rotter's, then Wheeler had likely been infected. He motioned to Wendy. "Come here."

She shook her head again, so he went to her. Tears coursed down Wendy's face and fell onto his hands, which lay on Kipp's shoulders. "I just want to see his mouth," Mike assured her. Knowing the P.O.'s politeness wouldn't last if she refused, Wendy slowly turned Kipp to face him. He touched the boy's mouth, parted his lips, examined his teeth, sighed.

"I think he was telling the truth."

There were a couple of short gasps. Voorhees was frozen beside the corpse. Beneath the shelf, Sawbones grunted.

Voorhees coughed into his fist and stood up. "We've got to keep moving." What Wheeler had said minutes earlier.

Mike began to ask, "Should we burn—"

"There's no time," Voorhees answered, and walked out the door.

So they left.

CHAPTER TWENTY-FIVE
Death in the Family

The afterdead made their way out of the shelter as the roof caved in, its collapse forming a maw with a thousand fiery tongues that belched smoke into the sky.

Aidan held his blackened fingers out in front of him and counted his siblings. He was three short. Three still inside, including Harry (but not Sawbones, as he'd fled earlier), and all of them were probably now covered in flames as Harry had been. There was some formality that Tetch had taught them to observe in such an instance, but Aidan had forgotten it. He searched the streets for Sawbones.

The man in black climbed down from his white horse and drew a scythe from his robes. Aidan's corrupt innards roiled at the sight of him.

Uriel had retrieved the rifle and loaded fresh rounds into it with his cracked, charred hands. He took aim at the man in black and fired.

The man flew back, struck the curb, folded over like a doll and lay still.

His flesh would not be tinged with smoke, this outsider. It was white and unblemished and Uriel's mouth watered as he shuffled forward, Prudence at his side, leading the pack.

David Dunwoody

Death stayed in the prone position and listened for their approach. The rifle hadn't left a scratch on him. He needn't have even reacted to the impact except to draw the rotters in. And now . . .

NOW

He rose, robes billowing out as he swept the scythe in a broad arc, black eyes rolling over white yet reflecting nothing in their depths. The setting sun played brilliantly across the blade as it glided toward Uriel, halving the barrel of the rifle, halving the zombie's torso, spraying a geyser of brown filth from dead arteries.

Uriel slumped into Prudence's arms. She dropped him and came at the man in black. He turned the blade flat and hit her across the face with a clap that shattered bone.

Sweeping his cloak around his back, Death swung the scythe under his arm like a pendulum. One of the rotters had circled behind him; its groin was skewered and the filleted remains emerged from its backside, on the bloody tip of the Reaper's blade.

Death gripped the scythe's handle with both hands and hurled the impaled rotter into the others. They fell in a heap of tangled, thrashing limbs.

Aidan struggled to his feet and reached into his suit jacket for his knife, taken from the butcher block in the manor kitchen. Its size was pitiful in comparison to the scythe, but this man in black wouldn't be able to kill him. Shouldn't . . .

Peering over Death's shoulder, Aidan saw that Uriel was still motionless in the road. He frowned.

The scythe pierced him beneath the chin and parted his tongue on its way up through his mouth; he felt foul liquids erupting inside his head, felt his limbs go numb as his brain was speared, and then nothing as Death lifted him off the asphalt and dangled him before the others.

The white-eyed specter glowered at them, at their senseless gaping faces. He jerked the scythe free.

"Come. Come at me."

They didn't. The remaining four stood together and stared but did not attack. They were wary of this new threat.

Why did these empty things seek to protect themselves? Death wondered. What purpose, what order was there in their existence? He knew now that the undead had existed as long as there had been life on Earth, but he'd not sensed them, not felt their cold blue flames until the plague began. Man had made the plague. Perhaps that was why he had finally been allowed to see them, and why he felt a responsibility to deal with them.

It was his responsibility, that was all. He wasn't angry at them. He wasn't vengeful. It wasn't possible. Death felt nothing.

But, watching the rotters as they stood their ground and stared that same blank stare—all four of them—impatience stirred within him. He wanted to feel his blade pierce their flesh, resistance yielding as their insides split, entire bodies torn asunder; he wanted to destroy them with his bare hands, but his hands couldn't extinguish their candles. No, he could only reap the miserable things using a scythe forged from their own bones. He who marked the passing of every life found his purpose defied and defiled by them, found himself forced to adapt to *their* laws, to meet them on *their* turf.

Walking corpses.

An absurdity.

He stepped forward and swung the scythe with the intent of cleaving each of them in two.

The first clapped both hands down on the blade, managing to stop its progress through the rotter's side.

The handle was yanked from Death's grip. He lunged at it, and one of the females raked her thin gray fingers across his face. His eyes rolled back and his flesh opened beneath every fingertip as if fleeing from the zombie's touch. He spun away, blind, clutching at his face; an arm snaked around his waist and hands began ripping at his cloak.

He tried to summon his horse, but its wounds mirrored

his own and it was folding over on the asphalt. He thought of a stillborn child he'd seen the morning before, ferried to the landfill by its haggard mother, another life in a world that shouldn't be.

In Mike's apartment, Cheryl was squatted on the toilet seat, clutching her abdomen. The dull ache was growing into something worse and there wasn't any sort of medication in the place. Maybe there was a little something stashed away back at Lee's . . . ? No, she shouldn't venture out alone, even with a gun. She could barely get around the apartment. Bunching herself up on the toilet seat, squeezing tears of pain from her eyes, Cheryl rocked back and forth and tried to think of something else.

No, not the baby. Think of . . . of what? Kittens? She'd once seen a litter in a cardboard box devouring their mother, long dead from the strain of labor. The kittens had been born infected, yes, but weren't dead yet. Maybe it was in their nature.

To give birth to an infected baby, the dying child of a dying mother, there could be no greater heartbreak in the world. Yet Cheryl had known women who'd insisted on carrying their pregnancies to term after being bitten. That wasn't human nature though, was it? Weren't people supposed to be more rational than that?

Maybe not. Maybe the plague had forced Man to acknowledge what was really true all along, deep down inside. What was rationality, in the end, but people turning their back on instinct?

Perhaps the spread of the plague and the decline of rationality had been the reason undead sideshows enjoyed brief popularity. Her brother had taken her to one such show in a foul-smelling circus tent, with hand-painted signs declaring HORRORS OF THE DEAD WORLD! COME FACE TO FACE WITH THE FLESH-EATERS ROAMING THE AMERICAN BADLANDS! CERTIFIED BY THE GOVERNMENT OF THE UNITED STATES OF AMERICA!

That last disclaimer meant that the sideshow organizers

didn't cultivate infected blood for their own use, nor did they display human rotters. Any group alleged to do so was classified as terrorist. No, this was an all-animal attraction promising wild beasts decaying before the audience's own eyes. Cheryl had protested all morning long but her brother wanted to see and, well, he sure as hell couldn't leave her home alone for an hour. So they'd sat in the hot tent amidst morbidly curious others and waited.

A spotlight coughed on and illuminated the sawdust-covered floor in the center of the bleachers. A man in a crimson top hat and suit vest paraded into the light. His face was painted white with black circles around the eyes. His grin was all too similar to that of a lipless rotter. The man plucked his hat from his head and bowed all around. "I am Eviscerato!"

Cheryl snorted at the name. Her brother elbowed her with a stern look. "What," she whispered, "am I supposed to show this guy respect?"

"Don't cause trouble," her brother answered in a low voice. "These people are—"

"AND NOW," Eviscerato bellowed, "THE FIRST OF OUR CARNIVAL'S MANY UNSPEAKABLE HORRORS, A FEARED PREDATOR TURNED GHOUL!" Handlers in blood-stained jumpsuits emerged from the shadows, pulling on chains. The chains were fastened around the neck and limbs of a grizzly bear, most of its face already eroded, leaving a fanged skull that emitted a warbling cry.

Cheryl moaned and grabbed her brother's arm. He ignored her, studying the animal.

Eviscerato danced around the bear and its handlers, shouting taunts. The bear seemed oblivious to his presence; indeed it didn't appear to have either of its eyes. All of its claws were intact, however. If she squinted, Cheryl thought she could see bolts keeping the grizzly's paws in one piece.

The handlers pulled the bear into a standing position. It made a sound of protest and its belly shifted. The thing's innards were sloshing around in there. Was it able to eat? Did they even feed it? What type of food? Unnatural as the beast was, Cheryl found herself pitying its condition.

Waving his arms like a madman, Eviscerato approached the towering grizzly. "Look!" he cried, pointing like a rude child at the distended belly. Then, another handler trudged out, this one holding a chainsaw. Eviscerato accepted it from him with a flourish.

"I want to go," Cheryl stammered. She squeezed her brother's arm until he shoved her hand away.

"It's just another rotter, Cheryl. Jesus."

"It's an animal. It doesn't know—"

"None of them know! Shut up!"

The saw came to life, and there were scattered cheers from the audience.

Eviscerato drove the saw teeth into the bear, just above the groin, and spilled its guts out onto the floor.

A short, squat man tumbled from the yawning wound and splashed down in a soup of gore and sawdust.

He rose to one knee, thrusting his bloody fists into the air. The audience laughed and applauded. Cheryl slumped against her brother.

"They just stuck him in there beforehand and stitched it up," he would explain later. "They probably reuse the same bear until it falls apart. It's not *alive,* Cheryl. Why the hell do you care? It's not like it's a goddamned puppy and even *those* things don't have feelings." She disagreed wholeheartedly with that, but it was pointless to try and argue. He'd try to rationalize it: "I wanted you to see once and for all that there's nothing there, nothing in those animals. I should've known you'd react this way."

Months later she heard on the radio that Eviscerato had been mauled and infected by a wolf during one of his "performances." He'd spent his last days doing illegal shows where he'd taunted human rotters, letting them bite him, even biting them back.

She hadn't felt sorry for him.

Cheryl was stirred from the memory by a knock on the door. Mike had a key . . . maybe it wasn't Mike. She reached across the sink for the pistol he'd given her and stood up.

Cheryl hobbled out of the bathroom and across the carpet to the door, quiet as possible, and she looked through the peephole.

There was a dead man there. He was holding a shovel.

CHAPTER TWENTY-SIX
Interlude: The King of the Dead

An oral tradition from the badlands . . .

The boy had never been to a circus before. The circus was a place where animals and clowns and magicians performed. It was rarely seen, traveling by night and in great, sweeping paths all across the land, but when the circus did come through a part of the badlands, all the people there were happy for just a little while.

The boy's father often told him about the last time the circus came to town, many, many years before the boy's birth. As the sun rose over the hills, a caravan had appeared, a train of brightly colored wagons and cages hauling all sorts of animals—some of them alive. For the price of a scrap of food, everyone had gone that night and seen dancing clowns, majestic beasts and other fantastic sights.

Almost every night the boy asked to hear about the circus. Almost every night, after his father kissed him and the world grew silent, the boy prayed for the circus to come.

One day it did, and it was just as the boy's father had described it. A line of wagons pulled by dead horses stretched far into the hills, full of colors and animals he'd never seen! Men with painted faces waved and smiled at him as they passed.

At the far edge of town, where there was nothing but dirt, they put up a giant tent that nearly scraped the sky. The boy sat and watched for hours as men and animals went in and out of the tent. He wanted to follow along, but his father wouldn't let him. "Not yet," the father said. "They're putting the magic in."

The boy knew that there were wonderful and secret things going on inside that tent. He desperately wanted to see, but knew he must behave lest he never see the circus at all, so he sat and waited until the sun began to descend. At twilight his father came and found him. "Now we can go in."

Each act that the boy saw that night made his heart thunder and caused a grin to spread from ear to ear. He clapped until his hands were raw and red. All the while, his father watched him with a smile as big as the boy's.

Then they brought out their most special act: THE KING OF THE DEAD. He was a dancing jester painted in a rainbow of colors. His limbs flew and spun and kicked up a storm of dust. His name was Eviscerato.

Other men, dead men, were brought out to stand around the King of the Dead. They were chained to posts in the ground. The boy's father told him not to be afraid, so he wasn't. His eyes followed every movement of Eviscerato's feet as the nimble jester came just within reach of each dead man, then pulled away from their snapping teeth. All the while he smiled and laughed and sang! Everyone in the audience applauded madly.

Eviscerato spun in a tight circle, in the center of the dead men, then stopped cold. He looked into the audience, right at the boy. He reached out a hand. One of the dead bit into it.

The crowd roared. The boy stood and stared as all the dead men grabbed Eviscerato and chewed and tore at his brightly colored costume. All the while the King of the Dead smiled! How could a man smile through such terror? The boy was mesmerized. Blood pooled at Eviscerato's feet and he danced in it. He nipped at the necks and fingers of the dead men, he continued to sing and laugh. Despite the horror of the scene, there was not a face in the audience that did not grin from ear to ear.

When the torches were extinguished and the crowd was ushered out, the boy climbed onto his father's shoulders and searched for his new hero. Eviscerato was nowhere to be seen.

It was late by the time his father tucked him in bed. They stayed up a while longer talking about all the things they'd seen. The boy kissed his father and settled down to dream about the circus.

When he awoke, it was still dark, but small fires glowed outside the window of the shanty, and the boy got up to see what was happening.

The circus was leaving. The tent was gone and the animals were motionless in their cages. As the caravan passed the window, the boy saw men without makeup sitting atop the wagons. He watched them until the last light faded over the horizon.

Then another wagon passed by the window and stopped. The King of the Dead was the driver. He smiled his painted smile and reached out a bloody hand.

"Come with me," Eviscerato said. "Come dance forever."

The boy took his hand and climbed out the window. The King of the Dead whipped the horses and pulled away. The boy's father awoke at the sound of horses, and chased after the wagon, crying out his boy's name, but the boy didn't hear him.

CHAPTER TWENTY-SEVEN
Interview

Four. Only four had come back. They were all disoriented, stained with soot and blood. Sawbones was not among them.

Tetch made them wait on the porch while he spread plastic across the foyer, then he brought his siblings in and locked up behind them. Aidan hadn't returned either; without him, there was little hope of getting specifics on what had happened. "Stay on the plastic," Tetch muttered. He nudged Prudence, whose eyes refused to meet his, and leaned in close. "How many of them were there?"

She studied the grime at her feet, the blistering on her burnt flesh. Standing on her toe, Tetch lifted her chin with his hand. "Use your fingers. How many?"

She raised an index finger and averted her gaze.

"No. No." Tetch stepped back and glanced at the others, only to have each one look away. "Not just one. I want to know how many there were to begin with, how many of them did this to you! Bailey! How many?"

The rotter shifted his weight from one foot to the other; he wasn't ashamed, he simply had nothing to offer. Tetch grabbed him by the hair and shook him around. "Tell me!"

Bailey raised one finger.

Tetch snapped it in his fist. The afterdead stood motionless.

"I sent all of you and only four came back! Why are you telling me this? Didn't you see any of them? Gerald!" Tetch backhanded the next in line. "Look at me!"

Gerald's glassy stare penetrated his brother. "Now," Tetch breathed, pulling a fountain pen from his jacket, "take this and write on your hand. You know numbers, don't you? Tell me how many people you saw, and if you put a 'one' down so help me . . ."

The rotter grasped the pen awkwardly and held it over his open palm. He wrote nothing.

"Gerald?"

Tetch's eyes widened as the pen, unused, was handed back to him.

He brought the pen up to stab it into Gerald's unblinking eye.

"Please don't!"

Tetch whirled to see Lily at the top of the stairs. "Go to your room!" he commanded.

"What happened?" she shot back.

He hurled the pen at her and missed by a mile. "Go to your room!"

A thought struck him then. He remembered catching Lily by the fence, how there had seemed to be a shadow in the swamp that fled from view when he'd come outside. He remembered that she'd said something the night before about a man with black eyes.

Tetch started up the stairs, and Lily backed away from him. "Don't be afraid of me," he said softly. "I take care of you. I love you. Don't you love me?"

She nodded. It was a quick, insincere gesture. Tetch lowered himself to her height and gave her a pleading look. "Lily, some-one hurt your brothers and sisters. I think the others . . . they're dead. Really dead. Who were you talking to in the yard earlier?"

The girl turned on her heel and tried to bolt; he caught

her arm and shoved her across the landing into the wall. Tetch pinned her there. She screamed, but he held fast. "Who are you screaming for, Lily? Who's out there that you trust more than me? Who do you love more than me? Don't say nobody, or you're a liar, Lily, and lying makes you an ugly little child and no one loves you then!"

"No!" She struggled against him until her face was bright red. "You're the liar!"

"I've never *ever* lied to you!" Spittle struck her cheek and Tetch raised his cuff to wipe it away. She flinched, going limp against him. His body's reaction was quite the opposite. "I've never lied to you," he repeated. She kept her eyes shut tight, face turned away. He pulled her into an embrace. "Lily . . ."

"You've never lied to me."

"But you don't really believe that."

"Yes I do." Like the others, she wouldn't look at him, but she said in a tiny voice, "I was just scared."

He kissed her on the cheek and gave her a bit of room to breathe. "It was the man with the black eyes, wasn't it? He came back."

She gave a reluctant nod. Tetch whispered "Good," and kissed her mouth, tasting her breath, his hands trembling against the small of her back. "What's his name, Lily?"

"He doesn't have one."

Tetch's grip relaxed. Opening her eyes, Lily backed away from his pale face, his slack arms. He didn't even look at her.

She went back to her bedroom.

Outside the burning shelter, under a dark sky, a pile of crumbled and mutilated remains lay in the folds of a black cloak. There was a sound like dead leaves rustling and Death reconstituted himself.

He sat in the street for a long time, his steed pacing around him, and he thought. These undead hadn't been like any others. They'd been taught to behave and interact in some semblance of mortality. They were the ones from the swamp.

The Reaper spent some time looking through the clothes of the corpses around him, then got back on his horse. The people from the shelter were still nearby, but some of them would be dead soon. Though he couldn't prevent that, couldn't add a single precious second to their flickering candles, he could at least see that none of them were added to the ranks of the undead.

Tetch lay on the floor outside Lily's door, ear pressed to the wood, until her breathing became deep and even. Then he returned to the foyer. The others were still standing there.

"Go out to the shed," he told Gerald, "and bring the crate inside. Be careful with it. Simeon, you help him."

He dismissed Prudence and Bailey as well, then went to the window and peered through the curtain into the shadows of the swamp.

"Can you hear me out there?" he whispered. "I know who you are."

There was a story a bum had told him once when he was a boy, one that he had never forgotten. Pressing his face to the cold glass, Tetch spoke. "I am the king of the dead."

THIRD STRIKE
Hand of God

"I know what I saw," Dalton repeated. Sergeant Gregory stared at him over a tin cup filled with lukewarm, reprocessed water, the last they had; they'd be distilling urine before they caught up with the rest of the troops.

"A horseman."

"One of *the* horsemen." The faint odor of smoke made its way to Gregory's nostrils and he looked toward the walls of Jefferson Harbor. "Why here, do you think?"

"Because of us," answered Dalton. "The Hand of God, placed here, waiting to receive the horseman's message. And the message is death, Sergeant. See, as the Army pulls back, Death is finally descending on the badlands to take what's left. I think it reaffirms our strategy."

"But you said you saw him, the horseman, kill a zombie."

"Of course. It makes sense that these living dead would offend one of the Lord's riders. They are the dark spirits risen from the abyss, taking hold of expired human bodies. Lucifer's lot, cast from Heaven and trying to come back. That's my theory anyway."

"How long have you been developing your own gospel, Dalton?" Gregory sniffed. "All that we know is what's written in the book each of us carries. We can't assume based on some hallucination you may have had that—"

"I didn't hallucinate it! I didn't dream it!" Dalton snapped. He almost blurted out the story Logan had told him, if only to make someone else look like the maniac; for Christ's sake he was only seeing what was written in the Holy Book!

"I think it was a sign that the world is being prepared for Christ's return," Dalton stammered. "Is it just coincidence that this squad was made to hang back and receive that sign? I think not."

"All right," Gregory said. "I'll bite. Let's say you saw the horseman. Shouldn't he appear to me too then?"

"Maybe he will."

Coates turned his binoculars to the northwest and saw a vague shape on the horizon, barely discernible in the dusk; he would've mistaken it for a tree if he hadn't already mapped every tree's location during the day. "I think there's a lone feral out there. You want to pick it off, Dalton?"

"Let it come," Gregory said. "'Cap it when it gets a bit closer. We'll use it for kindling."

Barry folded out a little canvas chair and settled herself with her battleaxe in her lap. "Sarge knows how to make the most of 'em."

"I wouldn't recommend relying on them for warmth," Gregory said with a smile, "but I was taught to survive using not only the elements of my surroundings, but those of the enemy coming at me and of the brothers at my side. When your comrades drop, remember, they're nothing but meat. Meat can be a shield, and meat can be used as a distraction. When a rotter goes down in flames, you can sling him into a horde and take the whole lot out. You can use the starving, weak, immobile undead in a pinch for barricades or fuel. I can see him now, Coates. It's fine, let the bugger come and we'll break him down for the fire."

Coates nodded, and positioned himself to blow the rotter's knees out once he came within range.

"You ever have to eat someone?" Ahmed asked.

The camp fell silent. Barry raised an interested eyebrow.

"That's what separates us from them," Logan spat.

Dalton laughed. "Is that it?" Logan glared darkly at him.

"If it came down to it, if you were starving and alone, and not infected—would you?" Ahmed asked. "It's a question they put to all new recruits."

"Do they, now?" Gregory asked. "Cannibalism in the field isn't as common as you may have heard, son. We have enough rations. We're not about to eat our dead. If we did, it would be an act of utter desperation. The Lord condemns what those—"

There was a pop.

Coates pitched forward.

Everyone else hit the dirt a half-second later, their eyes glued to Coates. The man's head showed purple and smooth in the dim glow of the flashlights. He'd been shot through the head, the cheap bullet erupting inside his brain and spitting out the top of his skull.

"God!"

"The fuck?"

"Did it come from the city?"

"Kill the noise!" Gregory hissed.

Dalton rolled to gather the flashlights. Lying atop them, he peered through his night-vision scope. "That rotter—it's got a gun."

Gregory, his heart thumping against the dirt, wormed through the campsite to the newly moistened spot where Coates lay. It had been a clean kill. The feral must have had some shooter's training in the remnants of its mind, some bit of skill that enabled it to pick off the scout from that distance in this light.

"God damn him," he breathed, pulling himself along the ground, inches from Dalton. "It might be one of the deserters who skipped out of the Harbor . . . there were six of them, they stole away in the night with a cache of small arms. Fucker."

Barry came up on the other side of Dalton. "I don't see him."

"He dropped to the ground right after we did. I think I see him now . . . wait. That's not . . . Shit. I lost him in the brush."

"We've got to go after him. What's out that way, Dalton?" Gregory asked. Coates had been assigned to map out the area, but he knew Dalton was constantly on surveillance.

"Not much. There's a little rock quarry about half a click out . . . we might be able to flush him into it." Dalton turned to look up at Gregory. "In a few hours, he won't have enough visibility to snipe at us. That's the time to move in and corral him."

"Rotter was stalking us, God knows for how long." Gregory was fuming. "It knows we're armed. It means to pick each of us off, then come in and feed." The sergeant sat up, wringing his hands. "Exactly what I've been talking about. They're starting to strategize."

"Maybe that isn't it," Barry whispered. "Maybe it's waiting to see what we do with the body. If we'll leave our dead behind for it to feed on."

"I won't give the bastard the satisfaction," Gregory said. It had to be a deserter who'd gotten infected in the badlands and turned tail, coming back to the city as an undead. A traitor to the end. "Ahmed, read Coates his Last Rites. Not worth much here, not now, but it might do his soul some good in its passage to the other side. We'll light him up when we move out."

BEFORE THE EMPIRE
"Walking Among the Dead"
by Mark Duncan

Published in Soldier *magazine . . .*

It's the first of April and a lot of soldiers around me are feeling the fool right now. The encampment is on the Oklahoma-Texas border, or what once was the Oklahoma-Texas border. It's a refueling station with a few beds and some supplies for the troops. The guys before us cleaned most of the place out.

I've spent much of my recent time with Sergeant Jose Fields. He's lost two brothers and two sisters in the last year—all of them serving in the Armed Forces—and is determined to see this last military operation through to the end. But waiting for his battalion's call to withdraw has begun to wear on his nerves. "At this point we're just waiting. Waiting and trying to keep each other alive."

Late last year I interviewed Senator Sam Gillies for the *Sentinel's* final issue. The entire interview was not published. Excluded from the *Sentinel* piece was a discussion about the military's plight in the badlands. What follows is from that discussion.

Mark Duncan: Rumors of a full withdrawal from the badlands region of the U.S. circulate all the time in the field. Is there any work being done to set a timetable, and what has the Senate done to address the concerns of servicemen and women?

Senator Gillies: We're doing everything in our power to secure the safety of civilians and soldiers alike. The real conflict arises from some Americans' refusal to leave areas designated as uninhabitable. We want to keep these people alive, or course, but how much of our resources can we be expected to expend when these individuals are essentially defying a federal order to get out of there? These places are not safe! The badlands are areas that have fallen to the undead. It's a sad but true fact. People are paranoid about the government's intentions. Why? What dark ulterior motive could we possibly have when we, with heavy hearts, pull out of these regions? We urge these people to trust their government in this most dire time and leave the badlands on their own. Then we can start pulling troops back.

You see, Mark, the problem with setting a timetable is that so many people would simply ignore it. Then the troops are gone and all those people are left defenseless against the growing hordes out there. It would be a hollow, meaningless gesture to set a timetable.

MD: Senator, many in the badlands feel that redrawing America's borders and declaring areas "uninhabitable" is just as hollow a gesture. They believe we should fight to keep the country intact.

SG: How? We'd be spread too thin, and once our military and federal aid resources are exhausted, they're exhausted. We need to gather together what we have left and use it to create renewable resources in a safe, contained region. I'm talking about a place with farmland, nuclear power, schools, health care, security—it's not out there in the badlands. We simply can't do it. Look, America isn't admitting defeat here. We'll only be defeated if we lose every last patch of soil and every last life to these undead. America is still alive.

MD: Is the Senate still investigating the possibility of a cure, or way to wipe out the zombies?

EMPIRE

SG: First of all, I don't refer to them as "zombies." I don't want to trivialize the threat we're facing here. By God, these are the walking dead, soulless things eating up the world we knew. I'm convinced this is because of sin and disorder. And I'll tell you one thing, ignoring the U.S. Government and trying to hold onto these badlands will only end in grave, gruesome consequence.

Now about a cure—we don't even know what the virus is. We don't understand what we're seeing under our microscopes. This catalyst, this thing that reanimates the dead—some scientists have speculated that it can bond to any common blood-borne virus. They've suggested that it isn't the virus itself which is the plague. Again I'm telling you this is something brought about by God's wrath. And are the people out there praying to Him? I know I am.

Is there a biochemical weapon that we can use to target only the undead? Not that we know of, and we simply don't have the resources available to try and develop one. You also have to remember that there are animals and other things that are undead, running around out there.

MD: You've made some references to God and to this plague perhaps being a sort of punishment—can you talk more about that?

SG: Well look, America was the greatest, strongest nation on this earth and it was a Christian nation. But we were still full of sin. And we still are! Sin and mistrust feed this plague and increase the numbers of undead. If we worked together and had faith in one another and in God above, we could begin to conquer this thing. I believe that.

MD: If you succeed in consolidating America's people and resources, will there be an election system put into place, or will you and the other members of the Senate remain in power indefinitely?

SG: We'll cross that bridge when we come to it. As is we don't have the confidence of the American people behind us.

169

We need that before we can begin talking about elections and balance of power and all this.

MD: You're the president of the Senate and, effectively, the leader of the country. What does that mean to you, to be the leader of this country?

SG: It means I'm doing everything I can with my two hands to hold this great nation together and restore its glory. It means I love America and all Americans, and I'm reaching out to each and every one of them right now. We need your cooperation and support, and then we can bring the troops home, we can bring you home, we can all have a home to come to.

When Sergeant Jose Fields reads the text of the preceding interview, he scoffs and sips his day-old coffee. "We're just running in circles," he says.

It's dawn on April 2nd. A pack of rotters attack the camp. Rocker Jenna O'Connell and her crew, here to offer the troops some much-needed eye candy, are ushered into a tent while soldiers line up on the perimeter. They drop the rotters at a distance by shooting apart their legs, then set them aflame.

Sergeant Jose Fields is nudging a smoldering body with the toe of his boot when it sits up and bites his shin.

"Goddamn it." He's sitting in the medical tent right now. The bite broke the skin, drew blood, and he knows his fate. His captain is talking to him about options as I look on.

"We can take you outside tonight, away from the camp. We'll go out past the rocks and do it quietly," the captain says. "You and I will do it, Jose. All right?"

"Goddamn it all," Sergeant Fields mutters, fighting back tears.

"You'll be with your brothers and sisters soon."

Fields has basically shut down. He spends the rest of the day in the tent, under suicide watch. That's what they call it when they're waiting for an infected soldier to die and rise again.

I was taken out later with a scout team, and didn't see what became of Sergeant Jose Fields. I'm told that he and his captain walked out past the rocks at sunset.

It's April 3rd and we're on the move. Texas is hot and empty. I'll finish this article tonight and dictate it by radio to the home office. Haven't seen many dead today; a few stragglers in the distance, nothing to worry about.

The convoy's lead driver is a drunk named Timms who tells filthy jokes and muses on life's little tragedies while we thunder across the desert floor. "Half of us will be dead before summer's end," he says. He's got some homemade mash in a flask on the dashboard and stops every few sentences to offer me a swig. "I guess I'm okay with it. I'm okay with the job, too, gives me something to do until the fuckers finally get a hold of me. You ready to die, Duncan? 'Cause I'll tell ya, God don't give a fuck one way or the other."

I might share Timms' words with Senator Gillies if we ever meet again. After I'm done dictating this piece, I think I might just hunt Timms down and have a drink with him.

—MD

CHAPTER TWENTY-EIGHT
Dawn

The East Harbor Mall on the next block had been one of the first large buildings to fall when the outbreak began in the early 21st century. Some old movie about zombies had sent dozens of townspeople fleeing to the mall, hoping to barricade themselves inside its stores and wait out the nightmare. Those who didn't kill each other were quickly cornered and ripped apart by the undead.

Clothing outlets, restaurants, a department store and a movie theater were among the empty husks within the mall. Everything from underwear to cash to theater seats had been plundered, and the bloodstained floors were eventually licked clean and the place was abandoned to the elements. Squatters were known to spend a night or two in malls, but the buildings were generally regarded as unsafe.

Voorhees led the group, checking each outlet to see if the entryways' security gates still worked. Most had been torn down.

Jenna and Lauren brought up the rear, holding each other to no effect. The terrified couldn't comfort the terrified, Mark Duncan observed. Still, he thought he'd give it a shot.

"We'll be okay. We're with these people now," he told the women. Neither responded. "We're better off than we were at Fetish," he continued. "That cop said we're on our way to the police department. He's got it secured."

"The cop who killed that man?" Lauren stammered.

"Here we go!" Mike called. They were ushered into a store with nothing on its walls to indicate what it had once sold. Voorhees pulled down the security gate.

"What good will that do?" asked Wendy.

"It'll do," Voorhees grumbled.

"I've got to get back to my apartment," Mike told him. "Cheryl, the girl I told you about, she's there. You continue to the PD and we'll catch up."

"Out of the question," Voorhees shot back. Then, lowering his voice: "You're the only one I trust. Probably the only one who trusts me, now."

"I'll take Shipley with me."

"Why would you do that?"

"What if Cheryl can ID him as her attacker?"

Cop instincts taking over, Voorhees considered it. He eyed Shipley, who was sitting alone in the back of the room.

"Take my gun, Mike. No one else knows it's empty."

Mike nodded gratefully and motioned to Shipley. "We've gotta go get somebody."

"What? Why me?"

"If you'd rather stay with me, just say so," Voorhees cracked.

Shipley narrowed his eyes and got up. "Fuck that."

Mike raised the gate, and Voorhees handed over the pistol. Shipley stopped in front of the senior P.O. before leaving. "You take care of these people."

"That's my job." Voorhees pushed Shipley into the corridor and slammed the gate back down.

Mike led Shipley back the way they'd come, and they scanned the mall parking lot for rotters. There were none. The shelter was being rapidly consumed by flames, filling the early morning sky with black smoke.

"Don't try running, or anything else," Mike told Shipley.

The other man snorted. "If I wanted to run I'd have already done it. If I wanted to do something else, I'd have already done that too."

Shipley had deserted the military, had run from his prison sentence, but with a purpose. He wasn't a coward. He was running *to* something, not *from* it.

He'd deserted with two other soldiers: King, a female, and Bish. The pair were in love and talked all the time about escaping the badlands and finding some lost beach to fuck on for the rest of their days. Shipley had thought they were both out of their gourds but kept his mouth shut.

They tromped across the dry, barren earth with a few stolen supplies. There was no safe cover under which to set up camp, so they each slept with one eye open. Tried to, anyway. More than once Shipley had been stirred from a foggy dream to spy King thrashing atop Bish like she was a porn star. More than once she was watching Shipley while doing it.

"I'm bit," Bish said one morning while picking the charred skin off of an unlucky lizard. He pulled up his camouflage tee and showed Shipley a bite on his side. It was old. "How long ago?" Shipley demanded. They hadn't seen a rotter since they'd deserted.

"A few weeks?" Bish shrugged. "I don't think I'm infected. The window's five to ten days before you croak, isn't it?"

"They don't know. They don't know shit about it, no matter what they say," Shipley replied. King was relieving herself behind a bush. "She know?" he asked.

"She's seen it." Bish bit into the lizard with a crunch. "She don't care."

Because she can just plant herself on my face once you're dead, Shipley thought. He took a tiny sip from his canteen. "Maybe I can't get infected," Bish mused through a mouthful of guts. "It's like Gerry, you know, how she can't get pregnant."

Bish was functionally retarded, Shipley decided, and went hunting for his own lizard.

It was a few nights later that Bish slipped into a coma. He'd just shot his wad, and King shook Shipley awake with a rumpled shirt held to cover what he'd already seen.

"Maybe it's heat exhaustion," she said while he looked over the unconscious soldier. She'd pulled on the bottoms of her fatigues and was walking around topless; Shipley ignored the swaying of her breasts as she took shallow breaths.

"He's dead," Shipley muttered. They didn't have anything to decapitate Bish with, let alone torch him. The cheap combat knives handed out to grunts by the Army could barely cut a steak. Shipley would have to saw at muscle and bone until the blade broke, then wrench the head completely off.

King wailed. "He can't be! How did it happen? Not the bite! It wasn't the bite!!"

"Of course it was the bite, you fucking . . ." Shipley spat and turned away. He pulled out his knife and she seized his wrist.

"Please don't do this to him! Just leave him in peace—"

"Cut the crap! You didn't love him!" Shipley plunged the knife into Bish's throat. King opened her mouth, but no sound came out. "I know what love is," Shipley said softly, and started sawing.

Bish threw him off with a gurgling cry.

Shipley lost the knife in the darkness. He scrambled to his feet and saw Bish sitting up, blood gushing down his bare chest.

"Oh God!" King sagged, sobbing hysterically. Bish turned to look at her and more blood spurted from his ragged wound.

"King! Get away from him!!" Shipley crawled in circles trying to find the knife. How far could the fucking thing have gone?

"I *do* love you!" King cried, taking Bish's face in her hands. He stared dully upward, and she knelt to kiss his mouth.

Shipley's finger found the tip of the knife. Cursing, he grabbed the handle, but not before King's muffled scream rang through the night.

Bish tore the girl's lips away, greedily gnashing at her face, one arm wrapped around her back and the other mauling her breast. Blood spilled over his face, into his gullet, and his wide open eyes stared into hers the entire time.

Shipley buried the blade in the back of Bish's head. There was no response from the undead; as the tip of the knife emerged from his mouth, he met the dying King in a hungry kiss.

Grasping the handle with both hands, Shipley threw all his weight against it. Bish's head was ripped from his neck.

King slumped over on the headless, spasming corpse of her lover. Shipley wrested the knife from the zombie's skull and stood over her, sawing into her throat. He screamed to drown out any sound she might make, and screamed and screamed and screamed until he was utterly alone with the soldiers' unrecognizable remains.

Gerry King was the first and last living person he'd ever killed.

"Here we are." Mike pointed up the staircase of an apartment building. The sun had risen a bit and, though the sky was slightly overcast, it cast its warm light down upon them. Things almost felt normal—normal meaning a Jefferson Harbor without a family of rotters prowling inside its walls.

Mike followed Shipley to the landing, then had him stand back. He rapped on the door. "Cheryl! It's me."

A series of locks snicked as they turned. Cheryl yanked the door open and wiped tears from her eyes. "There was one out here! It had a shovel, going from door to door, and I didn't think it could get in but if it had been here when you came back we would've had trouble . . ."

"It's okay, the coast is clear." Mike stepped into the doorway. "We've gotta go. There's a safer place downtown, with other people. I just need to grab a few things, then we can go."

Yet he didn't go in. He stood beside Cheryl, closing his grip around Voorhees' pistol. There was ammo inside the apartment, but the way she studied the man on the landing kept him at her side. "This is Shipley," he said.

Cheryl just smiled. "Hi."

CHAPTER TWENTY-NINE
Deconstructing the Dead

Just before noon, a series of explosions rocked Jefferson Harbor. Boiling smoke tore into the sky as tongues of flame licked heavenward; at the east end of town, the great gates set into the city wall were flung from their hinges like so much rubbish on the wind.

The medical plaza went up in an unimpressive smattering of flames, but by contrast the Donner Convention Center's entire roof swelled like blistering flesh and was ripped away by the explosions within. The city landfill ignited like a mountain of gas-soaked rags, spewing noxious black smoke that seemed to stretch its tendrils across the sky and swallow the sun.

Gene stood at the edge of the flaming landfill and studied the smoke tower. His cheek was scabbing over where the pipe had cut him before he died; gaseous rumblings in his lower organs had ceased and he felt less pressure inside his abdomen. He was regenerating.

Noon. Voorhees and his survivors were taking the scenic route to the police department. He led them into a long-abandoned construction site to rest. Duncan pointed out the numerous empty buildings across the street, but the cop just shook his head. "Don't trust 'em."

"But—"

"Did you not hear those explosions earlier? Look at the smoke out there. Let's stay out here a while—we can spot a rotter coming from blocks away in any direction."

"What if Mike and the others reach the station before we do?" Palmer asked. "Does he know how to get in?"

"He can figure it out."

"Wheeler—" Jenna began. Voorhees shot her a dark look. Staring right back at him, she went on. "He said something about the 'Addison estate'—a house in the swamp?"

"I said that. The house in the swamp part." Palmer sat on a concrete slab and peered up into the steel ribcage of an unfinished office building. "Addison was a doctor who lived out on the west end. That was years and years ago. He's got to be dead."

"Well, what about those rotters then? Wheeler said he recognized them. He called them kids."

"I'm hungry," Kipp mumbled.

Wendy patted his head. "We'll eat soon, honey."

"It looks like rain," Voorhees observed.

Jenna walked past him to Palmer. "Wheeler called the rotters kids."

"The children that Addison took in, the children of the wealthy," Palmer said. "I wouldn't be able to recognize any of them, especially if they were undead. I don't see how Wheeler could have."

"It's just . . ." Jenna sighed, picked up a rock, tossed it into an open basement. "It's something."

"We all want answers," Palmer replied, in a counseling tone.

Jenna flinched. "Reverend, don't start with that."

"I wasn't going to say anything about God, if that's what

you mean. If God wanted to share something with us, I'd sure as shit know by now. I ask Him every morning and every night. Look. We were all born into a world with undead. We've all spent our entire lives asking questions, and we each desperately want something to hold on to. An answer." Gesturing around the site, Palmer smiled bitterly. "You really think there's an answer in Jefferson Harbor?"

"Why are we still alive?" Lauren asked. She was looking at Kipp, who had knelt to follow a beetle's progress over the soil.

"Laurie, please. I want to find out about these Addison kids," Jenna said.

"Let it go," Duncan grumbled. "The Rev's right."

"They were working together!" Jenna shouted. Lauren went white and pressed a finger to her lips; it went unnoticed and Jenna went on. "I've never seen anything like that! And all of them looked *perfect*. Didn't you notice? They almost seemed alive. Not a mark on them! Those clothes . . . somebody keeps them. Somebody alive."

She pointed to the darkening sky. "Those explosions . . ."

"Okay, now you're grasping at straws." Duncan stood to face her. "I'm a journalist, Jen. I made a whole fucking career out of seeking answers, taking picture after picture of those things, searching for the words to describe them—all by myself, all in a blur until they all looked alike to me. They were here before any of us, and they'll be here after we're gone. All we can hope is that we're not walking among them."

"Very moving. You want to jot that down before you forget?"

"Jen—"

"Don't call me that, asshole."

"I think Kipp's getting sick," Wendy broke in, quickly adding, "from the weather. Looks like it could rain. Between that and the smoke don't you think we should be indoors, Officer?"

"There's shelter here." Grabbing a bit of plastic sticking out of the earth, Voorhees pulled an entire sheet from the dirt and shook it clean. "Let's get beneath the scaffolding, and if it does rain we can drape this over the planks. Okay?"

The group reluctantly gathered together, in stubborn silence, but thankful for the company.

In the auto shop behind the remains of the shelter, Sawbones had managed to work himself out from under the shelf. He rolled over, propped himself up and looked at his nearly-severed feet.

Carefully he took them, one at a time, in his hands, and he tore them off.

The damage done to the dog's-skull had loosened the wires fastening it to his head; he rolled over and slammed his face into the floor. The skull shattered, bone hanging in bits from the sides of his head. He tugged the wires out of his flesh.

Sawbones' exposed head was nothing but raw meat with patches of malformed skin. His jaw had been wired shut. He pawed at the workbench beside him until it spilled tools into his lap. There, pliers.

The doctor went to work.

When it was done, he parted his lips, breaking capillaries that had formed along the seal, and spat black blood. Reaching in, he felt a full set of teeth. Despite only being fed through an IV, he had eaten well. He massaged his jaw until he was able to open and close it without using his hands. Not much biting power, but there were ways he could work around that until he was stronger.

There was no going back to the house in the swamp. No more master, no more others. He grabbed the axe and began the process of standing on the stumps of his legs.

Rain started falling on the roof. He rose, fell, rose, fell, carved bits of meat and bone away from his ankles to improve his balance.

Finally, he stood and stayed standing. It required the support of the axe handle, like a crutch, but he was standing. Sawbones took slow, wet steps across the floor. Several times he grabbed at the wall to steady himself. He'd need a better crutch. Especially since the axe was needed for other things.

Sawbones walked out into the rain and opened his eyes and lips to receive it.

It felt good.

CHAPTER THIRTY
Under

"What about food?" Wendy complained.

Voorhees dragged the plastic sheeting over their heads. "It can wait. None of us is starving yet."

Standing over an unfinished basement, Lauren watched rain pool at its bottom. Jenna gently brought her away from the edge. Duncan watched them confer in hushed tones.

"What's with her attitude?" Voorhees asked the photographer. "She's not a goddamn rock star anymore."

Duncan was surprised at his own words. "Don't pigeonhole her as a spoiled bitch. She wasn't making demands, she was looking for answers. Like the Rev said."

"Doesn't matter. You'd better take her aside and let her know that she better listen to me, for her own damn good." Voorhees pressed a finger into Duncan's chest. "Unlike the rest of you, I still have a job."

Duncan stared silently at the finger between his ribs. The P.O. removed it, saying "I'm not trying to come off like a son of a bitch here. But I won't compromise anyone's safety. Got it?"

"Tell her yourself," Duncan muttered.

Lauren pulled away from Jenna and walked out from under

David Dunwoody

the scaffolding. "Come back here!" Voorhees yelled. He grabbed Jenna's arm. "Go get her!"

"For fuck's sake—"

"I won't tell you again."

Jenna threw his hand off. "We made it long enough without taking crap from people like you."

Palmer wedged herself between the two of them. "This isn't accomplishing anything."

"No shit," Voorhees snarled through gritted teeth. Then he saw something, from the corner of his eye: Lauren stiffened and came to a dead stop in the rain.

Climbing over a concrete abutment, Zaharchuk, the dealer, trained his Desert Eagle on her.

"Stay there," he coaxed, hands trembling, the gun jerking from side to side. Lauren whimpered, but remained still until he was able to slip his arm around her and turn her to face the others.

Voorhees' hand flew to his empty holster. "Fuck." He reached behind his back for the widowmaker.

"Leave it, old man," Zaharchuk called. "I've seen you, I watch you when you're not watching me. I know all of you."

"He's crazy," Duncan whispered. Voorhees stepped out from under the plastic.

"Stop!" Zaharchuk barked.

"Okay." Voorhees held up his hands. "I'm unarmed. Why don't you lose the gun?"

"I know you've got a cleaver strapped to your back, shit-heel." The mouth of the Desert Eagle dug into Lauren's neck. She closed her eyes. Zaharchuk pressed his cheek against her shoulder, peering at Voorhees as if from a foxhole.

"Tell me what you want," The patrol officer said. There was silence in response. "We don't have any food or drugs. We don't have anything to offer but shelter. Safety. Is that what you want? Do you want to travel with us?"

Zaharchuk's eyes narrowed, but still he said nothing. He adjusted his grip on the rain-soaked pistol.

184

"We're all in the same situation here," Voorhees continued. "If you want our help, you need to let that girl go. Put that gun away."

Jenna stared hard at Lauren, trying to send her strength through her eyes. Just hold on—don't move, don't cry, don't make a fucking sound.

Zaharchuk wiped his nose on Lauren's shoulder. "This is my gun! I'm the one who's safe!"

"Then get out from behind that girl."

Zaharchuk's fried logic had put him in a corner, Duncan knew, and the maniac would only try to shoot his way out.

Wendy screamed from the back of the group. Zaharchuk yanked Lauren's hair back and pressed the Eagle to her chin.

Voorhees, glancing back, saw Wendy teetering on the edge of the unfinished basement; the zombie had come up and grabbed her by the ankle. The zombie, the one they'd left behind, the one they'd crippled, had her leg. She shrieked and reached for the others.

Then she lost her footing and dropped into the cellar.

"What the fuck was that! *What the fuck!*" Zaharchuk shoved Lauren forward. The gun was trained on her head. He was going to shoot.

Voorhees whipped the widowmaker through the air; it buried itself between Zaharchuk's eyes, and he flopped back into the mud without so much as a squeal.

Palmer dragged Kipp away from the edge of the basement. Down below, Sawbones was on top of Wendy, tearing at her clothes, her flesh. He pressed his gaping maw into her throat, and the puddle beneath them turned dark crimson.

Voorhees tore off his trench coat and made a running leap into the basement. Pain stabbed through his legs as he landed with a splash. Sawbones, the horror under the mask revealed, turned and grunted.

He had the axe. Voorhees was driven back by a wild swing. Clambering over the earth like an infant, Sawbones swept the axe through the air, scant inches, then millimeters from Voorhees' knees.

Duncan landed behind the rotter and ran to Wendy. Her throat was an open wound brimming with blood. Her eyes, unblinking, collected rainwater.

Voorhees moved in a wide circle. Sawbones followed. Did he remember the cop? Of course he did, and he knew that Voorhees was his greatest threat. Nothing would stop the undead from taking him out. Except . . . "Get the widowmaker!" he screamed at those standing topside. "The blade!"

Jenna ran past a sobbing Lauren and wrenched at the handle jutting from Zaharchuk's face.

Duncan grabbed Sawbones' leg and pulled it from beneath him, sending the rotter face first into a puddle. Sawbones sputtered and rolled over, heaving the axe with both hands.

It spun past Duncan, and searing heat lanced his thigh; he saw the bloodless gash open wide and turn red in the space of a second.

Voorhees fell upon Sawbones and locked his arms around the rotter's neck. SNAP-SNAP-SNAP-SNAP went vertebrae and still it clawed at the cop's eyes.

Jenna jumped down. She saw Duncan lying in a red-and-brown paste. "Mark!"

"Kill it," Duncan groaned through white lips.

She ran at Sawbones. "Move, Voorhees!"

He released the rotter and rolled through the mud.

Sawbones stared up at Jenna, at the widowmaker, followed the gleaming steel through the rain and into his throat.

She straddled him and hacked away at his face, driving the blade all the way into the ground, again and again, blending the pulverized remains of Sawbones' real skull with the earth under him.

Voorhees ripped a sleeve from his shirt and tied a crude tourniquet around Duncan's leg. "She's still . . ." Duncan sat up and pointed at Jenna's frantic chopping. She was chopping nothing. Voorhees eased Duncan back down on his back. "Don't talk."

"I could hear you from a block away!" Someone shouted over the edge: Mike. Then the scope of the carnage below hit him, and he fell silent.

"Wound's not that deep," Voorhees said to Duncan. He heard a slapping sound and turned. Sawbones' head was gone. Jenna was attacking a slick of gore.

She fell into the mud and screamed.

A moment later, Shipley's voice rose even above hers.

"Where's the kid? Where's Kipp?"

Had any of the survivors scaled the skeleton building and stood at its peak, they would have seen the boy stumbling out of the construction site, heading west toward the Jefferson Harbor Museum.

To the east, they might have also seen a cloud on the horizon. Not in the sky, but on the ground—feral undead converging on the pillars of smoke that rose from the city.

CHAPTER THIRTY-ONE
Daddy

Mike pulled Shipley away from the others. "Cut the hysterics!"

"He's my *son*," Shipley gasped. "They took him when I went to prison. They took him but I kept track of him, I knew where he was, I came here for him, don't you fucking get it? Where is he!"

"Jesus." Mike glanced at the dead guy a few yards away, a local dealer he'd seen in Voorhees' files. The Desert Eagle still lay in his hand.

Retrieving the gun and checking its magazine to find it full, he trotted to the edge of the basement. Voorhees was standing between an unconscious Duncan and a weeping Jenna. He himself seemed to be in shock.

Mike gestured for him to approach and lowered his voice. "I think Shipley and I should go look for the boy."

"What?" Voorhees turned the words over and over in his head, but could make no sense of them. He was still seeing blood, pools and geysers and clouds of blood. The rain on his head felt like blood and he swatted angrily at it.

"I'm going to take Shipley to look for the boy," Mike repeated.

"No, no. We all need to stay here. That kid's a goner."

"I know . . ." Mike leaned into the hole, whispering ". . . Cheryl ID'd him. It's *him*."

He showed Voorhees the Eagle, and the man understood.

"Don't do anything stupid," Voorhees mumbled. "Don't waste any bullets. One shot."

Mike nodded and lifted his head out of the basement.

"W-what happened?" Cheryl stammered. She was still standing away from the others, an outsider, not sure if she wanted in.

"It's all right now." Palmer took her hand and led her beneath the scaffolding.

Mike gave her a smile as he tucked the Eagle into his waistband. "I'll be back in a little while."

"We'll be okay," Voorhees called to the group as he climbed up. "That rotter was alone. We'll just wait for Mike and Shipley and Kipp, then we'll get the hell out of here." He patted Cheryl's shoulder. "It's all going to be okay now."

She nodded absently. "I mean," he said, "Shipley won't be coming back."

"Huh?"

"Mike told me. We've been hunting for this bastard for more than a month." Still getting a questioning look from her, Voorhees sighed and said as softly as possible, "Mike told me Shipley's the one who raped you."

Cheryl's frown melted away into a horrified, gaping stare.

"I . . . I never told Mike that . . . I never even told him I was raped . . ."

Mike tossed Voorhees' gun to Shipley as they walked down a slope. "Here. I've got the Eagle."

"This one ain't even loaded," scowled Shipley. "You really think I didn't know?"

"You're a smart guy." Mike smiled at him. There was something wrong about it. The Eagle, turning playfully in his hand, came to rest aimed at Shipley's chest.

"What is this? What are you doing?"

"You know I could kill you right now. I could. Shoot you where you stand and leave you for the rotters."

"Whoa, whoa." Holding his hands out placatingly, Shipley dropped his gruff tone. Only way to deal with cops when they started losing it. If you fought back, you got swatted down and maybe never got back up; he'd seen it a dozen times in lockup. If you rolled into a ball and started begging, they kicked you while you were down. Shipley steadied his tremulous voice and spoke. "I'm not this guy you've been looking for. I'm not a bad guy. I know I've fucked up before but I've never, ever hurt anyone like that. I came here to get my son out of this hellhole and head north. I know where the troops are headed, I know where the cities are. You could come with us! We'd all be safer. But what's important to me—the only thing—is that Kipp's safe. That's all."

"You were serious about that?" Mike laughed, the pistol never wavering. "He's your kid? I'm starting to see the resemblance." As he wielded his power over the other man, Mike seemed to be lost in the moment; but rushing him would break the trance and end in death, Shipley knew.

"How're you going to explain to that retard where you've been? What Daddy did? Sorry son, Daddy liked little girls, not little boys."

"I'll explain as best I can."

"You won't explain shit—you won't tell him a thing, and you know it. He's better off out there with *them.*"

Shipley looked around in desperation. Kipp could be blocks away. He could be in the hands of an undead, another clown . . .

"Just let me go. I'll go myself. We won't come back, we'll leave you alone. How about that? Just let me go, Officer?"

"Ohhhh. 'Officer'. You can go then. I'm sorry." Mike sneered and leveled the pistol with Shipley's head. "Don't condescend to me, cocksucker. Ever."

"Okay, okay."

"Turn around, Shipley."

Knives of ice drove deep into Shipley's veins.

"Offi—Mike . . ."

"Turn. Around."

Shipley's eyes studied the ground. There had to be a rock, a pipe . . . he could run, just run. Now! No, the cop wouldn't miss. The falling rain drummed maddeningly on his head.

"I want to tell you," Mike called genially, "one thing before we do this."

"Tell us both."

Not Mike's voice.

Voorhees kept his distance from the other P.O. He let his presence sink in before saying another word.

"What are you doing here? I've got this," Mike growled.

"She got pregnant, Mike. With your baby. She miscarried."

In a half-second the entire scene shifted. Mike was exposed, he had no way out, no excuses, no lies. He kept the gun trained on Shipley and looked at his partner. "Cheryl."

"Yes." Voorhees scratched his stubble. His stomach mewled. Mike lowered the gun slightly, just slightly, the barrel still pointing at Shipley, who stood stock-still.

"How did I miss it?" asked Voorhees, sighing. "You could hardly wait to start once you'd arrived in town." Then, angrily, "You interviewed each of those victims. You comforted them, held them, sent them north 'for their own safety' with their boyfriends or sisters or, if they had nobody left, nobody. Why'd you really pressure them to leave the Harbor? Did you think something might click, that they'd hear the perp's voice in their heads and realize it was yours?"

"They always do," Mike answered, "eventually. I wish I could be there when it happened . . . but I wanted to stay here. I mean, I like it here. Just the two of us working the case, the only cops in town, the only ones they had. And then this guy—"

Mike pulled the trigger. Shipley flew back. The gun was pointed at Voorhees before he could draw a breath.

"With him I could stay even longer. There wasn't any need to convince you, was there? You liked him for it the second you saw him!"

Shipley twitched in the mud. He'd taken a gut shot. It was a wonder he wasn't screaming. Voorhees glanced over and saw that the man's eyes were locked on the two cops.

"I think I know how this is going to work," Mike murmured. "That first shot was Shipley. He popped you with your gun, the one I gave him. The second shot is me killing him."

"Is this what you wanted all along?" Voorhees asked. The widowmaker's sheath on his back was unclasped; he feigned shivers and tried to drop the blade into his hand. "You wanted to take control of the group? Have those women relying completely on you?"

"Well, I didn't plan it out like this, but it works."

"Sure it does. You'd need to get rid of me, of course, wouldn't you, Mike. Because I'm stronger than you, because they listen to me even if they don't like me. That's real power, isn't it?"

"Oh, fuck you," Mike spat. "They'd turn on you just like that. I could turn them—"

"We'll never know, will we? You're gonna kill me and go back there with some bullshit story that makes you look like a hero. Bullshit, bullshit—"

"Shut up!"

"Bullshit, Mike. You're full of it. Cheryl knows you raped her. What're you going to do about that? How're you gonna walk away from that a hero? Think fast, Mike!"

Voorhees hurled the widowmaker. It glanced off Mike's knuckles and he dropped the gun with a howl. Just as quickly, his other hand dropped to scoop it up.

Voorhees delivered a knee into Mike's forehead with a CRACK. Weisman went sprawling and Voorhees grabbed the Eagle. His knee gave out from under him and he rolled toward Shipley.

Mike got up, screaming, and found the widowmaker.

There was a thunderclap, and he spun wildly through the air before landing facedown.

Shipley could barely hold the gun. He dropped it in his lap.

Voorhees cradled his kneecap and fumbled through his pockets for a handkerchief. "Hold tight, Shipley."

"No." Wheezing, the man rolled over and struggled to a standing position.

"What are you doing?" Voorhees demanded.

Slipping the Eagle into his jeans, Shipley pointed west. "I'm gonna get my boy. Then we're gone." He staggered off.

Voorhees fought to get back on his feet. "I'm sorry!"

Shipley gave him half a glance and a dismissive wave.

Jenna came over the hill where Mike's body lay. She took the widowmaker from him and, searching her surroundings for any sign of the undead, descended toward Voorhees.

Shipley left the construction site. He crossed the street and headed up the steps of a museum with its doors hanging open. About halfway up, he stopped to catch his breath, to stem the pain radiating through his entire body, and he saw Kipp come out.

The boy's gaze, which once had bespoken nothing but love, was now only hungry. He shuffled down the steps with arms open to receive his father.

CHAPTER THIRTY-TWO
Empty Places

Down a set of stairs at the rear of the police station, through a locked door and into a dark tunnel beneath the three-story structure, Voorhees led the others to the PD's only non-barricaded entrance. The door had a new lock and four bolts, for which he had all the keys.

The others were silent. They'd heard the gunshots, heard Jenna and Voorhees' accounts of Mike Weisman's death and what had preceded it. Shipley and Kipp were gone. Cheryl was in shock, and Palmer drew her coat around the girl and held her close.

The only light in the lobby came from a shattered skylight overhead; the many doors and windows had been covered with boards, desks and shelves. Rain pooled on the floor and Voorhees led them carefully around the water. "Up those stairs." He tossed his keys to Lauren. Jenna was supporting Duncan, but Lauren turned and handed the keys to her anyway.

"It's the first hallway, first door on the right. My name's on it." Voorhees walked to the barricades and reached between two overturned desks, pulling out a pump shotgun. "There's a first-aid kit up there too, in my desk. Clean Duncan's wound."

"How?" Jenna asked from the bottom of the steps.

Voorhees sighed. "Hold on."

Leading them upstairs, he unlocked a room marked EVIDENCE and went inside. A second later, he appeared with two jugs of distilled water. "One of these is for drinking. Conserve it." He handed that to Palmer. "Use the other one to clean his leg. I'm gonna have to stitch it up."

"Whoa, whoa." Duncan swayed in Jenna's arms. "Let's just dress the leg and call it a day."

"It needs to be closed up."

"Just bandage it. I don't want stitches."

Voorhees reached back into the darkness of the evidence room. He pulled out a dusty plastic bag with pills in it, some crushed. "You'll forget all about the pain. Deal?"

Duncan shrugged helplessly. Voorhees stuffed the bag in his pocket and locked the room up. He brought everyone into his office: a chair, some overturned buckets stacked with files, a water jug and a can which purported to hold coffee beans. Sure enough, it did. Voorhees popped one into his mouth and gestured to the open can. "Eat up."

Cheryl stared blankly at the can. "Sorry, fresh out of roast duck," Voorhees grumbled.

"Leave her be," Palmer said sternly.

Duncan was helped to the floor, back propped against the wall. Voorhees handed him a few pills. "What are those?" Jenna asked.

"You don't recognize these babies?" Voorhees answered. "I thought you kept bowls of them backstage." Before she could retort, he said to the others, "The squeamish need to wait outside. Don't leave this floor, don't mess with locked rooms. Okay?"

Palmer took Cheryl out of the room. Lauren looked from Jenna to the door. "I'm staying, Laurie," Jenna said quietly. "Just hang out in the hall. Okay?"

Lauren nodded glumly and left. The door clicked in her wake, and the room was silent.

Duncan took the pills with a mouthful of water and closed his eyes. "How long?"

"Ten minutes and you'll be under. You'll feel like it, anyway." Voorhees fished the first-aid kit out from under his files and, removing the tourniquet from Duncan's leg, pressed a wad of gauze against the wound. "O'Connell, there's a little bag under the chair. See it? Needle and thread are inside."

Jenna opened the bag. "Are you kidding?"

"What?"

"These are for mending socks."

"You got another idea? Kiss it better maybe? We need to close this gash up before it gets infected."

Infected . . . what a choice of words. Jenna threw the bag to Voorhees.

Duncan's breathing had relaxed, and he looked like he might be slipping into unconsciousness. Jenna sat in the chair and watched Voorhees thread his needle. "I don't know what kind of person you think I am, but I was never a drug-addicted slut."

"Every professional musician since the plague has been a drug-addicted slut," the cop replied flatly. "It's their escape from the world."

"So what's yours? Playing policeman in a ghost town?"

He didn't say anything for a few minutes. Duncan moaned slightly, then his head fell onto his chest.

"I stayed here to help the residents who refused to leave. It's their right to stay and it's their right to be protected."

"Did you ever ask yourself why I came out here?" Jenna felt something rising in her throat, a sob maybe; she choked it down and went on. "Why would I come to a coastal city under martial law if I was just a party girl? I thought maybe . . . I don't know, I thought I could make people smile a little. There's nothing wrong with forgetting about the hell we live in for just one day. If all we're doing anymore is surviving, what's the fucking point?"

Voorhees removed the gauze from Duncan's wound and

shifted to sit beside the unconscious man. "You've got me there."

In the hallway, Cheryl and Lauren stood quiet while Palmer rummaged through another office. She came out with a pair of gloves. "Anyone cold?"

The girls shook their heads. Palmer went to put the gloves on, and a crumpled cigarette pack fell from the left one.

She knelt and picked it up. There were smokes inside.

"Mother of God," Cheryl whispered.

She leaned forward eagerly, and Palmer handed her one. She stuck a second cigarette in her own mouth and went back into the office. "There must be a light in here. Lord, let there be a light."

A cry of triumph, and she came out holding a tiny flame to her lips. Cheryl ran over to light up. They both inhaled slowly, filling their throats, their lungs; they sighed happily.

"You smoke?" Palmer asked Lauren. She shook her head no.

"I never, ever, ever dreamed I'd smoke again." Cheryl held her cigarette out before her, as if it perhaps weren't real. "I haven't smoked since I was seventeen. And just one cost you the shirt off your back! This . . ."

"It's a blessing." Palmer spoke through a gray cloud. She propped herself against the wall. "It'll help with the hunger pangs. Are you sure you don't want one, Lauren?" Another shake of the head.

"Where did you come here from, Hon?" the reverend asked Cheryl.

"The badlands."

"Really? How'd you end up here?"

"Long story."

"We've got plenty of time."

"I was with my brother, and he was dodging the draft. There are thousands of people out there in shanty towns. It's really not that bad, about the same as it is here . . . just no walls."

"No cops either."

Cheryl shuddered at that.

"I'm sorry," Palmer gasped, "I didn't mean—"

"I know, I know. I can't even bring myself to think about that right now. But my brother . . . well, as we moved further south he started dropping hints that I should stay with my cousin here in the Harbor. He was only trying to look out for me, but I felt like I was a burden or something. I got more and more difficult . . . those last weeks together we fought constantly. I cursed him for running away from the Army and taking me with him, even though I knew Portland had fallen. Portland, Oregon, our hometown."

"Ah."

"Anyway, we weren't too far outside the city gates when a couple of rotters hit us. They must have been wandering all around the walls, because as soon as I screamed more of them came stumbling out of the night. There were . . . there were runners. Have you ever seen them?" Tears welled in Cheryl's eyes.

"I have," Palmer nodded. "You're lucky to be alive."

"I'm not lucky. He saved me. He pulled them off of me and onto himself . . . he laid there, and they took the easy prey while I ran."

"If he hadn't, you wouldn't be here now, and I know you'd say that's not much consolation, but you can't blame yourself. You can't tell yourself that you weren't worth saving. If you do, that means his death was a waste."

Cheryl stubbed her cigarette butt out on a windowsill. She didn't speak. Palmer gave her another one.

"Maybe you're right," the girl finally said.

A few hours later, Duncan was awake, though groggy, and he was carried by Voorhees and Jenna down the hall to a dark room. They placed him on a cot. The door closed, and Duncan stared into blackness.

He heard a weight shifting beside the cot.

"Someone there?"

"It's me." Jenna's voice. "How does the leg feel?"

"I don't feel much. A dull ache, I guess. Ugh, I'm fucking stoned."

"How's your head?"

"Iffy."

Her hands, on the edge of the coat, moved to touch his side.

"Jenna?"

She kissed him on the cheek. Her breath smelled like coffee. "Is this okay?"

"What?"

"I want to do this. Do you?"

"Jenna—"

"If you can't, because of the leg, it's all right." But she began undoing his jeans. And, though he could have stopped her, could have done more than say her name, he didn't.

Water sloshed. A wet cloth slipped into his pants and massaged his crotch. His loins throbbed and he nearly came. "W-what are you doing?"

"I want to be clean." Her pants rustled, descending to her ankles. "I want this to be good. I don't want to fuck, Mark, I want to feel good." She was still massaging him with the cloth, and he rolled slightly, searching with his hands. "You have another?"

She handed the other rag to him. Steadying himself on his elbow, he found her in the dark. Feeling her through the cold cloth, seeing nothing, hearing only his own labored breath—despite it all he somehow felt closer to her than he'd felt to anyone.

She sucked in a deep breath. "Are you crying?" he asked.

"Is it okay if I am?"

"It's okay."

He drew her onto the cot, Jenna carefully straddling his legs, easing herself down. He felt her bare breasts brushing his shirt and he unbuttoned it. Their lips met in a single sigh as their flesh touched.

"Oh God."

"You don't have to hold back," she breathed.

"No, it's not that." He pressed his mouth over hers, tasted her, moaned again. She moved slowly and twinges of pain, of anxiety, gave way to warmth. Outside the room, in the light, in the world, were the dead and the almost-dead. She felt alive, so fucking alive that the tears streamed down her cheeks onto his. He kissed them away and her fingers traveled the rough contours of his face. Getting close, she buried her face in the crook of his neck and let instinct drive her rhythm. He pushed his face against hers, groaned in release.

Shuddering waves erupted through her and she pushed herself back, arching her body to feel it in her back, her toes, her fingertips.

Wary of his thigh, she slipped off of him and found her clothes.

"Jenna?"

"Mark, don't."

He touched her shoulder and plied her back to the cot. "Just stay. Just a while."

"I want to, but . . ."

"Then stay."

She touched his face again. It was the face of a stranger. Jenna fought back the tears this time.

Down the hall, Voorhees stood outside his office. The others were inside; he knew Jenna had stayed in the room with Duncan, so there was only one explanation for the soft footfalls coming from downstairs.

He crept out of the hall and panned the lobby with the shotgun. "Come on up. I've got something for you. All of you. Come get it."

"Don't shoot . . . ?" A man in a soiled dress shirt and slacks poked his bearded head over the banister. "I'm Thom. I work for the city?"

CHAPTER THIRTY-THREE
Silent Running

"I thought that tunnel was sealed off," Voorhees muttered into his fist.

"What tunnel?" Palmer asked, studying Thom's ragged form.

"There's a security tunnel running from the PD to City Hall. Few people outside the mayor's office knew about it. Of course, that was before the mayor jumped." Turning to Thom, Voorhees asked him, "I've never seen anyone going in or out of that building. Every door's barricaded to the max. How many people are over there?"

"Oh, it's just me." The man's voice was timid, quiet. He was used to speaking in whispers, or perhaps not at all. His hands trembled excitedly as he described his situation. "There were other staff staying there, but some left . . . and others . . ."

"Others what?"

"They just didn't make it. There's no food, not much water except what leaks in when it storms like it is now. Do you have any food?"

"Not much, but we'll get you something," Voorhees replied. The man, hugging his emaciated frame, smiled gratefully. "I was a clerk in the mayor's office. The mayor was writing a biography, you know. I've spent the last few months proofreading the manuscript."

This guy was just a little mad. Palmer offered him a cigarette, and he refused it with a wary look. "Terrible for you. Can't fight or run with emphysema. Some of my colleagues were heavy smokers. That's what got them in the end. It eats you from the inside out. Cancer, I mean. It's like a rotter growing inside you. Makes you ashy." Thom grimaced.

"How did you know we were in here, Thom?" the reverend asked.

"I saw you going in. They saw you too, I think. That's why I came over, through the tunnel. Thought you ought to come with me to City Hall."

"Wait, who's 'they?'"

Thom gestured toward the lobby entrance. Hefting the shotgun in his arms, Voorhees climbed onto the barricade and peered through a paper-thin slit in the damaged doors. "Christ Jesus."

Jenna clambered up beside him. He directed her to another crack looking out onto the city plaza.

Dozens of rotters were pouring out of the suburbs that lay beyond Greeley Park. They must have broken through the east gates. But why so many at once—why a horde? She could see why they were congregating around the plaza: if some of them had seen the survivors going into the PD, the rest would follow that group's frenzied activity. Still, that didn't explain why they'd entered the city in such numbers to begin with. The undead population was reportedly sparse around the Harbor . . .

She thought back to the radio broadcast she'd heard, the senator claiming that zombies were migrating to coastal cities as the military withdrew their forces. It didn't make any sense. This many rotters had no way of knowing that military support was gone; it wasn't like they were camped out in the badlands, watching the city. Even if they were picking up federal radio frequencies in their fucking fillings, they couldn't understand the transmissions.

Could they?

Mark appeared beside her, making an effort to prop himself up. "How many?"

"Too many."

"It's the smoke." He slumped down on the barricade. "I've seen mobs of them drawn to fires before. Burning trash or bodies always requires extra security . . . those explosions all over town caught us off-guard and they saw it for miles around."

Grabbing Jenna's hand suddenly, Mark sat up. "What were you going to say back in the construction yard? About the fires?"

"You mean before you cut me off? Told me I was grasping at straws?"

"Yes, before that."

"Don't start this that again," Voorhees yelled. "It doesn't matter right now, we just need to get the hell out of here. Thom, you're sure that City Hall is clear?"

"Absolutely, officer."

"Lead the way."

They went to the rear of the lobby, to a small room adjacent to the defunct elevators. Thom opened a hatch set into the floor and started down the ladder there. "Be careful, it's pitch black in here."

"Great." Lauren pressed herself against Jenna, who embraced her. "We'll go together."

Thom was telling the truth; the tunnel was absolutely dark. His voice echoed off the damp walls. "Just walk straight ahead, keep your arms out. There's some crud on the floor so be sure of your footing. Easy to slip. Plus it smells."

"We noticed," Voorhees grumbled. He was bringing up the rear. Shutting the hatch and securing it as best he could, he dropped into the passage. "Everyone all right?"

"I felt something! On my leg!" Cheryl cried.

"There's nothing down here but us," Thom assured her, but his frenetic tone didn't calm anybody.

There was a dull thudding overhead. "What's that?" Lauren asked. They group stopped moving.

"I think they're in the PD," Voorhees said softly.

"We've almost reached the end of the line," Thom called. "We can seal the hatch once we're out, keep 'em from following us. Just have to keep moving. It's not like they even know—"

A shaft of light appeared back from the PD end of the tunnel.

"Run!" Voorhees dropped into a crouch, facing toward the encroaching threat, and the others rushed toward the hatch that led into City Hall. The others' screams bounced off the walls, made their way down the tunnel and into Voorhees' head, rattling him, but not as much as the silhouettes interrupting the shaft of light. The undead began coming down.

He fired a shotgun blast straight down the tunnel, briefly illuminating the gray-and-green forms of the rotters. It did nothing to slow them down. Voorhees turned and ran.

Thom threw open the City Hall hatch and pulled himself up into a room almost as dark as the tunnel itself. He knelt to assist Cheryl, and they in turn each took one of Palmer's arms. "Hurry!" Lauren cried from below.

The rotters were dropping into the tunnel from the PD hatch at a horrifying rate. Voorhees fired another shot. A rotter, now only scant yards from him, was caught and thrown back into the horde; they swallowed him and kept coming. Voorhees pumped and fired again. Curdled brains sprayed the tunnel's ceiling.

He lunged for the ladder and the others yanked him up, nearly tearing his arms from their sockets. The hatch clanged down and Thom dragged a shelf over it. "We need more!" The rotters beat on the underside of the hatch. Locked as it was, it still jostled in its frame.

Jenna opened the closest door and found herself in a narrow hallway lined with offices. She seized a file cabinet just inside one of the offices and wrestled it back toward the hatch. Voorhees helped her throw it atop the shelf. "More!" he yelled.

They grabbed a second file cabinet and a desk, shoving as much furniture as they could into the tiny room. Then Thom locked the door to the hallway and they began to pile more things in front of it. "Follow me to the fire stairs," Thom said when they had run out of barricading materials.

"The top floor's the most secure," he said breathlessly, taking the steps three at a time. The others could barely keep up. "The other floors are bad. People died there, I haven't been able to get 'em out with the windows all boarded up. You'll notice the smell." It was like a guided tour of Hell.

The fourth-floor corridor was lit by candles. "Not a safe idea," Voorhees commented.

"Oh, I hardly ever leave. I just had to get you guys." Reaching the end of the hallway, Thom moved a shelf away from a window, and they were able to look out over the plaza. "See, this is how I spotted you. I just sit here most days." He gathered a pile of papers and shoved them into a box. "That's the mayor's book."

"What sort of supplies do you have here?" Voorhees peered down and watched the rotters cram themselves through the doors of the police department. Pieces of the barricade in front of the station's main doors spilled down the stairs and were stomped to bits.

"Well, candles and matches, obviously." Thom was pacing around. It made Lauren uneasy, and she sat down on the floor. "Lots of paper. Pencils too, plenty of stationery in general. Weapons . . . well, there are scissors and letter openers, things like that. The guards took all the guns when they deserted us. They left even before the Army did, but the mayor refused to leave."

"Yeah, then he threw himself off the roof," Muttered Voorhees.

"That was a terrible day." Thom nodded solemnly to the others, as if he weren't the only one that cared. "His secretary died that morning. I think they were in love. He told me he was going to do it, too. 'The only place where the dead no longer outnumber us', he said, 'is on the other side.' It was a sad moment, but as far as last words go . . . I'm going to include that in the afterword of the book, I think."

"There are runners down there," Cheryl said. She pressed her face to the glass. "Stand back," ordered Voorhees, but Thom laughed idly. "They can't see us up here, especially on this side of the building with the way the light hits it. Besides the barricades here are better than the PD's—no offense Officer. Oh God, I can smell rot coming up through the vents. I'm going crack a few windows, all right? Nothing they'll notice down there." Without waiting for an answer, he left.

"He's more than just a little mad," Palmer thought aloud.

A lot of the running dead were poorly coordinated, stumbling about, some of them moving sideways like crabs. Their muscular build gave them an edge over the walkers, and getting to the meat first kept them healthy, kept them fast, superior to the other rotters, but their faces remained dull and lifeless. There was no primal aggression, no snarling or baring of teeth. They were just as blank and silent as the rest. To be chased down by them was . . . Cheryl saw her brother's face, covered in bloody bites, telling her to go, to leave him with the runners.

"I'm sorry," she whispered.

Runners clambered over the backs of slower zombies and into the PD. Palmer took Cheryl away from the window.

Lauren covered her nose and mouth with her hand and left the hallway. The odor of decay in the stairwell was even worse. She could see a door standing open on the landing beneath her. That must have been where Thom had gone. She wanted to offer him some help with the windows, but she couldn't bear to see any bodies.

Do it, Lauren, she told herself, snap out of this. She began descending the stairs.

Thom emerged from the doorway with a severed hand in his mouth. He glanced up at her and stopped.

The hand had been removed with surgical precision, and bites had already been taken from it. Thom's lips were dark red. He said something through a mouthful of meat. Lauren screamed and turned to run.

He caught her ankle and hurled her down the stairs. The hand fell on her face, and she screamed louder. "No, no!" he cried. "It's not what you think. Be quiet!" A long pair of scissors plunged into her abdomen. Her scream bubbled away.

Voorhees ran into the stairwell and saw Thom trying to pull the scissors free. "She fell! She fell!" the man was yelling, stringy bits of muscle falling from his mouth.

Voorhees didn't think. He only saw what he saw, and reacted.

The shotgun blast tore Thom's arm off and peppered his chest, his shirt opening up and spitting out flesh. Flying into the wall, he sank wordlessly.

Voorhees dropped the shotgun and ran to Lauren. She was in the grip of abject horror and crippling pain, blood pooling rapidly around the scissors. The cop pressed his hands over the wound, around the blades.

Jenna shrieked from the top of the stairs. She grabbed the shotgun. Mark wrested it away.

"I'm not, I'm not a zombie," Thom whispered. "I didn't even kill them. I just needed to eat." The blood pulsing from the stump of his arm diminished. His face was bone-white, and he shook as he spoke. "I told him, the mayor, I told him it wasn't her anymore, it was just meat. I told him we could eat her together and the rotters would never have her. He'd see her on the other side . . ."

Thom shrugged and died.

"She's still alive. Help me." Voorhees kept one hand on the wound and slipped the other beneath Lauren. "Help me!"

Jenna came down and blinked her tears back to look into Lauren's eyes. "You'll be okay. She'll be okay, won't she?"

Voorhees said nothing.

Outside, the faintest of screams had caught the attention of a few rotters. They looked around hungrily. Others were exiting the PD, having found no sustenance; one of them gestured toward the street with a moan. The others in the plaza shuffled to follow its gaze.

A man on a horse galloped toward them. A scythe glistening with rain swept over his head, and they realized that, in fact, he was no man at all just before he cut them all in half.

CHAPTER THIRTY-FOUR
Like Moths . . .

Baron Tetch caught a snarl of fencing around his pickaxe and tore it down with a roar.

At the swamp's edge, he and his remaining afterdead had nearly opened up all of the west wall's vulnerable areas, the places where there was no concrete; the ferals would soon be entering the city from all sides. Addison's explosives, old as they were, had been even more effective than Tetch had anticipated. The doctor's journals suggested he'd collected the dynamite in hopes of loosing more energy from within the ground. Everything had been a surgical procedure to Addison, hadn't it? Flaying away flesh and earth in search of answers. All his tools could never have found the knowledge that Tetch now possessed.

Simeon was helping him in this area. He saw the rotter eyeing his flesh with furtive glimpses. "Are you hungry?" he asked. Simeon nodded. Tetch held out his hand.

Simeon stared, confused, gnashing his teeth behind closed lips. Hesitantly he reached out, took hold of the hand, and opened his mouth.

Tetch jerked it away and slapped him across the face with resonating force. Simeon staggered back and fell over the fencing.

"Without me, you never eat again. Do you understand? You don't know how to hunt, and even if I taught you, you'd forget. No, I bring you the meat! Without me, you'll simply waste away. Is that what you want? Or are you patient?"

Simeon understood maybe half of the words, but he got the message, and nodded. He could wait to eat.

Tetch was still hoping that Sawbones would come back with something for the others—he was tougher than any of them were, and maybe he'd stayed back to field-dress his victims—but as the storm abated and the sun began to descend, hope had faded with the light.

He wasn't concerned at all about the survivors' presence in the city (not anymore), but he *was* preoccupied with thoughts of Lily's dark man. He had strong suspicions as to who the specter was, or at least what it represented, but its motives were unclear. Perhaps it had targeted Lily because it could exert no influence over Tetch.

"Simeon," he said suddenly, "go back to the house and check on your sister."

The rotter licked his lips. Tetch threw down the pickaxe. "Never mind! I'll have Prudence do it."

Back at the manor, Lily sat alone in the foyer. She stared at the back door. It was locked, as they all were, but she knew how to get out. It was just a matter of having the courage. She'd believed that she did, but here she was, sitting and staring.

She wished the man in black would come back and take her, but he didn't seem to want her. No one wanted her—not her parents, not Daddy Addison, not the man in black, no one but Baron. And Baron . . . he had taken notice of the fact that she was growing up. He kept telling her that she was becoming a woman, and the way he said "woman" made her uneasy. There was something about the word when it came from his mouth, as if to Tetch it were a key that opened the door to a bad place.

The doorknob rattled. She ran to the staircase and crouched behind the banister.

Prudence entered, a husk of a woman with spindly legs that could barely carry her along, thin as her frame was. Her face was sunken and empty, searching the foyer, waiting expectantly for Lily to emerge from a room or come down the stairs.

The girl stepped slowly into view. Prudence's head on its twig-like neck turned in the shadows and settled on her. The afterdead didn't move. "Here I am," Lily said uneasily. Prudence had a large house key grasped in her fingers. It pointed accusingly at Lily, who had been thinking of running . . . still was . . .

She ran. She ran at the towering zombie whose weight was probably equal to her own, and hit its body with a thud, and there was no resistance. Prudence slumped to the floor with a papery sound. Lily stumbled over her and out the door.

It was hard to see and she braced herself for the grasping hands of the others, of Baron, but she heard nothing—no one else was there! Lily ran for the gates, praying Prudence had left them open.

She had.

The child ran free into the swamp.

As the sun's light bled from the clouds and sank into darkness, her feet plunged through lush grass, soft earth. She scraped her palms, pulling herself along on gnarled trees, and stubbed her toes on huge roots jutting from the mud. She didn't care. Exhilaration overtook Lily and she ran even faster.

Glowing beads of light began to emanate from the trees—clusters of fireflies, some of which whispered past her face. There were so many! She'd never seen such a thing. A few stars became visible overhead, and though the sky was smoky, she could see tree branches threaded through one another and birds scuttling through them. The swamp seemed so alive, in stark contrast to the house and its inhabitants.

A bird landed on the grass before her with a soft slap. She stopped in her tracks and peered down at it, able to discern its pointed beak and glittering eyes. Lily knelt. "Are you all right?" She rolled down one of her leggings and pulled out a cigarette lighter she'd concealed there. It had been Daddy's (she'd taken it from the study), and sometimes she'd use it to navigate the corridors of the house in the dead of night. Now she could see a bird up close for the first time, one that wouldn't take off and leave her trapped inside the gates. Lily thumbed the flint and a small flame sprang up.

The bird's breast was wet. Touching it, her fingertips came away red. "Oh, no—"

Several other birds flew toward her, squawking dully. Their wings beat at her face and she fell back with a cry. They descended voraciously on the fallen one.

"No! Stop it!" Lily swatted at them, losing the lighter. She felt through the grass for it, wincing as she heard the weak cries of the victim.

There! She found the lighter and struck it. One of the birds looked up from its feeding, beak crimson, eyes black; feathers and flesh were missing in patches from its body. She could see the tiny bones in its thighs, pushing through well-worn holes in dead flesh as it stamped its feet. She'd led it and the others right to the wounded bird, to their living prey. Screaming, Lily kicked them all into the darkness.

A man pushed through the trees and groaned at her.

He was dead. A chain dangled from his hand. He had no lips, and his bare genitals had been flayed. He clicked his teeth at her and advanced.

Lily ran a wide semicircle around him and continued through the trees. She just had to get out of the swamp, to the city. There were people there, she knew that now. She knew Tetch had tried to kill them. He was a liar and a bully and if there were people in the city that he hated that much, then they must be nice people.

Now running, emerging onto a paved road, she saw only a few scattered rotters, and when they saw her they began running.

She looked down a side street and spied something beyond

the swamp's silhouette: a huge bonfire. That was the source of all the smoke. There had to be people there! "Help!" Lily screamed, pumping her legs until they were numb, until she felt like she was about to pass out. She stole a single glance over her shoulder and saw the rotters gaining. The one with the chain was using it to knock the others back. He wanted her all for himself, like Tetch. "No!"

Lily careened breathlessly over a sand dune and came to a stop at the edge of the burning landfill. A foul odor swept into her nostrils. She nearly threw up, but then she saw the other rotters milling about the flames.

The man with the chain grabbed her shoulder, then pain rang through her skull as he struck. He brought the chain down again, on her back; she pushed away from him, turning, and was hit in the chest. The world spun and roared around her. Sand caught in her nose and shoes and the other rotters were coming. A fierce heat came off the burning garbage, making it hard to keep her eyes open. The chain man swung and missed. THUMP. He gathered the chain up and prepared to strike again. She ran into the fire.

There was a smoke-filled path between the mountains of refuse. Her lungs about to burst, she couldn't help but inhale deeply, and was wracked with crippling coughs. The chain man, stepping through the flames, watched dumbly as his legs caught fire. He spied Lily and resumed his shambling pursuit.

She ran again. Slammed into something solid: a wall, a shed. The door was open. She fell in, pulling the door behind her and grappling blindly with the deadbolt. Something brushed her legs and she shrieked through a scorched throat scorched, but it was only a cot.

The chain crashed against the door. Her mind stopped working then.

Outside, Gene watched the ferals swarm over the flaming hills and writhe as the fire consumed them. He knew what the fire could do, both to himself and to the child—meat. He also knew that there was a place in the landfill where the child might think herself safe.

Starting forward, he searched through his pockets for the key to his shed.

"She's going to die," Voorhees said. He tried to take Jenna out of the stairwell but she pushed him off. "Didn't you hear what I said, O'Connell?"

"I heard. I'm staying."

Voorhees gave Thom a last look, the madman's dying words echoing in his head. The last time he'd served as a juror—on one of the last cases to be tried in a criminal court in America, before the judiciary hung up their robes and deferred to the military's swift brand of justice—Voorhees had heard the case of a cannibal. Cristan Mellon, the boy's name was. Two decades past and he could still remember the hateful way the boy spat out his own name. He'd butchered and eaten his parents, along with three other residents in their apartment building, then paraded around downtown Chicago in their bloody skins. He demanded to be recognized as a "zombie with human rights." "They're us, they're us!" he'd screamed before being found in contempt and hauled out of the courtroom. As the legal system crumbled around them, the farce of a case had ended with the defense all but giving up and Mellon found guilty on five counts of murder. Upon being sentenced to life in prison, he only laughed. "What life, what prison?" he sang, before taking a bailiff's gun and shooting himself in the stomach. "It's just meat!" Mellon cried, pulling at his guts on the courthouse floor. "Who cares, who cares," sang Cristan Mellon as he rolled down the steps to the lobby, where a P.O. shot him dead.

A blanket of coats had been placed over Lauren, and she lay on the landing near Thom's corpse. Her glazed eyes stared at nothing. Her lips moved, but she wasn't saying anything, at least not that Jenna could hear.

"Yes, I can hear you," Death said. He knelt beside Lauren and studied her face. "Not long now."

"I don't . . . I don't want to die," she whispered.

"It won't hurt anymore."

Tears welled in her eyes. "I know. But Jen . . . she's going to be alone. She needs me."

The woman in question was standing on the stairs; a young man with a bandage around his leg embraced her. The specter realized something, though he wasn't sure what it meant, and looked back at Lauren. "It's *you* that needs her."

"Yes."

"Do you love her?"

"Yes."

"What does it feel like?"

Lauren met Death's black gaze. "It . . . hurts."

He thought at first she was talking about her wound, but she could no longer feel that. She was slipping away, a pinprick of flame sputtering in a pool of wax.

"It's an ache. A beautiful ache. God, I love her . . . please take care of her. Just . . . just don't let her suffer."

There was nothing he could say. But he did. "I will," he lied.

The light in her eyes went out and didn't come back.

Jenna buried her face in Mark's shoulder. Voorhees grimaced, pumped his shotgun and walked out. Reverend Palmer stepped silently past the couple on the stairs and whispered a prayer over the departed. Death wondered if there was anyone who heard such things.

Maybe they did, and maybe they lied too, telling humanity, "I will."

He had to return outside and hold off the undead. It was the only thing he could do. The Reaper melted into the shadows.

CHAPTER THIRTY-FIVE
A Pale Horse

Gene navigated the flaming refuse until he saw the shack, surrounded by hammering undead. He shook the keys in his hand, but the sound was lost amidst crackling flames and incessant groaning. The girl had to be inside. With the shovel in his other hand he began to beat and pry at the backs of the other dead. Many simply stumbled away, disoriented by the smoke. Reaching the door, Gene worked the keys into the lock with awkward hands.

Throwing the door open, he glanced in and spied her under the cot. She tried drawing her legs further in, but it was no use. Gene dropped the keys and gripped the shovel handle tightly, lowering it in order to drive it into her body and tug her into the open.

The girl did something unexpected then; rising up, she overturned the cot onto the shovel, then screamed and ran at him. She tried to duck around him, but he caught the collar of her dress. The others had seen her and lunged forth as one. Gene let her go and stabbed at them with the shovel.

The girl ran brazenly into the zombie horde. Their stiff arms swept over her, tearing out handfuls of hair and fabric, then smoke poured into the shack and Gene lost all sight of her.

216

Rotters pressed against him in the doorway as if the child hadn't just escaped. Planting the shovel's head in the chest of the nearest one, Gene threw them back and set off in pursuit of his meal.

A soft, steady sound, like a wind, led Lily away from the landfill, and she saw for the first time in her life waves gently crashing against the beach. The sight was horrifying and liberating all at once—she couldn't swim, which meant she was trapped unless she braved the waters and kicked her feet and prayed that the ability to stay afloat came naturally. She could swim and swim and swim and never see Jefferson Harbor or its ghouls again.

There was one standing in the sand, looking out on the water; it turned, and she stopped dead in her tracks.

It had a gun. It pointed it at her. She screamed.

"What?" it spoke.

It lowered the gun and walked toward her, then broke into a jog; it was a he, a living man! "Little girl? You're alive?" he cried. He took her arms and looked at them, then at her singed curls, and her face, smudged with soot. "Are you all right?"

"They're just over the hill, in the fire," she stammered. "They'll come!"

He nodded and, taking her hand, led her briskly down the shoreline. They both watched over their shoulders, but there didn't appear to be any pursuers; Lily hoped they'd all been burned up.

"Are there more people?" she asked the man. He stopped and mulled the question over.

"Yes," he finally answered, "and they can help you. I can't . . ." Turning his arms over, he showed her a series of bites on both and palms filled with blood.

"I'll take you to them," Shipley said quietly. He looked back at the dark waves, the beckoning sea. It could wait. He could still save a child tonight.

He took her hand again, and then a shovel crossed the

beach like a missile and punched through his chest, clearing it of bone and muscle with a THUK before exiting out his back.

Lily ran with a shriek that split the calm of the beach and restored the world to its nightmare order. Gene retrieved his shovel and shambled after her.

"Lily!"

The girl turned. She hadn't told the man her name. Was the zombie calling her?

The man in black tore down the shoreline on his horse, scythe held high.

Gene turned and raised the shovel just in time to block the blade, but was thrown back into the sand. Horse and rider continued unabated toward Lily. She opened her arms and let him sweep her up.

And so it was that they came to sit on an outcropping of rock far from the Harbor wall. Death gathered his robes around his feet and watched the ocean's ceaseless dance. Lily, picking bits of ash from her hair, gazed up at him until he returned the look.

"Who are you?" she asked.

"I am the angel of death."

"Am I dead?"

"No. It's not your time yet. That's why I was able to intervene back there."

"But if it was, you couldn't have saved me?"

"No."

She frowned, and so did he. It was difficult enough explaining this to an adult, especially the ones who thought they could bargain for their insignificant lives.

"Couldn't, or wouldn't?" Lily asked.

He opened his mouth to deliver the standard response, the clinical, unfeeling response, to tell her that he had no influence over her insignificant life; but as he thought of the undead, particularly the one that had been after her, and as he thought of the fate that might await her, suddenly Lily seemed . . . significant.

He had no answer for her. She nodded and looked out at the sea.

On her other side, the horse lowered its head. She nuzzled it and watched its eyes close, its posture relax. Death's eyes closed, and the contours of his face smoothed.

"Does your horse have a name?"

"I . . . it's me. My essence, like everything else about me, except for the scythe." He opened his eyes and said flatly, "I am the horse."

She giggled. "I thought so." Then she turned and nuzzled it again. It seemed like she was doing it for his benefit, and it was wholly unnecessary, but he let her continue. For her sake.

"How many people are still alive?"

"Many. Most of them are far from here."

"If they get bit by those wild rotters, do they die right away?"

"No."

"How long does it take?"

"Sometimes it takes a short while, other times not. I'm not sure why. It might have to do with their spirit."

Turning from the horse, Lily moved to touch Death's hand. "Cold."

"Yes."

"If you're the angel of death, why can't you make them all go away?"

"I don't know." He waited for the next question, but the girl was silent. Eventually it was he who spoke, in a voice that nearly trembled. "I hate them."

"Daddy Addison wasn't my real daddy. My real one, I don't remember him at all. Or my mom. Do you know who they are?"

"I can see your lineage. I could tell you their names." But it wouldn't much matter, nor would it matter if she knew the name they'd given her at birth.

"Are . . . are they rotters?"

"No."

"They're alive?"

"No."

"What happened to them?" He set his jaw and stared hard at the water. She prodded him with her bare toes. "I wanna know."

"You shouldn't . . . it'll make you sad."

She tried to look tough, but she spoke barely above a whisper. "Did they get eaten?"

"Yes. But there's more to it than that. It's about Baron, it's about why you can never go back to that house."

"What does Baron have to do with it?"

"Your parents came back to the house a few years ago. They wanted to take you away. Addison was already dead then. Baron killed him, just like he killed your brothers and sisters."

"Did . . ." Tears filled her eyes and they looked black as his. "Did Baron kill my mom and dad?"

"Yes."

"I hate him!" she shouted. Death flinched away. She grabbed his robes. "You have to kill him. Please!"

"I can't. It doesn't work that way."

"You just don't want to! Why not? Why won't you do anything!"

"I'm not a judge."

She balled her hands and beat on his shoulder. "I hate you! You're just like him!"

He grabbed her arms and tried to steady her. She shrieked and thrashed in his grip, and her curses turned to sobs, and she fell against him.

The horse stepped forward and pressed its muzzle against her shoulder. She threw her arms around its neck and cried long into the night.

And in the house in the swamp, Baron Tetch raged.

CHAPTER THIRTY-SIX
Bait

"Just listen for a minute. Just let me walk you through it," Duncan said quietly. He and Voorhees sat by the window at the end of the fourth-floor corridor. The sun was coming up behind a miserable-looking cloud cover.

"I suppose I've got nothing better to do," muttered Voorhees. "Shoot."

"Addison's got 'domesticated' rotters, like the ones that attacked the shelter, like the one with the skull that followed us. We managed to kill some of them and get away. Then, you've got these explosions all across the city, and ferals start homing in on us. Now do you really think it's all a coincidence?"

"Of course I don't," Voorhees said sharply. "But what you're saying is ridiculous. If Addison was still alive, and had trained up these zombies, why would he send them to kill us? Why would he lure the ferals into the Harbor?"

"He wants us out," Duncan replied. "Simple as that. I don't know why—and I'm not saying this guy is thinking rationally either—but that seems to be the answer."

"Let's say for a second that you're right, Duncan."

"Jenna's the one who put it all together, you know that."

David Dunwoody

"Fine. Let's say for a second that O'Connell's right. What, then, do we do about it?"

"You're a P.O."

"I'm not going to make anyone here any safer by running off into the swamp to arrest a guy who might not even exist. That's assuming I get past the horde in the plaza."

Duncan shrugged. "I'll go with you."

"Forget it."

"Look." He tapped his bum leg. "You remember what happened here? The axe?"

"Yeah."

Duncan's face fell, as if he was reconsidering what he was about to say. Voorhees looked from his eyes to the bandaging, then it clicked.

"Duncan, that's unlikely. What you're getting at is unlikely."

"How do you know?" The man's voice was a soft, scratchy whisper. "You used that axe to take the rotter's feet off. The blade had his blood or whatever it is all over it . . . I could be infected."

"Very, very unlikely," Voorhees said. Even as he did, he was studying Duncan's pallor. How long did he have left if he was right? Should he be quarantined? Or would it be better just to . . . no. No, there wasn't any way to be sure. Voorhees had never seen the infection transmitted by touch, or sex, or toilet seats, and this here was simply outside the realm of possibility.

Almost. Almost outside the realm of possibility. The cop still had room to be skeptical.

Palmer was alone in the stairwell, sitting above the remains of Lauren and Thom. Voorhees had removed the heads and intended to get rid of the bodies later. How? Throw them out the window and confirm the survivors' presence to all the rotters? Maybe set fire to them on the roof? That'd be brilliant.

"Lord," Palmer said, "what do you want me to do? Anything? Do I just keep praying for the dead until I'm dead, too?"

222

The door to the third floor was still slightly ajar. There was an infinitesimal movement. The reverend didn't notice. She folded her hands together and let out a long sigh.

"I'm okay, I guess. As okay as I can be. My faith is my faith. But these people don't have anything to hold on to except each other. I have been ministering to them, through my works— right?—but I'm not about to start preaching. If this is the end of the world, no one cares.

"Do you understand? Whether you meant to or not, you've answered the question of what comes after death. We see it all around us. No one looks for God anymore.

"I just don't get it. If you don't have anything for me, I suppose I'll just keep doing what I'm doing."

Eyes closed, she listened intently with her heart and mind. She thought that maybe, somewhere out there, she sensed a slight shrug.

Then she cursed in pain.

A few moments later the reverend returned to the fourth floor. Jenna and Cheryl were sitting in a vacant office, and Voorhees and Duncan were in the hall. They each glanced at her, and the look on her face was enough to hold their attention.

"There are rats on the third floor," she said.

"Dammit. Did you close that door?" Voorhees asked.

"Yes," she replied.

"Good." He nodded.

"I got bit," Palmer said. She wriggled the toe of her shoe.

"Is it bad?"

"The rat was dead."

Jenna and Cheryl came out of the office. The men rose to their feet. Palmer gave them a pained smile. "I asked for it."

"No, no you didn't," Cheryl exclaimed.

"I can still run. I can lead the rotters away, to the west. You all have to clear out of here. You need to leave the city."

"No. No to all of it. Never." Taking her arm, Voorhees shook his head insistently.

"What then, stay and starve?" Palmer snapped. "The city has fallen! It's done!"

"You . . ." Voorhees bit back his words and stamped his foot.

"I get it," Palmer told him. "This is your city. You want to die here, then fine. But don't bring the rest of these people down with you under the pretense that you're protecting them."

"You don't get it at all!" the cop bellowed. "I don't want to fucking die! I don't want anyone to die! The last thing I'm going to do is let you walk out of here!"

"H-he's right," Cheryl stammered.

"I'm already dead," said Palmer.

"Are you sure," Jenna asked, "that the bite broke the skin? Here, take off your shoe—"

"I'm going out there. Period," Palmer said. Voorhees tried to grab her again. She shoved him across the hallway. "If you don't want to use this opportunity to escape, don't."

"Leave, stay, leave, stay, what's the fucking point?" Cheryl cried. "Why are we arguing over *where* we want to die? Why do you *want* to be eaten alive, Reverend?!"

"Because the alternative is that I become undead!"

"I can take you out right now," shouted Voorhees, "without any suffering! You want to be a fucking martyr, that's all it is!"

"My leg—" Duncan began. Voorhees slugged him in the stomach to cut him off. Jenna threw herself on the cop's back.

"Stop it! Don't!" Duncan gasped, pulling at her.

"I'm trying to help you, Voorhees!" Palmer beat her fist against the wall. "I'm trying to help you do your damn job! You cannot save these people *and* save Jefferson Harbor!"

"All right!" Dumping Jenna into Duncan's arms, Voorhees grabbed the shotgun leaning in the doorway nearest to him. The others froze, watched him pump it and dig shells from his coat pockets.

"I'm taking you out there. Rear entrance on the first floor should be relatively clear. We've got to make it quick, and we need a distraction. O'Connell, check all these offices until you find Thom's stash of matches. We need fuel—Duncan, grab a box of paper from the copy room. Then you can help me break down some chairs."

Voorhees turned to hand Palmer the shotgun, but she shook her head. "You'll need it more than I will."

"Right." He tried to think of another order to bark, but remained silent. He looked back at the reverend. "If I was the last one . . . but I'll never be the last one."

"You're too good at your job," she replied.

Twenty minutes later, a series of blazing torches flew off the roof of City Hall and landed out front in the middle of the plaza. The rotters searched the sky to see where they'd come from, then staggered toward the flames.

The rear door flew open; a jawless zombie cocked its head at the sight. A shotgun blast sheared its torso off at the waist.

Voorhees hustled Palmer out the door. Without a word, she ran for the street. The cop went to shut the door, but he saw something coming from the south.

A man on a horse.

As the horse neared the plaza, a rotter emerged from behind an overturned bus with a shovel in its hands. It cleaved right through the stallion's front legs as if they were clay. The rider tumbled forward Voorhees saw the little girl clinging to the man's back. He heard her scream and ran to her.

The rotter's detail came into view, and by God he recognized the son of a bitch. "Gene!" Voorhees shouted. The garbage man turned and caught a blast right in the chest.

The ferals were swarming around the City Hall building. Voorhees skirted them and ran to the man and girl. When he got to them, the fallen rider looked up. Without reason, Voorhees knew immediately who he was.

"Take her," Death rasped.

The cop grabbed the girl and slung her onto his back. "Hold onto my neck," he instructed her, and loosed a hail of fire from the shotgun into the oncoming horde. They stumbled and spun and continued forward in a deranged dance. He sent the butt of the gun through a rotter's gnashing teeth and tore its throat open. The door he'd come through was wide open. If he could reach it before any of them saw . . . please . . .

"I'm over here!" Holding a torch over her head, Palmer screamed at the top of her lungs.

Another rotter ate shotgun pellets and its cold brains showered over the rest as the undead abruptly changed course and went after the reverend.

Voorhees ran into the building and slammed the door, throwing every bolt and pushing the furniture back into place in front of it. The girl hung on him like a corpse. He glanced over his shoulder at her just to be sure she was still alive.

Palmer's feet pounded the asphalt until she couldn't even feel them, just a vibration in her head, just the cold wind. She looked back and saw even the runners falling behind. She slowed her pace. "Don't give up on me now, you assholes!"

Their expired bodies writhed as they pushed onward, driven only by hunger, driven only to survive. They would never know why her death was so much more than that. In that moment, she found a God that she hadn't realized she'd lost.

Then the ones coming at her from the side grabbed her. One of them rolled back the cuff of its jacket and pointed a revolver into the horde.

It was Addison's child.

Palmer screamed as the other Addison children appeared and carried her toward a pickup truck with a landscaper's faded logo stenciled on the side.

FOURTH STRIKE
Hand of God

The rock quarry was a quarter-mile in diameter, a shallow crater cut into the earth and peppered with medium-sized boulders and scraggly brush. Somewhere down there, Gregory knew, the rotter had slithered away and was waiting for his men.

It had taken a full thirty-six hours to make it to the quarry. They'd spent the previous day lying in the brush, drenched in rain; unable to track the rotter's movements, unable to risk exposing themselves until the weather calmed down. Gunshots and explosions from the direction of the city had kept everyone on edge.

Then, in the night, after creeping along the ground for agonizing hours, Logan had spotted the rotter hunched at the edge of the crater and taken a chunk out of his shoulder, sending him over the edge. Gregory wished Logan had waited and let Dalton take the shot, but at least they had the bastard contained now, and were preparing to enter the quarry from all sides and finish him off. The tables had been turned.

The sun had risen, chasing the shadows from the maze of boulders; Gregory pulled out a pair of binoculars and searched for any sign of their prey.

On the other side of the crater, Dalton inched down a

David Dunwoody

rocky incline on his stomach, rifle clenched in his hands. A few pebbles clattered down ahead of him and he froze. He felt like he was up against another mortal man, something he'd never faced before. But did this rotter really have any marksmanship, or had it been lucky to kill Coates with that shot? Something told Dalton that it was the former. If this was indeed one of the deserters from Jefferson Harbor, then it was newly dead, and retained some mental faculties that made it a unique threat.

He wondered if any of the other deserters lurked about, or if this one had feasted on them.

Barry entered the quarry from the south. She went down on her back, sliding up behind a boulder and planting her boots against it so that she could rest her shotgun across her legs. She snapped the battleaxe attachment on. A close-range shotgun blast among these rocks could send a thousand tiny daggers every which way. If she was going to be the one to take the target out, it would be with the axe.

The crater's layout was going to throw her auditory senses off; she'd have to rely on her sharp vision and the shadows creeping across the sand.

Ahmed thought back to what Gregory had said about using all the elements to one's advantage. From a pocket on his shirt he plucked a small bag containing a dozen dead flies. A fresh, well-fed afterdead was said to have an aura about it—a strong energy that could stir the tiniest of organisms to life, if the rotter was close enough. He tied a shoelace around the bag's opening, making a necklace of it, and draped it over his head. Down in the crater, squeezing through those boulders, he might be only a few feet away from the rotter and not know it—but the buzzing of the flies would alert him. Maybe.

Some of the instructors said that tricks like that were "old wives' tales"—but they didn't put their faith in Christ, either. Ahmed had come from non-practicing Muslim parents who told him to look at the world and decide for himself if there was a God. He felt that there had to be something—otherwise,

228

what was the point of this fight? Of life? Maybe it was just the fear of dying that kept people going. But when he'd heard the teachings of Jesus, of resurrection and judgment, he couldn't help but look at the world and think: surely God is among us.

Sergeant Gregory was a strong Christian and a good leader. He'd barely shown any emotion when Coates was killed, but later there would be time set apart for mourning the fallen warrior, Ahmed was sure. That was why he'd been ordered to read the Last Rites over the private's body before it was set ablaze.

Descending into the crater from the north end, he patted the bag around his neck and wiped sweat from his brow. He began to whisper the Lord's Prayer. "Our Father in Heaven, let your holy name be known, let your kingdom come, and your will be done, on earth as in heaven."

He sat in the shadow of a boulder and pressed his face to the cold rock. "Give us today the bread that we need, and forgive us our wrongs, as we forgive those who have done wrong to us." With the rotter, the soul that had departed the body was not at fault. It was just meat now, driven by an ungodly force to kill and rend flesh like itself.

"Do not lead us into trial, but save us from evil." Ahmed felt a fluttering against his chest, as if the Holy Spirit were embracing him; then he heard the buzzing of the flies.

The gunshot rang through the quarry like a lightning strike. Barry fell to the ground. There was no way to know where it had come from, or who had fired; she had to call out. "Sergeant!"

"Who was it! Dalton!"

"No sir!"

"Logan!"

"Not me sir!"

"Ahmed! There was a pause. "Ahmed!"

Ahmed did not reply.

Logan threw himself into a narrow passage where two large boulders leaned against one another, crouching in darkness. He was the closest to Ahmed. At the other end of this passage would be the area where the soldier had come down. If Logan was lucky, he'd come upon the rotter at feeding time and get the drop on him. But if the sarge was right, this fucker was smart.

He slowly made his way forward, machine gun at the ready, eyeing the sliver of light at the end of the passage. "Bite my dick," he breathed. The fucker was waiting for him.

He sprinted into the sunlight and somersaulted to the ground, letting off a spurt of gunfire to either side. He spun to find Ahmed's corpse plastered to one of the huge boulders, his throat torn out. No rotter. A trail of blood led around a small boulder and deeper into the crater. Rather than following it, he hopped onto the rock and crawled to its peak.

There it was, right in the center of the crater—dressed in fatigues, with long, clotted hair and blood hanging in front of his ugly face. The rotter saw Logan and raised its gun. The soldier felt a chill paralyzing his limbs.

"Got 'im!" Barry cried, vaulting over a boulder and burying the battleaxe in the rotter's back. She drove it to the ground and yanked the blade free, cleaving into the undead's skull with a crack like another gunshot. Blood pooled around her knees. She twisted the shotgun, prying the skull wide open and shaking gray matter out onto the ground. "Let's get a torch down here!"

Gregory, Logan and Dalton rushed to join her. "Ahmed's gone," Logan wheezed. "I knew he was too green for this gig."

"He's gone home to God," Gregory muttered. "If we could all be so fortunate."

"We'll have to burn them both," Dalton said, heading in the direction Logan had come from.

"Read him his Rites," Gregory called, scraping bits of brain off of his boot.

"We should catch up with the convoy," Barry said. "We've lost two men just sitting out here, and we haven't seen any packs roaming about."

"Not just yet." Gregory looked skyward. "I want to see Dalton's horseman."

"What's that?"

"It's why we're really here," Gregory answered. Barry stepped close to him, and he inhaled her musk. The fight always got her hot. He felt a twinge of guilt at wanting her like this, out here in the field, when they'd just lost a good man; but all was forgotten as she pulled his hands to her hips. "Ian," she whispered, "why are we really here?"

"Dalton says he saw a horseman at the gates. He thinks we're here to receive a message."

"What do you think?"

"I was brought out here to do God's work. We all were." He slid his hands around her waist and pressed his erection against her belly. "If He has a message for us, then by all means I'll receive it."

Logan looked on anxiously. Pulling his hands away from Barry, Gregory addressed the other soldier. "We'll head back to camp. Another day of this and I say we pack it in."

They headed back toward Jefferson Harbor, unaware that in their absence a horde of undead had descended upon the city.

BEFORE THE EMPIRE
Harvey Powell Interview

As told to Anita Lunden on April 15, 2112 for Living History *magazine . . .*

My name is Harvey Powell and I'm the oldest living survivor of the outbreak. I was born in 1995. I was twelve years old when the plague broke out, and I lived in Wales with my father at the time.

He was a doctor and they called him to America to deal with the plague. He brought me along, and we arrived in New York City in August of 2007. At that time, the outbreak was confined to the south and there was only a bit of trouble on the Mexican border. My dad was sent to Louisiana to see the infected. I went along because my dad didn't want me out of his sight. He said he thought this might be the End Times, and I should be at his side all day and night. As such, I saw a lot of the early victims, the ones who'd been bitten after a riot at some military base down there near Jefferson Harbor. They had them in plastic tents outside of the city hospital. It was hot as hell in those tents, and we had to wear special suits that made it even hotter. I clung to my dad's hand and he led me around, from bed to bed, looking at these many soldiers.

Some of them had already died and come back. The Army

knew they were undead, and I saw them, the very first zombies, strapped down to stretchers inside these tents, thrashing about and spitting blood. They lay right beside the other infected, the ones who were still alive. The living victims tried to talk to them and just got a bunch of spitting and gnashing in response. The dead were starving animals. The Army started to take over the highways and the cities in that area, but it was too late. I guess a lot of infected people had fled the military base right after the outbreak and had gotten the bug into their friends and families. As soon as the next day it was reported to be on airplanes; zombies were attacking passengers and bringing overseas flights down. It was Hell on earth, just like that. End Times, like my dad said.

He was a smart, smart man. Doctor William Powell. While world leaders were wringing their hands and trying to decide who to blame, he sat there and studied the first undead. I sat alongside him and I stayed quiet like he told me to, just watching. I loved my dad so much. He was a hero to me and to everyone else there. Everyone hoped he would find a cure in those early days. He really tried, but outside the plastic tents the world was going insane. The plague had already reached Europe. Presidents and prime ministers were talking about bombs. The terrorists from the East were saying that God had finally brought His hand down to end the great conflict. Martial law took hold in major cities. A lot of people started killing themselves. Cults formed for that single purpose, to die en masse in tenements with blood bubbling from their lips. The media ate it up. They camped outside the White House while the President said nothing.

I don't know how he got infected, the President, but he did and it was a public spectacle. When he finally sat down before the cameras to address the nation, to try and fool them into thinking he had some idea of what was going on, he seized up and died right there. Me and my dad watched on a little TV in Louisiana as the President of the United States rose up with dead eyes and started uttering gibberish. The Secret Service fell upon him and we knew that the world was over. A new age had come.

Naturally, there came to be talk of the President's infection being an assassination. Our government started to collapse. Meanwhile my dad just sat in the tents and toiled away with these early infected. Soldiers stood outside and shot anyone that approached the hospital, living or dead. I think it was the Russians that began the genocides, the mass killings, to try and bring some sort of order to their crumbling reality. It was madness. So the calendar rolled over. It was 2008 and most of Eastern Europe had become a killing field.

Everyone had expected the Middle East to blow up first, but most people in those parts fell into the dirt and started praying. They just prayed and prayed and prayed, for months, being picked off by the undead, begging their gods to come down and take them away. It was a quiet end for them.

Africa, the birthplace of humanity, was overwhelmed with guerilla warfare, desperate men trying to seize a parcel of land and become princes in the last days of mankind. Errant missiles washed them away. I honestly don't know what became of Australia. I'd like to think that maybe some people over there are still okay. It's always been a unique place. I think maybe they got off okay. I like to think that.

My dad took me out of Louisiana and back to New York in 2010. I was fifteen. "We should go north, or south, to a cold place," I remember telling him. "My work isn't finished," he'd always say.

New York's fall has been documented more times than I can count. I don't ever wish to revisit that. It was a nightmare.

Me and Dad fled to the Northwest. People weren't talking about a cure anymore. It was now about survival. But my dad always kept hoping, kept writing in those journals of his. America continued collapsing in on itself.

Dad got bit in December 2012. We were caught in a storm

of undead carrion in Washington state, and he got nipped by some bird. We hadn't seen birds in a long time. It was a terrible surprise.

"I need you to kill me," Dad said. "There is no arguing about this. You need to kill me and you need to get the hell out of here. Go north. As far north as you can. The cold slows those bastards down. Find somebody, somebody like me, and they'll take you. There are still good people out there."

He always believed that.

It was a sawed-off shotgun with a violent kick. He told me how to brace it against myself, and that it would hurt terribly, inside and out. "But you'll be all right," he said, "I've taught you how to survive out here. Take my stuff. Find somebody. If you see a rotter, run the other way. Always."

The blast from that gun kicked me right out of the Jeep we were living in. I remember landing in a snowbank and seeing my dad spill out the other side of the vehicle. I took the Jeep and drove north until it died on me.

So it was 2013, and I was eighteen, and I met up with Wolf Brunner, a big bear of a man who preferred to describe himself as a canine. He had a monstrous diesel truck that could chew through Canadian ice and we pushed farther north.

Wolf felt that we were chosen to endure the plague and combat the undead. "When all this is over," he'd say, "we'll rise up and start anew. We're just good, honest people on the run. Isn't that right?"

Wolf reminded me a lot of my dad, just without the scientific interest. But he was a philosopher all the same and I liked him a lot. We rode together for a long time.

Radio broadcasts came through now and then, different governments pleading for people to settle down and move into designated areas. Sometimes preachers came on and told us that we all had it coming, that this was the big spanking they'd been promising for decades. Good for them. Ham radio operators came through once in a while and they were nice to talk to. They'd guide us to a safe house where we could gas up and sleep. Then we'd continue north.

And why were we going north? Well, we just figured the zombies would freeze before they could reach us up there. Sure it was a miserable place to live, but you could *live* there, that was the bottom line.

Wolf had a heart attack one night in 2014 and rolled that truck into a group of snowy trees. We hung there, upside-down, suspended by our seat restraints, and we talked while Wolf's life ebbed away.

"Where do you think we are?" He coughed.

"Pretty damn close to Alaska, I reckon," was my reply. The blood rushing to my head made me tired. After a bit I slipped free and fell to the ceiling. "No one will ever find us out here."

"Well, that includes the rotters."

"I guess it does."

"I'm ready to go, Harvey. How about you?"

"No, I've got something to do. I have to do something with my life before it's over. You and my dad always said there was something more to be done and I've gotta do it."

"We're in the middle of nowhere, son. How're you gonna make it another day?"

"That's my problem. That's my something to do. How're you holding up, Wolf?"

"I'm about done for." He shivered, snowflakes falling from his hair and beard. "Do me a favor?"

"What's that?"

"Shoot me."

I didn't want to tell him that I'd already shot my dad, and that was supposed to be it for me. But I didn't want to turn away and leave him to freeze, or worse. So I loaded the sawed-off and aimed it into the cab. I said goodbye to Wolf.

Over the next ridge I found a camp. Ex-military guys trying to make it work in an ice cave. We did make it work, for a while. But it was just too damn cold. There was nothing to hunt, to eat, to fuck—can I say that? I'll say it. There was nothing there, no way to perpetuate the species up there in the frozen north.

It was 2016 when I got back to the States. The Army was drafting again, more like begging, to try and drive back the rotters. I didn't want any part of that. I went out into what was being called "the badlands" and found some people trying to hold their towns together. And it was a long, bloody struggle, and we often lost—but that was living. I felt like a homesteader striking out, claiming new land. That's how I lived out my adult years. I ignored the government broadcasts and fought for territory with the undead at my heels.

But, eventually, a man gets old and just can't fight anymore. I figured I could ask someone to empty that sawed-off into my face, or I could settle down and tell the story of my fathers. I'm not certain that we'll be able to sustain our species, but we have to at least leave something behind. So I tell this story and I hope someone younger learns from it. I hope they go out there and fight for what's theirs.

Don't be afraid of the undead. I think Wolf was right. I think there's a place for Man after all this is finished. So don't ever give up, and don't try to seal yourself up somewhere and pretend that the plague never happened. Fight it. The people that fight it are the ones that will shape the new age.

(Harvey Powell died of old age on April 27, 2112.)

CHAPTER THIRTY-SEVEN
Twenty Questions

She awoke in Hell.

The room was so red, so deep red, so overpoweringly monochromatic that it struck Palmer's senses like a wave, all sight sound and feeling. Then the prickling of her flesh gave way to an oppressive heat. Sweat stung the corners of her eyes; she blinked through the pain and tried to discern shape or depth in the room.

The heat faded. So did the light, and it was soon replaced by a soft glow from behind her. She tried to turn and couldn't. She was in a chair, and her arms and legs were bound.

"I told them they might taste you later, if they behaved," a voice at her back said; it was malicious, but youthful. "I'm not entirely disappointed. They couldn't find Lily, but they did fetch one of the maggots that conspired to take her from me."

The speaker stepped around the chair and pulled another from the shadows for himself. He turned it backwards and straddled the seat, resting his chin on the back of the chair. "What's your name?"

"Reverend Palmer. What's yours?" She felt swelling in her mouth, where one of the rotters had cuffed her. The last thing she could remember was being thrown in the back of a truck. If they were Addison's "children" then this was Addison's house. But the man before her wasn't Addison . . .

"My name? Don't have one," he replied with a glib smile. "Like the dark man. He has no name, does he?"

"I don't know what you're talking about. Where am I?"

"You helped the dark man take Lily, isn't that right? Or is it the other way around? Did you people summon him here?"

She had no idea who this guy was, what he was talking about, nor his relation to Doctor Addison, but he looked like he was on edge. Scared for himself or someone else. This "Lily" maybe. If she asked the right questions, she might be able to get some answers and even get these ropes loosened. "Where's Addison? Isn't this his house?"

His face paled. "No more questions from you. I ask the questions!" He slammed his fist against his chair.

"I'm just trying to understand why I'm tied up," she said firmly, "and why I'm in this house. You sound like you need someone's help. Maybe we can start over—"

"I'm not untying you," he snapped. "Your mouth still works. I suggest you use it to tell me what I want to know, rather than trying to fuck with my head."

"I don't want to make you tense." Palmer lowered her head. "Ask away. If I know anything, I'll tell you."

"Where's Lily?"

"I don't know who Lily is."

The man rapped his knuckles on the back of his chair, humming discordantly. "What does she look like?" Palmer asked, then, "Is she one of the rotters—"

"She's *not* a rotter. And you know it!" He stood and cast the chair aside, leaning into the reverend's face. "If you think the dark man can protect you, you're wrong. I will tap into forces that . . ." Stepping back, he smiled again. It was worse than the first time. "You say you're a reverend?"

"Yes I am."

"So you must be praying with all your heart right now for God to come down from the clouds and save you. Are you?"

"Should I be?" she retorted. Her boldness surprised him, but he seemed to enjoy it. His posture changed and he began to pace around her. "I don't pray to the Old Ones. They don't want lowly supplicants. Your god is a petulant child, so insecure . . . my tribute to the Old Ones is to realize my own greatness. You rummage through this ghost town, praying for enough to get you—little, pathetic you—through the next day. I look out there and see an empire for the taking.

"Men can be the new gods, you know. We can take what is ours—we only need the will to do it! But no, not you. You can't. You'd rather die on your knees and awaken a zombie. I'll be your new god.

"I think Addison knew all that, in the back of his mind, but he was afraid. He wanted to give us as offerings to the Old Ones."

Palmer studied the man's face as he spoke. So he was one of the children the doctor had adopted? What had really gone on in this house?

"Addison," the man continued, "was too frightened to accept that what the Old Ones really want is for us to take for ourselves! The groveling supplicants with their pitiful offerings will become the walking dead! As they should! As *you* should!

"But not Lily."

The man opened a folding straight razor in his palm. "My name is Baron."

Palmer strained against the ropes. "I don't know who Lily is. I don't know where she is!"

"Then you're no good to me."

"That's it then? You were so convinced that I had the answers you needed, and now you're just going to—to—"

"Cut your throat? Mm-hmm." The razor danced in the light

before her eyes. "I'll deal with the dark man himself if I have to. I'm not afraid."

"Yes you are," Palmer spat. Baron held the blade a hair's breadth from her eyeball. She blinked rapidly, trying to hold her gaze steady. She thought she could feel the cold steel against her eyelashes. Her bladder failed her, and Baron laughed.

"I think I'd like to show you something, Reverend . . ."

He walked past her. She heard him ascending a creaky flight of stairs.

So this is it, she thought, this is the end. After everything, this room is the last room I'll see, his face is the last face I'll see? Was it all worth it?

Somehow, prayer was the farthest thing from her mind. Speaking to God, pleading with Him in her last moments and hearing nothing in reply would have eroded the last bit of sanity she had left. Instead she thought back to the beginning of her spiritual journey, decades before—to the Seminarium Vita, a compound far from Jefferson Harbor. It had been a collection of cabins on a mountainside thick with evergreens. Every morning the sun rose and bathed the compound in warm light, and the Seminarium's leader, the Reverend Jordan, would walk outside to greet the new day with his people.

Palmer had been part of a group that fled a town at the base of the mountain. A pack of ferals had taken the town, and though the rotters were still down there, feeding, it wouldn't be long before they were on the survivors' trail. Sleeping in short, fitful spurts beneath the trees, hunger gnawing at their bellies, Palmer and her companions began to accept the hopelessness of the situation. That was when they came upon a hastily-erected chain-link fence, patrolled by men in robes, and saw the cabins beyond—that was when Palmer first saw the kind face of Reverend Jordan, and felt an odd sense of comfort.

He had taken them in and explained that Seminarium Vita was not just a shelter from the cruel world below, but a "place of higher learning." The men and women who lived there lived under Jordan's religious tutelage. Though his faith was great, he would say, he wasn't a fool—he didn't expect the hand of the Lord to sweep down from the clouds encircling the mountain's peak to swat away attacking undead. No, the Seminarium was equipped with high-powered rifles and flamethrowers. The weaponry was in limited supply but it was rarely needed. And Jordan, a former soldier, knew how to use it. He proved as much when the rotters finally showed up, severing their heads from their bodies with a crack of the rifle and piling their remains into a great pyre that burned for days.

Eventually, most of Palmer's group would leave the Seminarium and go back down the mountain. She stayed. A year later, she was ordained.

When the occasional infected came to the Seminarium, Jordan instructed his clergy to pray over their bodies. They prayed not for a miraculous cure, but for the soul to be free and at peace when the corrupted body finally turned. The bodies were incinerated in solemn ceremonies, in a fire pit lined with stones; then the ashes were taken up the mountainside to be delivered into the wind. Only one man, Reverend Hardeman, argued that they should be praying for divine healing. "I did just that, in my youth," Jordan would reply. "But if it was indeed God who delivered this plague unto us, He meant for it to take its grim toll."

Hardeman, a handsome, charismatic man Palmer's age, slowly became estranged from the others. He'd sit on the roof of his cabin and pray all day to the sky, asking for God to bless the rest of the Seminarium with a renewed faith and understanding.

One morning, Palmer joined him on the rooftop. "Haven't we all asked God to take this plague away, at one time or another?" she said. "And didn't we mean it with every fiber of our being? But here we are, Hardeman."

"A handful of believers aren't going to stop this nightmare," he snapped. "We need to come down from this mountain and preach our truth to the rest of the world. Staying up here and burning bodies and thanking God for the dirt we wallow in isn't going to bring peace." His eyes were alive with righteous anger, his hands gesticulating passionately as he spoke in his sermonizer's voice. "We need to draw a line of faith."

It wasn't long before Hardeman's chance came.

After a burn ceremony, smoke still lingered in the air over the compound. It drew a pack of ferals. Their distant groans could be heard coming from the trees, coming up the mountain. Reverend Jordan stood at the fence while rifles were handed out. Hardeman prayed loudly on his rooftop, calling for others to join him. A few looked anxiously at Hardeman as his voice carried into the woods. "It doesn't matter," Jordan said. "They're coming one way or another. Just be ready."

A few undead began to appear among the trees. The marksmen began to pick them off. The cracks of the guns seemed to excite the other rotters, and as they surged forward Palmer realized that there were dozens upon dozens of them. Perhaps they had been gathering for days or weeks at the base of the mountain as pillars of smoke rose into the sky. For the first time since coming to Seminarium Vita, she felt terror.

Jordan ran along the fence with fresh ammunition for the shooters. He shouted orders, shook his fist at the rotters as they crowded against the fence and started tearing it loose. He never saw the runners climbing into the trees. He didn't see them until they leapt onto him, tearing his face off and driving him into the dirt. A flamethrower-wielding clergyman screamed and fired a jet of blinding heat at Jordan and the writhing undead. Then he was tackled, and the stream of fire was turned on the marksmen, and the fence collapsed and the compound was overrun.

Hardeman jumped off his roof and grabbed at the remaining men and women. "Draw a line of faith! Here! Now!" he cried, raising his hands to the advancing horde. "Father in

Heaven, we call upon you now to smite these beasts! I call upon you! Don't you hear me, God? God!"

He was mowed down.

Palmer ran to the rear of the compound and pulled herself over the fence, scrambling into the woods. Behind her, the cabins had caught fire, and the dead and the living ran helter-skelter among one another, bathed in flame. She was one of the few to escape the Seminarium and the forest fire that followed its destruction. They found a craggy path a half-mile from the compound that led down the mountainside, and they escaped while the mountain burned.

And now . . . this room. This room, the last room, the last moments of her life. She was as cold and alone now as she'd been back then.

Palmer lowered her head and began to pray.

Inside City Hall, Voorhees took Lily to the window at the end of the fourth-floor corridor. They watched the remaining undead shuffle about.

"Her name's Lily," he told the others. "Lily, this is Jenna, and Mark, and Cheryl." Lily didn't take her eyes away from the plaza.

"Where is he?" she asked.

"The . . . man you were with? He told me to take you. I didn't see what happened after that."

"They got him," she breathed. "How can that even be?" She stared hard at the glass, at the tears forming in her reflection's eyes.

Jenna touched the girl's shoulder. "Where are you from?"

"I won't go back."

"You don't have to. I promise." The girl turned and Jenna offered her a warm smile, something she hadn't thought herself capable of. "We won't make you go back."

"Daddy Addison's house."

"In the swamp?" Voorhees choked.

Mark Duncan nodded grimly at Lily. "Who else is there? Addison?"

EMPIRE

"No. Baron killed him. Baron killed my mom and dad. He's all alone in that ugly house."

"Who's Baron?" Duncan asked. Kneeling down to her, he added, "He never has to know that you told us."

"He's my brother. He killed all the rest of them. He made them into rotters and now they do whatever he says."

She'd been around the same undead that had attacked the shelter? Voorhees tugged at the sleeves of her dress. "Have you been bitten?"

"Sometimes," she jerked her arms away.

"Wait, what?" Voorhees exclaimed. "You mean you've been bitten before and you're not sick?"

"They aren't like the other rotters. They didn't get bit either. The swamp made them come back."

"All of them?" Duncan felt a twinge of hope—maybe he wasn't infected after all—but the girl's impression of how things worked was probably skewed. What she was saying might not be true at all. "Even the one who wore the skull on his head?"

Lily nodded. "The swamp makes everything come back. Bugs and frogs and birds. Just magic, I guess." She held up her fist, showing them each the scar of a bite below her thumb. "It's not like the city." Baron had been truthful about that, at least.

"Okay, I need to think about this." Voorhees slouched down on the floor and rubbed his temples.

"What's there to think about?" Duncan shrugged. "Everything we've been arguing about makes sense now."

"Lily," Jenna said, "I'm so sorry about what happened to your friend out there. But you'll be safe with us. We're going far away from here."

"He can't be dead!" Lily cried. "He's an angel!"

Jenna looked questioningly at Voorhees. The cop wouldn't even lift his head.

Out on the street, Death's ambushed body, having been fallen upon and ground up like so much refuse, was but a crumbled ruin. Gene dragged his shovel through the chalky remains. Neither horse nor rider had been able to fight him off, as if he'd crippled both when he ambushed them.

But the girl was gone. The girl was meat and this wasn't. Gene took a mound of the pale quasi-flesh in his hand and studied it. Then he packed it into his mouth.

It tasted like nothing. It fell apart between his gnashing teeth, and he tilted his head back to force the dry mass down his throat.

Then every muscle in Gene's body seized, and black blood spurted from his eyes and nose and he fell stiffly on his back. A paralyzing rigor had taken hold of him. He stared blankly skyward, unable to move even his eyes.

Beside him, a disembodied figure curled and rolled onto its back.

CHAPTER THIRTY-EIGHT
Empire

"This," Tetch said as he descended the steps into the cellar, "my afterdead found when they were laying the explosives in the garbage dump." He was carrying a small bundle in his arms. Palmer craned her neck to follow his progress across the room.

"I want to see what you think." Tetch brushed specks of dirt from the blanket and uncovered what was inside. There was movement within; Palmer steeled herself, assuming it was some sort of animal. "I brought it back in the swamp. Now, you take a look at it, and you tell me whether or not I am a god, a god without fear of death."

He thrust the premature infant at her. Its toothless mouth opened and let out a gurgle; thick red bile spattered the reverend's face.

Palmer wailed and turned her head away, but the vile smell of the baby surrounded her and she retched. Tetch danced around her, pushing the bundle into her face every time she turned. Palmer cried to her lord, but there was only the stench of the dead thing in the blanket and Tetch's earsplitting laughter.

Then, with a howl, he turned and hurled the baby into the brick wall. A wet smack, then silence.

The razor swept across Palmer's throat in a flash. Her

screams drowned in a torrent of blood that spilled over her lap and pooled at her feet.

Tetch straddled her, letting the blood soak his abdomen and groin. Taking her limp head in his hands, he pressed his face to hers. He threw open the conduits in his body and called her dying breath into his lungs.

Tell me, he thought, tell me everything.

He saw others in the city and saw that their number was four. They had slaughtered as many of their own as his after-dead had. They were hiding in the police house—no, the city hall. He strained to catch a glimpse of Lily among them, but there was nothing of her there in the reverend's memory.

Yet they must have her, he thought.

Shaking the scraps of Palmer's subconscious from his mind, he refocused and tried to locate the dark man. Nowhere to be found. Only the feral undead wandering the streets. Hundreds of them.

This was his empire. And these brainless rotters could be educated. Yes, they could be trained, but he would go further. Before long they wouldn't just be going through the motions of people in a proper society. The dead would come to comprehend their role in his empire. They would fill his court and worship at his feet and would be far more sophisticated than the living that struggled to subsist in this new world.

He'd considered moving his home to the old bank, but ultimately decided he would stay here in the swamp, the source of the energy that permeated the virus, the so-called "plague." Dealing with these infected rotters instead of his murdered siblings would be a new challenge, but he welcomed any opportunity to prove himself.

On each new day he would rise and survey his kingdom, all his subjects. "What a morning indeed!" he whispered, imagining himself pulling on a silken robe offered by one of the servants. "Lily, let's get up and go out to the garden. You'll want to plant some new colors in there, won't you? It does look lovely already but you want it to look even better. It'll be the most beautiful garden for miles, for continents! The servants will help you if you like. Prudence will make tea and bring it out. We'll spend the morning sitting outside, it's a lovely day. You're so lovely. I've had the women stitch up some new clothes for you and themselves and the rest of the house staff—they're starting to look like a proper lot, aren't they? Healthy too. The hunting parties bring in mounds of fresh flesh every night for them to root through. I think maybe a few of them could take voice lessons and learn to sing. Even if they can't quite form words I'm sure they could manage to carry a simple tune, something to listen to at dinner. Maybe we can find some old instruments in town and have them take those up. It's possible, under my guiding hand. Doesn't that all sound lovely. Lily?"

Lily.

He needed her now. *Lily. Lily! Where are you!*

(I gave you pretty dresses and I watched you dance. I gave you warm food and watched you eat. I gave you a warm bed and I watched you sleep)

He concentrated hard, gathering the energy that ebbed from the reverend's body, and sought Lily's spirit. He knew intimately her heart and mind

(and you will know her flesh)

and might be able to sense her innocence out there, burning bright amongst the primal fear and hunger of the city. So he rocked atop the corpse in the chair, overturning every grain of sand in Jefferson Harbor.

There!

Yes, she *was* with the living! He tasted of her hatred for him and nearly fell to the floor.

"The dark man . . . how has he poisoned you against me? Lily . . . I love you . . ."

The reverend's blank face seemed to mock him. He backhanded her, spilling more blood from her throat.

He called for his siblings. They came down the stairs and fixed their eyes on the corpse.

"Eat," he told them. "Then clean up and meet me in the yard. We're going to get her."

The bundle lying against the wall squirmed. Creeping closer, Tetch pried the blood-caked fabric back and saw there, in that corrupted flesh, a tiny hand. Its webbed fingers clenched and unclenched without purpose. He covered it back up and stepped away. "I'm not your god."

The others had descended on Palmer. Tearing thick ribbons of skin away in their teeth, they paused only to yank bits of clothing and hair from their mouths, pushing at each others' hands to get to the best parts first. Her breasts were ripped off and gnawed on for a few seconds before being discarded. Simeon pushed his hands down her throat and tugged at her innards while the others groaned in anticipation.

Tetch stared in disgust. When Palmer's ribs began to crack he went upstairs.

CHAPTER THIRTY-NINE
Mine

So it came to be that, as Voorhees dragged the headless bodies of Lauren and Thom to the roof of City Hall, he found a man waving to him from the roof of the police department.

"So you're the city's policeman?" the man called.

Voorhees, who was carrying the corpses by their bound feet, let go and hissed, "Quiet!"

The man shrugged. "They're all busy." He gestured downward, and Voorhees peered over the edge. In the plaza, a pickup truck was making lazy circles. The rotters still in the vicinity had gathered around and were lurching feebly at it with each pass.

There was a goddamn rotter behind the wheel.

"I'm Baron Tetch," the man said.

"Senior P.O. Voorhees," came the reply. The cop gritted his teeth. He'd left the shotgun inside.

"The last of a dying breed," Tetch remarked. He studied the sky, still stained with smoke.

"I'm not dead yet," Voorhees called back.

"You found my little girl, didn't you?" asked Tetch. "Saved her life. I can't thank you enough. I'd offer you a ride out of town with us, but there isn't any more room in the truck."

"There would be if you dumped that corpse out of it."

David Dunwoody

Two gunshots rang out. Voorhees stumbled toward the edge again.

A well-dressed rotter, standing outside the entrance to the PD, had kneecapped another one that tried to get inside. Voorhees watched in horrified fascination as the gun-toting undead reloaded its revolver.

"Those corpses mean a great deal to me," Tetch said as he followed Voorhees' gaze.

"Of course. They're your brothers and sisters."

"So Lily's been talking." That cold smile never left Tetch's face. "You want to bargain, then?"

"There's no bargain to be made." Voorhees let his voice rise in volume. If it attracted any attention from the ferals, Tetch's little helpers could presumably deal with it, and keep the other rotters at bay. "You're responsible for more deaths than I can remember. You think I'm going to hand over that girl to you?"

"Going to arrest me?"

"Doesn't seem like there'd be much point."

Tetch clasped his hands and cocked his head. Waiting for Voorhees to exhaust his bravado and realize that he was the lesser man. To give up the child. Instead, the cop stepped to the edge of the roof.

"She's talked about other things. You like 'em young, don't you, Baron?"

The young man's arrogance drained from his face and he became the pathetic little worm that Voorhees had seen all along. The yawning space between them seemed to contract, Tetch's shoulders dropping, his stance changing from threatening to threatened.

"I can see why you prefer the company of those maggot-eaten retards. They don't judge you, do they? They don't care what you do in your house out there in the swamp. Out there, you're the only man Lily needs. Isn't that right?"

Tetch's lip curled as he glared in the cop's direction, but he wouldn't look directly at him.

252

Voorhees pushed further. "I've been here a long time. I know people like you. You think you can do whatever you want. But this city still has a cop." He slipped his hand into his trench coat. "And no, I'm not going to arrest you."

Tetch shook his head angrily. This wasn't going the way he'd planned.

Voorhees grinned, even though the hand in his coat was closed around nothing but a belt loop. "I don't think I even have handcuffs. Lost 'em at the shelter. You hear about that? Did your dogs report back to you about the bang-up job they did?" He stifled a chuckle. "Speaking of which, we hacked that skull-faced rotter to pieces. Was he your favorite doggy?"

It was Tetch's turn to chuckle. "Not really," he said. Then he shouted *"Kill!"* and the doggy guarding the police station snapped the revolver upward and fired.

The bullet missed Voorhees by a hair. He threw himself to the rooftop as another shot grazed the edge of the building, spitting dust into the cop's eyes.

"Pull out your gun and shoot me!" Tetch laughed. He clapped his hands and turned away. He was leaving. Leaving without Lily?

No.

Voorhees began a frantic crawl toward the access door. "Duncan!" he bellowed. "They're inside!"

Down below, the undead gunman, Gerald, walked across the plaza to the de-barricaded City Hall entrance. Prudence and Bailey were already making their way across the lobby.

On the fourth floor, Jenna heard Voorhees' voice bouncing down the stairwell. "What's he saying?" she asked Duncan. He didn't hear her; he was letting Lily see the shotgun, warding her curious hands away with an attempt at a stern look.

Cheryl poked her head past Jenna into the stairwell. "Voorhees? He's saying something about 'inside.'" Cheryl yelled up, "Voorhees!" The two women stood in the doorway and listened for a response. It came.

"That sounded like a moan. Like he's hurt!" Cheryl whispered.

"That came from downstairs," Jenna gasped.

A thin woman appeared on the landing below. Cheryl was halfway down the stairs when she realized the woman was dead, but she ran into its arms anyway, senselessly, shrieking all the while; and Prudence, embracing her, clamped rotted teeth down on her cheek just beneath the eye.

Duncan shoved Jenna aside and took aim. Cheryl turned, her face a bloody screaming hole, no longer human, and in his horror he blew her away.

Then Gerald staggered into view on the landing and fired wildly. Duncan and Jenna fell back. The shotgun clattered at the rotters' feet. Bailey passed Gerald as the latter emptied the revolver and reloaded from his pocket.

"God! God!" Duncan stammered, covering Jenna with his arms, protecting and restraining her at the same time, watching Bailey come up—but the zombie simply made a left into the fourth-floor hallway.

Lily let out a terrible cry.

"No!" Jenna tried to thrust Duncan off of her. A bullet whined past the pair as they struggled. "Stay down!" he yelled.

"Lily!" Jenna wailed.

Bailey emerged with the girl writhing in his grip. Gerald clumsily ascended the stairs and trained the revolver on the two adults. Lily strained at them from over Bailey's shoulder. "Don't let them take me! Pleeeease!"

Voorhees stumbled down the stairs from the roof. He saw Gerald and leapt to the next landing just before a flurry of gunshots chewed up the wall where he'd been. "Shotgun," he breathed, slapping at Duncan, "shotgun—" Then he realized it wasn't in the man's hands.

Gerald continued to lay down suppressing fire. There was a hollow click. He lowered his rotted head to reload.

Voorhees leapt over the stairs and slammed into him,

dashing Gerald's skull against the wall. They fell in a mess of thrashing limbs. He heard the others coming down after him, saw Jenna tear the revolver from the undead's hand. She rushed downstairs after the others.

Ferals were entering the lobby. Bailey swatted them out of his path. Simeon and Tetch waited right outside in the idling truck. "Hurry now!" Tetch yelled encouragingly.

Jenna burst into the lobby—and right into a feral. They went down with a crash. The revolver flew into the shadows.

Bailey and Prudence crawled into the back of the pickup, holding Lily down, and it sped out of view.

Jenna went limp with horror as the feral she'd collided with straddled her.

Duncan smashed its temple with the butt of the shotgun. As the zombie sagged, he jammed the gun into its desiccated belly and blew it in half.

Gerald's twitching body, head crushed beyond recognition, thundered down the stairs. Voorhees followed, shattering another rotter's fractured grin with his fist on his way to the doorway. "Oh God."

He turned to the others. "Back upstairs now!"

They fled past the shambling dead, who stared blankly at one another as they tried to process what had just happened. The halved rotter lying on the floor blinked at its smoking innards.

CHAPTER FORTY
Lies and Consequence

Once the manor gates had been closed behind the truck, Tetch pulled Lily out of the back and wrestled her into the house. She screamed and kicked all the way up the stairs, but once they reached the study she fell silent. He deposited her in a chair by the window and glared at her sullen face.

"What the hell is wrong with you?"

He slammed the door and locked it, then paced back and forth in front of her. "You've seen the city now—happy? Was it everything you'd hoped? If I hadn't come and gotten you, do you have any idea what those people might have done?"

She had closed herself off to him and stared at the carpet. He stamped his foot on the spot where she was looking. "So there are people in the city. So I lied. But now do you see why? It's Hell out there!"

"You killed my parents," she mumbled.

He dropped to one knee before her and clasped her hands. "Who told you that?" She tried to pull her hands free, but he tightened his grip so she just gave up and looked at the wall. "I'll ask you one more time. Who told you?"

"It's true," she replied.

"No. Before I say anything about that I want to know who

256

told you! Was it the man in black? Where is he? Has he left the city?" She bit her lip anxiously. Tetch smiled grimly. "You don't know where he is. He's left you. Of course he did. But I came looking for you."

Voorhees' words from the rooftop bored into Tetch's mind. He winced and pushed them back.

"Your parents—if you can call them that—they abandoned you too. When they came back it wasn't because they cared about you, Lily."

"Then why?" she spat. Her hands trembled inside his.

"Because," he pleaded, "they just wanted to have you so they could make people feel sorry for them! I mean, first you're a liability that they have to get rid of and then you're a meal ticket. I've never treated you with anything but love, you know that. I didn't tell you about them because I thought it would hurt you. To know that they were like that."

"Is that what they said?" Her eyes were dark with mistrust. Her hands still trembled, from rage Tetch realized.

"Of course they did," he answered.

"You let the others eat them."

"What was I supposed to do, Lily? Bury them in the swamp? Think about it. I just didn't want you to see them . . . now that you know, do you feel any better? No. You feel awful. And I don't know what the dark man told you about it, but he wasn't there."

"Yes he was. He's the angel of death."

"I know," Tetch said. It had a sobering effect on her. For the first time since he'd brought her back she made eye contact. "I know," he repeated, "and it doesn't matter. He has no place in the world anymore. I can bring the dead to life, Lily." He stroked his fingers along the back of her hand. She shuddered. "He doesn't understand things like I do. Neither did Addison. Neither did your parents."

Her lips parted, she wanted to argue; but there was no argument. He leaned in to kiss her.

She jerked her hands free and drew herself into a tight ball on the chair. "Liar!"

He slammed his fist against the nearby desk. She whimpered. He wanted to take her into his arms and comfort her, but she wouldn't let him. She wouldn't let him love her when he was the only one who could.

(You're the only man Lily needs—isn't that right?)

"I'll prove it to you. You'll see. Soon." He left the study, relocking the door from the outside.

Addison, Death, Jesus—all hopelessly irrelevant, hopelessly wrong. Cut from the exact same filthy cloth. Tetch pocketed the study key and headed up to the third floor. The servants' quarters up here had been mothballed years back, and a thick skin of dust coated the bare wood beneath his feet. He stood in the silence of one of the front rooms, at a window, and contemplated the encroaching swamp through a film of grime.

There were ferals out there. He could see some of them, eyeing the house from the shadows.

In City Hall, Jenna stood at the window in the fourth-floor corridor. They'd barricaded the stairwell entrance, and could hear the ferals that had followed them shuffling outside. "We can't just forget about that girl," Jenna muttered.

"I know," replied Voorhees. He toyed with the shotgun in his lap. "We could make a clean break if we had that truck."

Jenna turned to face him. "Are you suggesting we go to the Addison house?"

"I think we're both suggesting it."

"Make that all three of us." Duncan stood uncertainly on his leg. He was paler than he'd been before the attack. "Maybe we can use the sewers to get across town. At least part of the way."

Voorhees shook his head. "Sewer access is all sealed up. We're going to have to take our chances on the streets. I think . . . well, frankly, I don't think we'll all make it. We might all reach the house, but . . ."

"Someone will get bit," Jenna finished.

She pulled down the collar of her shirt. There was a gash on her collarbone. "The one that pinned me in the lobby."

Duncan let out a long sigh. "Jen."

"All that matters is that somebody gets that truck and gets Lily out," she smiled sadly. "As for me . . . honestly I just don't care anymore. But she hasn't lived life long enough to be sick of it."

"I'm infected too," Duncan lied. "The axe, it had that rotter's blood on it. I can feel it inside me." Duncan gave a mild shrug. "I wouldn't know where to go anyway. I spent my life chasing the dead, not running from 'em."

"I know the Army's withdrawal route." Voorhees kneaded his hands. "They briefed us before they pulled out. I'll take her to them. There might be refueling sites along the way, but if we end up running out of gas or just breaking down, we'll hoof it. If I can just get her out of town, I know I can keep her safe."

"We're really doing this," Jenna whispered. "Okay. When?"

"No time like the present," said Voorhees. "We've gotta get to the house by twilight."

"Okay." Jenna motioned toward an open office. "I'll make some more torches to throw the rotters off."

Voorhees turned to Duncan. He knew in his core that Duncan wasn't infected, that there was nothing coursing through the man but his feelings for that woman. He'd seen Duncan's photography of the undead hordes. There was always an intimate quality to the images, to the way he framed both soldiers and rotters, unlike the stark, gore-laden pictures snapped by most freelancers. Mark Duncan was a romantic. It was a stupid way to live. Maybe, though, a nice way to die.

CHAPTER FORTY-ONE
What You Sow

Death stood in an endless tunnel with candles set into niches in the walls, their halos of light constricted so that he himself was in complete darkness.

He began to reconstitute his body in the living world, but stopped. He knew Lily was alive—her flame still burned bright—but did it even matter? When her candle went out, it went out. As they all eventually did. He watched the tiny fires around him flicker and jump in life's dance.

I don't want to do this anymore, he thought.

(Then quit.)

Who are you?

(Don't worry about it. So are you quitting?)

This is all I am—my purpose is my being. If I quit, I cease to exist.

(No, not really. I've never made anything that didn't eventually find its will. Will becomes being, purpose becomes secondary. That's life I guess.)

You made me?

(I sure did. As I made others before you, and as, if you quit, I'll make another one.)

I'm not the first Reaper?

(Humanity was around long before you were. Don't feel bad for being

so presumptuous—you've been nothing but an ego for so long, you weren't meant to ponder things like that. But you, my friend, have begun pondering. Can I ask a question?)

Of course.

(What was it? What woke you up?)

It was . . . a child. A little girl.

(But for thousands and thousands of years you've seen a parade of children living and dying. What was it about this one?)

It wasn't just her. It really started with the afterdead. I have to ask— did you make them? If so, why?

(Maybe I did. I don't remember. Doesn't seem like my work though, does it? No will.)

That's it?

(If I knew more I'd say so. Sorry. But back to this girl.)

She doesn't have much time left. But to just let her die . . . It's not . . . it doesn't seem . . .

(Doesn't seem right.)

Yes. Exactly. But as you said I've seen billions of young flames snuffed out. I don't remember a single face or name. I don't know what's different about her.

(What's her name?)

Lily.

(Lilith? I like that. How do you feel about her?)

It makes me angry when I think about what might happen to her.

(Anger. That's fear, really, did you know that? You're afraid of what might happen. And what might happen is her death. You see, she made you look at yourself and you didn't like what you saw.)

I suppose that makes sense. Actually, that makes a lot of sense. Perfect sense.

(Yeah, I can be fairly perceptive sometimes. So you are going to quit, right?)

Yes. I am.

(Do you have any more questions before I cut you loose?)

I can go back to the living world, can't I? And help her?

(Sure. But you won't be able to reconstitute yourself again after this next time. When you're done, you're done. There's no Heaven or Hell or anything else waiting for you. If anything, I guess you're about to enter your afterlife.)

My scythe.

(You made it, it's yours. I like it by the way, novel idea to forge a tool from their bones so that you could affect them. Did it ever occur to you that the concept was born of your own imagination?)

It didn't.

(See, it was only a matter of time before you found your will.)

If I'm not the first—and not the first to quit—that means there are others like me out there?

(Hmm. Well, there were. Like I said, you'll be a wholly corporeal being. Your existence will become temporary. Theirs were temporary, too.)

Do you know what happened to them?

(I can't go down this road with you. That sort of knowledge and foresight is one of the things you're surrendering. You won't be able to see Lily's flame anymore, but you will be able to intervene in her life. You won't know how much time you yourself have left, but you'll have a life of your own. You're trading certainty away. Do you understand?)

I understand.

(Anything else?)

Do I . . . have a . . . name?

(Not until you pick one.)

That's it then.

(Farewell.)

And just like that, it was.

On the thoroughfare south of the city plaza, the nameless being stirred and rose to his feet. His steed rose with him, and he stepped over Gene's prone body to climb atop the horse's back.

Most of the afterdead had cleared out of the plaza. The sun was going down, filling their eyes with light, and they shuffled blindly amongst themselves.

He backed cautiously toward a strip mall across the street.

None of them appeared to have noticed him—then one let out a baleful moan . . .

And was knocked down by a crushing blow to the head. P.O. Voorhees stood over the rotter and swung his widowmaker into its face. The skull split like an overripe fruit.

He handed the cleaver to Mark Duncan, who nodded in understanding and took it, giving Voorhees the shotgun in return. Jenna O'Connell had the revolver that Tetch's zombie had dropped in the City Hall lobby. The fallen rotter continued to flail its limbs as they walked past it, but it wasn't getting back up, nor could it moan.

The man on the horse, sitting motionless in a long shadow, saw that Lily wasn't with them. He decided to follow. The horse's hooves were eerily quiet on the asphalt.

The living moved quickly from block to block, staying behind businesses to avoid the intermittent clusters of undead that stood in the streets. Just after they left the cover of a small building, a rotter stumbled out the back door and saw them crossing the road. It opened its bloody mouth—

And a scythe exploded through its chest. The travelers continued on without looking back.

Duncan had taken point and was ready to quietly dispatch anything that got in their path. Voorhees wielded the shotgun like a club; firing it was his last option. Jenna tucked the revolver into the waistband of her pants.

"Please. Please," a voice called.

A man, shirtless, walked toward them. He held out a grasping hand and repeated, "Please." His tone was flat, without urgency or emotion.

It was a rotter, parroting something it had probably heard from one of its victims. Voorhees motioned for Duncan to hand him the widowmaker, but the latter shook his head and approached the talker himself.

"Please," the undead said mechanically. Saliva ran in thick gobs down its chin.

Duncan swung the blade into its neck and wrestled it to the ground. He sawed frantically through meat and bone until the gurgling head fell free. Its eyes stayed focused on him.

Voorhees touched his shoulder. "Leave it."

They were nearing the construction site. Bad memories, recent ones. Duncan silently vowed there wouldn't be any more.

CHAPTER FORTY-TWO
House of the Dead

The dead had surrounded the house.

Standing along the fence, studying the crumbling manse with its dark, broken windows, its ivy-covered stone walls, studying what for all intents and purposes appeared to be a home abandoned to the elements.

Yet, they knew that wasn't the case.

The front door opened. Simeon came out and stood in the yard.

He examined each of the undead that stood silently before the gates. A female with half her scalp missing, a scrap of fabric caught between her teeth. A squat rotter that had died in his teens, his muscular arms purple and streaked with cuts. An adult male barely holding himself together—his hands clutched at a ponderous bloated stomach that wept dampness through his button-down shirt.

They were out there, Simeon was in here. They weren't to be allowed in. If they did come in, they would take his meat. And Tetch would be angry; he wouldn't help Simeon find more nourishment.

On the other side of the house, Bailey emerged from the back door and surveyed the yard before him. Rotters were crammed into every available space along the fence. Some of them had wrapped their thin fingers around the iron bars and were tugging.

Tetch was still observing from the third floor. He heard feet scraping behind him and turned to see Prudence's silhouette. She tilted her head, expecting an order.

"Just go downstairs," he told her, in a strangely reserved tone. "Stand outside the study. Lily isn't to be let out. Is that clear?"

With a half-nod, Prudence left him.

"Prudence!" he shouted. She reappeared. "Bring Bailey and Simeon inside."

Another slight sway of the head. Tetch returned his attention to the yard below.

Deep in the swamp, huddled beneath the sprawling mass of an ancient tree, Voorhees whispered, "Shit."

"We'll never make it past them," Jenna breathed. They could see the undead milling around the Addison house. They must have followed Tetch's truck into the swamp. For one terrible second she considered the possibility that Lily had been pulled—or thrown—from the back of the pickup and into the ferals' grasp.

There was a rustle behind them. She yanked the revolver from her pants and spun, but Duncan was in the way, and she couldn't see what was threatening them in the dying light.

Voorhees whispered again. "You."

The man on his horse stood before them like something out of a fairy tale. Duncan had become accustomed to describing things as something "out of a nightmare," but he wasn't frightened at all.

Death—called so now in name rather than occupation—read little more than curiosity in their faces. He was no longer able to disappear from the view of mortal men, and along with that ability it seemed he'd also lost his overbearing presence as the Grim Reaper. He was just a strange man.

"I can help you get inside," he said.

Jenna stepped out from behind Duncan. Remembering what Lily had said, she asked, "Are you an angel?"

"Not anymore," the man answered.

At the gates, the dead began rattling the bars with fervor. They knew there was something in there; as to whether or not it was meat, there was only one way to find out. They rocked against the gates and moaned.

The man in black swept the scythe through the crowd, turning his steed sharply in the soft earth and making a second pass. Before they knew what was happening, several of the undead found themselves falling, legless, armless. Then the scythe swung low and burst their skulls.

The horse collided with the horde and the man in black fell. He landed in a crouch, severing the feet of rotters as they crowded in around him, then rose to open their chests and spill their guts. They collapsed against him, gnawing madly—but they could not do any damage as their energy abated.

Voorhees watched in disbelief as the undead were killed by the dark man's simple weapon. The horse reared up and drove its hooves through the hearts of rotters, pinning them down so that the scythe could slice their throats with ease. Those who hadn't already fallen victim to the dark man began staggering away from the gates.

The scythe struck a padlock, and through a brilliant rain of sparks, the chains locking the gates fell away.

The undead grabbed at the horse's kicking legs and over-turned it. They plunged their hands into its clay-like flank. The man who was once Death turned away as a part of himself—this majestic animal—was torn to pieces.

Voorhees slapped Duncan's shoulder. Duncan sprinted through the gates, swiping the widowmaker at any rotter within range. One of them grabbed the back of his shirt; Jenna filled the zombie with bullets, giving it pause long enough for the dark man to split its body from groin to gullet.

Tetch saw it all from the window. He ran across the hall into a room filled with boxes and tore through them. A pearl-handled .22 fell into his shaking hands. Hearing a commotion downstairs, he instinctively cringed behind the boxes.

"It's *him*," he was saying, over and over again.

Voorhees entered the foyer and caught Prudence at point-blank range. The shotgun kicked her waifish body into the stairs with a roar. She sat up. Her head was pulverized by the second shot. Tiny fragments of bone fell over her convulsing body as it slid to the floor.

"Lily!" Jenna hollered. Duncan started up the stairs.

Bailey kicked open a door behind the staircase and heaved an axe over his head as he charged. Jenna pulled the revolver's trigger. Click-click-click.

Voorhees shoved her aside and blew a chunk out of Bailey's side. The rotter stumbled forward, bringing the axe down. Voorhees blocked it with the shotgun. They both fell.

Duncan turned at the top of the stairs to see if Jenna was following. A hand closed over his shoulder, and Simeon groaned.

He hurled Duncan into the opposite wall. The world leapt out of focus as Duncan's head smacked off the wood, and he felt Simeon grappling with him. The widowmaker—where the fuck was it?

Jenna grabbed Bailey around the neck. He bit into her wrist and she closed her teeth around his ear. Prying him up off of Voorhees, a scream building in her chest, Jenna walked her fingers up the rotter's papery gray face and plunged them into his eye sockets. They went in much easier than she'd expected. Bailey began flailing as he fought to see.

"Get off of him!" Voorhees cried. "I don't have a shot!"

"Don't need one!" Jenna growled, and she brought Bailey's head down on the marble floor with a sharp CRACK. Then another, and another—brackish brain matter erupted from his skull, and he stiffened. Paralyzed and blind, Bailey spat up a mouthful of bile and lay silent.

Duncan let out a cry from upstairs. He was lying on the widowmaker, its cold steel digging into his back as Simeon tried to bite his throat. He heaved the rotter down the stairs and rolled over to retrieve the blade.

Simeon sat up. Voorhees pumped the shotgun. Duncan whipped the widowmaker down the staircase and into Simeon's eye. A good third of the undead's face was sheared away. Voorhees blasted him across the foyer.

He and Jenna headed upstairs to join Duncan.

Outside, the dark man was trying to hold the gates closed, but was being forced back by the undead mob. They came at him en masse. He stepped back, scythe in hand, to face them for the last time.

CHAPTER FORTY-THREE
The Cavalry

On the second-floor landing, Voorhees stopped the others and pointed downstairs. Ferals were entering the foyer. Their glassy eyes met those of the living.

"I've got this," the cop muttered. "Find Lily, and stay with her."

It was then that Tetch rounded the corner and emptied the .22 into Duncan, who in turn spun and slumped over the railing overlooking the foyer. He looked into the eyes of the ferals below. Somewhere in the recesses of his mind, Jenna was screaming. Suddenly feeling heavy, he dropped to the carpet.

Voorhees, halfway down the stairs, fired a shot and opened the wallpaper beside Tetch's head. He retreated to the hall whence he'd come. Jenna heard his feet on stairs as she fell beside Duncan; she saw that Mark was dead, and she felt the last of the terrible scream scraping through her throat and past her teeth.

Then it was quiet, for a second, in the house.

Voorhees broke the silence. He whirled around and blew a rotter's chest open. It caught hold of the banister and held its ground. Voorhees dug through his pockets. No more shells. "I'm—"

Jenna was gone. After Tetch.

The rotter grabbed his arms. He threw it down the stairs and swung the shotgun like a club into the next zombie's skull. The widowmaker was down in the foyer. More undead were crowding through the front door.

He steeled himself and charged down the stairs.

Up on the third floor, Jenna's feet clapped down in a layer of dust. She searched the darkness: there were several doors, all of them slightly ajar. She recalled distinctly the clicking of Tetch's empty pistol before he'd fled the scene of Mark's death. "You don't have a gun," she whispered, a sob threatening to break her voice.

He threw open the nearest door and flew at her.

They slammed into the opposite wall with a fearful racket, dust falling in torrents; he slapped her across the face, grabbed at her neck, pressed all his weight against her.

She bit into the webbing between his thumb and forefinger. He howled, trying to jerk his hand back, but she clenched her jaw as tightly as she could and gave his entire body a shove. His hand tore open like crepe paper, blood following him across the hall in an arc. His head cracked off the wall—

And he was on her again. He shouted incoherently and snatched her throat in his good hand. She slammed a knee into his groin. He grunted, but held fast. She felt her head crashing into the wall over and over and over, and the world began swimming away, leaving an oppressive blackness. Tetch roared distantly. She fumbled with his arms, his chest—he was hard like a tree and his roots were snarled viciously about her windpipe.

She grabbed his balls through his pants and twisted with the last of her strength.

He released her as his mouth fell open; no sound came out. He seized her wrist. She put her weight into the twist. She could feel his balls squeezing together in her palm. Tetch's eyes filled with tears, feet dancing on the floor. "Murderer," she rasped.

Something gave.

Tetch fell back, and upon impact he let loose a thousand screams. Her foot caught his gut as he tried to roll into a fetal position. She pried him open and kicked him in the sternum. Fell atop him, raked her nails over his face. Blood beaded on his crimson cheeks, and he let out a tortured cry. She drove her fist into his teeth. Again. Again. His lips were swollen purple and he couldn't scream. His hands swatted feebly at her. She parted them and hit him again. Again and again, and she was going to beat him to death, she knew it—

But

Lily.

Jenna grabbed Tetch's hair and yanked his scalp until he cried. "I will ask you once," she said through her teeth. "Where is she?"

Tetch gave her a broken smile. A senseless, red-and-black broken smile.

It bought him the half-second he needed.

He seized both her breasts in a vise grip and dug his claws into her flesh. Jenna shrieked, and he threw her to the floor, scuttling away like an injured spider. Tearing a poorly-nailed 2x4 from the wall, he put everything into the swing.

It split over her shoulder with a CRACK. Pain exploded through her mind. He grabbed her hair and slammed the broken board over her taut stomach. WHAP! She grabbed at her hair, her abdomen, she kicked her feet—her legs went limp as he hit her again. WHAP!

"You came for my little girl?"

WHAP!

"You think you can take her from me?"

WHAP!

"You think you can take *anything* from me?"

WHAP!

He dragged her across the floor. Shock gave way to burning pain across her torso. Pulling her through a door into one of the empty rooms, Tetch twisted her blonde locks around his fist. Every inch of her scalp screamed with agony. She was sure that it was all about to come off—that he'd rip the skin from her head with his bare hands.

He let go. He let go and kicked her in the back of the head. She slumped forward. The remainder of the 2x4 snapped in half when it struck her forehead.

Tetch straddled her. "Oh. Oh God." He saw the blood soaking through the crotch of his pants. More blood dripped from his nose and mouth onto her face. He smeared it over her eyes. "Kill you. I'll kill you. Right now." He grabbed her breast, clamped his fingers around her nipple. She groaned, eyes half-shut. He twisted and they opened wide.

She slammed her palm into his chin. He spit on her, and she elbowed him off, bringing both fists down on his back. He coughed up blood and began a desperate crawl across the room. She followed relentlessly, beating on his head, until he stopped, about to collapse.

But he wasn't. He turned and slugged her in the nose. It popped audibly.

As she stumbled, Tetch leapt back onto her and began pummeling her face with renewed vigor. Each strike brought a flash of light, and she let her hands fall to her sides, thinking of Mark dead downstairs. Her head was thick with blood and pain and she wanted to be free, with him. Tetch's gleeful cries faded.

The floor yawned and gave way beneath them.

One floor down, she landed flat on her back, knocking the wind from her lungs—he landed on his knees and felt knives erupting through his legs and spine.

They'd fallen into a vacant bedroom. Tetch wrapped his arms around a bedpost and tried to get up. Jenna jumped onto his shoulders. With a pained cry, he staggered back and struck the edge of a vanity—the mirror exploded behind Jenna. Glass rained over the floor as they both went down again.

He grabbed a shard and slashed at her legs. His entire face was red, his eyes bloodshot. He pushed the glass dagger into her thigh with deliberate slowness, nodding along as she screamed. She tried to stop the glass and flayed her fingertips wide open. He leaned into it. "Does it hurt yet! Tell me it hurts!"

"Yeeeeeeesss!" she shrieked. He roared, drove it deeper. She battered his grinning face, but he fed on the pain; he laughed and spat, "Bleed me. Bleed me!"

Jenna flailed her arms above her head and found the leg of the vanity. She brought it down on him and he fell away.

"Why are you even trying anymore?" he gasped. "You want to be dead. You want it! Let me give it to you. Tell me you want it." His fingers picked up another long shard of glass.

Her entire body was throbbing with numbness. She lay there and stared at him, his chest heaving with exhaustion. She could barely breathe. And she did want it to be over.

"But not from you," she whispered. "Not you."

She lifted a thick shard toward her throat.

He heaved himself at her, and she thrust it at him; the glass chewed deep into her palm and she thought maybe it hadn't penetrated him at all.

Tetch sat up. It had.

He coughed up a gout of blood, spattering both their faces, and fell against the bed with a groan.

"Where . . . is she?" Jenna asked.

He sneered. "'Where is she? Where is she?' She's dead. Dead!"

Jenna's eyes fell to Tetch's waist, just below where the glass had embedded itself, and she smiled grimly. "No. You wouldn't kill her, not ever."

Crawling to him, she pulled a ring of keys from his pants pocket. He clutched pleadingly at the air. "Don't take her. Please . . ."

Jenna made her way to the door. She could barely see it through the blood blisters swallowing her eyes.

"I'm begging you!" Tetch howled. Meat tore and wept inside

him. He couldn't get up. He beat his head against the mattress. "Ple-ea-ea-ea-ease!" He heard the door open, then quietly close.

In the foyer, Voorhees yanked the widowmaker from one rotter's face and buried it to the hilt in another. The undead's neck cracked with a sharp twist, and a second turn ripped its head clean off.

Still they were coming. He'd been forced to retreat up the stairs, and every rotter he dropped was replaced by three more.

Behind him, Jenna was knocking on the walls. "Lily!"

She heard the girl's cry two doors down from the bedroom.

Voorhees met her at the top of the stairs. "It's no good. We can't . . ."

The man in black cut a mighty swath through the foyer, sending corpses through the air. The scythe skewered rotter after rotter and sent them reeling, lifeless, just ugly dolls scattering across the marble.

"Let her out," Voorhees shouted. Jenna unlocked the study door and collapsed at Lily's feet.

"C'mere!" Voorhees cried. He waved to Lily, who was staring in horror at Jenna. She began to kneel and Jenna pressed the keys into her hands. "Go, baby."

Voorhees scooped Lily up and rifled through the keys. The truck key was there. He leapt down the stairs as the dark man pushed the undead wave back.

"Where's the truck?" Voorhees yelled as they ran into a dining room.

"In the back," Lily said, staring back at the foyer, longing to catch another glimpse of her angel. Wasn't he coming? Wasn't he—

A rotter careened into the door and it slammed shut.

Voorhees cut through the kitchen and found a back door. He backhanded a shambling ghoul on the back porch and raced to the truck, some twenty feet away, covered in mud, dust and bits of gore. He threw open the truck door and helped Lily

David Dunwoody

clamber inside. Voorhees plunged the key into the ignition; for one awful second, it wouldn't turn it. Then it gave.

Headlights illuminated the zombies coming around the back of the estate. Some of them came out the back door of the house. He gunned the engine and swerved around them, not willing to risk a breakdown just to splatter their gaping faces. Lily covered her eyes and pulled her seat belt around her.

Out the gates and a sharp turn left, going back around the manor, heading for the west wall. With the wall's condition, and this many undead, there wouldn't be much of it left standing. No point in speeding eastward through the city.

His eyes checked the gas gauge; it was one-quarter full. Not much point in speeding anywhere.

The truck bounced over fallen slabs of concrete and out of Jefferson Harbor. Lily raised her head and let the belt pull snug against her chest. She glanced, once, over her shoulder, then out into the endless expanse of the badlands.

"Where are we going?"

CHAPTER FORTY-FOUR
Out

Mark was still warm.

Jenna pulled herself to him and kissed his face. There was no feeling in her lips. She nestled her head in the crook of his neck and sighed.

The man in black was still fighting in the foyer. After a few more mighty swings of his scythe, the fighting ceased. Save for a few murmurs, an unusual silence once again crept over the house.

He threw the bolts in the front door and ascended the stairs. Jenna looked hopefully at him, her eyes pleading.

"I don't do that anymore," he said. But he knelt beside her, gathering his robes to cover her broken body.

"Will Lily be all right?" Jenna mumbled.

"I'll keep watch over her," he answered. She nodded and turned to caress the dead man beside her.

"A beautiful ache?" he asked.

Jenna smiled. "I wrote a song that said that." Her final words. She lay her head down and died.

Death went into the bedroom, looked at the man on the floor. Tetch's eyelids fluttered. Heavy with drying blood, they lifted, and his red gaze took the specter in.

"Are you here to kill me?"

"In time," the dark man said.

An hour later, the ferals outside were drawn into the house by a long, tortured scream. When they reached Tetch, he was dead. They sat around him and used broken glass to cut away his flesh.

Hundreds of them crowded inside, searching every room on every floor, packing the house. It groaned madly around them. Then it all came down, wood and flesh and stone, all crumbling down into the cellar, into Addison's Hell. They lay pinned in the wreckage and pawed at one another, a cacophony of groans filling the night sky.

"Where are we going?"

"I'm not entirely sure," Voorhees finally replied. "North, I can tell you that much. That's where all the other people have gone."

"What people?"

"There used to be a lot of people in Jefferson Harbor. They left when the Army did. There are cities, safe cities, in the north. And I don't know how to get all the way to those cities, but I think we can catch up with the Army."

"Why did they leave?"

Voorhees frowned over the steering wheel. "They decided it wouldn't do any good to keep fighting for this place."

Lily stared at her hands, folded in her lap, and said, "I guess they were right."

"We tried," Voorhees snapped. She cast a frightful look in his direction, and he tried to soften his tone. "The people who died back there at the house, they didn't die for nothing. They died saving your life."

"I'm sorry," she pleaded.

Pursing his lips, he offered her his best facsimile of a smile. "You'll get it when you're older."

In the middle of the night, they reached a military fuel station. Voorhees whispered a silent prayer that there'd still be gas beneath the cement slab; he slipped the pump into the truck and waited.

The gentle sloshing brought a genuine smile to his face. Looking toward the cab, he saw Lily watching him through the rear windshield. She returned the expression.

The headlights caught the faintest hint of something moving on the horizon. Voorhees leaned into the cab and flipped on the high beams. It was a single rotter, a good thousand yards away, moving on a broken ankle.

He pulled the widowmaker from its sheath. "I'll be right back. Keep the doors locked."

"You could just let it go," Lily said. He fixed his eyes on her naive little face and shook his head. "Be right back."

He strode across the barren soil toward the undead. It lifted its bloody head to study him. He stopped, waiting to see what it would do.

It opened its mouth and moaned for his flesh, then came at him.

When it was finished, he replaced the fuel pump and got into the truck. Lily was silent.

"I didn't do it because of what he is," he told her. "I did it because of what he used to be."

Back in Jefferson Harbor, at the city plaza, Gene was standing. He felt the night wind picking up and let it caress his face. Something inside him tugged gently, pleasantly, and he didn't move a muscle for several minutes. Just stood there, feeling.

He knew one thing: he had tasted the flesh of the man in black, and he was no longer what he had been. His stomach still yearned for meat, and he kneaded his palms as the nagging, maddening craving made his mouth water. But there was something else, too. A new purpose.

He picked up his shovel and started walking.

In his flesh he felt a new vitality, a strength he hadn't known since he'd begun this sojourn among the dead. In his mind's eye he saw the man in black. He saw where the man was, and he hungered. The man had to be destroyed and devoured.

Long live the new flesh, his mind whispered. It was a strange, alien phrase, but one he suddenly and keenly understood.

Up ahead, another rotter staggered toward him. Gene stopped and, driven by some instinct he hadn't known before, leveled the shovel blade with the zombie's throat. Then he struck, severing the maggoty cords of tissue that connected the head to the body. The body dropped, the head bouncing away without so much as a gasp. Gene fell upon the torso and tore out two huge handfuls of rotten flesh.

He stuffed them down his gullet.

Though the lifeless tissue shouldn't have done anything to replenish his own health, he felt an odd surge of energy. He was consuming more than meat—he was consuming the dark force inside of the other undead . . . becoming so much more than just a shambling rotter . . . coming to understand it all so quickly . . .

He had to find the man in black. Now.

Gene rose, tearing away more dead flesh and pushing it into his maw, his jaw cracking as he fed voraciously. He would need to be strong for the hunt. He would need to be at his peak when he made the kill.

He broke into a run.

FIFTH STRIKE
Hand of God

They had heard the truck tearing through the west wall, and only caught a glimpse of it as it vanished over the horizon. The city was silent now.

Dalton led an excursion through the wall, into the swamp. He leaned against a sprawling, mossy tree and raised his fist. Groans could be heard.

There was a wrought-iron fence up ahead, visible through his night-vision scope. He saw the remains of a house beyond, and a few indistinct limbs swaying among the ruins, poking through holes and broken windows.

Barry took point and scaled the fence. What she saw was a writhing mass of dead flesh among a mess of stone and beams, dozens of hands grasping desperately at the night air; they were all trapped inside the collapsed house.

A few had wriggled out, breaking arms and legs in the process, and now wormed their way through the grass toward the soldiers. Barry discharged her shotgun into one's head. The others stopped and murmured at her.

"We ought to burn the whole thing down," she said.

"Right," Gregory replied. He lobbed a couple of incendiary bombs over a half-crumbled wall. They were simple detonators packed with napalm; the jellied gasoline erupted among the squirming undead, sending guts heavenward, and waves of fire washing over row after row after row of the ghouls crammed into the Addison house. They moaned their feeble protests as tongues of flame ate their eyes and mouths, and the soldiers walked around the property, vaporizing those who had escaped the house and watching the rest burn and melt into one another in a grim orgy.

Logan pulled a gaunt female to her feet, her back charred and blackened, and slapped her across the face. She swayed in his grip, and he drew her close, his lips brushing against hers.

"You didn't run out of that room," Dalton said from behind him.

"No," Logan answered, and cut her in half with machine-gun fire.

Gregory looked back toward the swamp to see if there had been any rotters lurking within.

He saw the man in black, not on a horse, but on his bare feet, scythe in hand. Gregory knew who he was just the same.

Barry turned and dropped her gun. "Lord."

"I know who you are," Gregory stated, putting as much volume into his voice as he could, even as he trembled like he was again a boy in Sunday school.

"Do you?" asked the man.

"Death."

"I was." The man looked past the sergeant, at the house. He watched the rotters burn.

"We'll get them all, eventually."

"Will you?" The man seemed bemused. "Or will you run to the next walled city and hide?"

Gregory lowered his head. The withdrawal. Was that really it, why the horseman had been summoned here? "No, we don't mean to hide, we mean to protect our children."

"The children." The man nodded in understanding. "Yes."

Gregory smiled and nodded back.

The man pointed to the west. "Did you see a truck?"

"It left the city. Headed north."

"Are you an angel?" Logan called. The man looked at him and he cowered.

"No."

"God, He'll come for us, won't He? When this is all finished? He is coming?"

The man studied each of their faces.

"I don't know God," he said. Then he walked into the trees, and was gone.

Dalton ran forward but Gregory grabbed a handful of his shirt, hauling him back. "How can that be?" Dalton cried. "How can he say that? How can that be!"

"Stop it!" Gregory snapped. Dalton tore himself away. He ran off beyond the flames.

"We'll move out at sunup," the sergeant said, "to catch the convoy." He turned to find Logan and Barry staring at their feet. Barry knelt and started to cry. Hadn't she been lifted up by the encounter?

"What." His voice trailed off. It had been one of the horsemen, there was no question. That the horseman didn't know God wasn't faith-shattering, he was just another soldier, carrying out his task. "And we *saw* him, for Christ's sake!" Gregory shouted. "You *saw* him, with your own eyes! How can you be shaken? What is it you're doubting?" Barry continued sobbing. Logan didn't say anything.

"Secure the perimeter." Gregory sat against the fence and opened his pocket Bible. He could read by the firelight until dawn, if need be. The others could be trusted to watch the trees while they considered their encounter with the horseman, and what he'd said to them; then, once they were over the initial shock, Gregory would talk with them.

His faith hadn't been shaken at all. It had been reaffirmed. He settled back and read to himself until he fell asleep.

EPILOGUE
To Dream

Chicago's security wall, three stories high, was manned by dozens of armored troops that paced atop it. The one gate that cut through this concrete and steel was surrounded by guards, and a fenced quarantine center was just inside. The city proper was still a few miles off.

A young Latino soldier, maybe twenty years old, sat on a stool with a laptop propped on his knees. Behind him, a canvas tent flap whipped in the wind. "You want some water?" he asked Voorhees.

"God, yes," came the reply.

"And you're a cop?" The soldier pecked at the computer keys with inexperienced fingers. Voorhees felt a little resentment at being interrogated by these kids, but as he looked toward the city in the distance, as he watched a female solder kneel to chat with Lily, he figured it was worth the hassle.

"I'm a P.O. out of Louisiana."

"Once you're approved and entered in the system, it'll kick your record out to Employment Services. They'll help you get work. We need cops. You'll probably end up doing exactly what you did back in Louisiana."

I hope not, Voorhees thought.

"Is she your daughter?" The soldier motioned to Lily at the other end of the tent.

"No, we're not related."

"Legal guardian?"

"No." Voorhees narrowed his eyes. "She's a refugee like anyone else."

"I know, I know. Don't worry about it." The soldier, hunched over the laptop, kept pecking keys. "I just mean they'll probably put her in foster care." The boy looked up and quickly added, "You can probably apply for custody. Honestly, I don't know how it works—"

"I've only known her a few days." Voorhees brushed dirt from the sleeves of his coat. "Am I going to get the widow-maker back?"

"The . . . oh, the cleaver? Doubt it."

"How about that water?"

"Right! Sorry. Just a sec."

Voorhees nodded and settled in for a long wait.

In the badlands, two ferals, staggering side-by-side across the parched earth, saw something on the ground ahead. Through shimmering waves of heat, their pus-encrusted eyes discerned a man's body lying on its back.

They increased their pace. The sun beat on their bare backs, blisters running over raw red flesh. They teetered on bones, stomachs aching, and lunged at the corpse in its ragged gray suit.

It sprang to its feet.

The scythe halved the first rotter diagonally and lodged itself in the second's skull. The man in the suit yanked the blade free and watched the undead collapse into rancid piles.

He'd broken off part of the handle, making the blade easier to wield. It slipped into a makeshift sheath inside the suit jacket. He'd taken these clothes off of another zombie; it made his own "corpse" all the more authentic, as he'd learned over the past few days.

285

His recent time among the dead had only made him yearn for the company of the living, of one little girl in particular. She was somewhere out there dreaming of him. He was sure of it, because he'd begun to sleep, and dream, and all his dreams were about her.

He hoped Lily was still with the policeman. He remembered that, at one time, the policeman's flame had been close to burning itself out; that was before he had intervened. Maybe he'd given Voorhees a new lease on life. He would never know for sure. Someone else knew, and that same someone knew Lily's remaining time on this plane, recording it without a second thought.

He'd find her. He'd carve a great bloody canyon through the plague-ridden badlands to do it.

That was settled, then. Now all he needed was a name.

The man stood over the remains of his prey and thought for a moment.

Then he continued on his way.

BEFORE THE EMPIRE
Excerpts from the Journal of Dr. Steven Addison

September 12, 2086

I've found a real Source this time. This swamp in Jefferson Harbor—it bleeds dark energy. I can hear their songs in the waking hours. We'll build the house here.

September 13, 2086

It's Friday. Yesterday's entry was brief because I was so excited; speechless, and barely able to write. The swamp seethes with an aura—the echoes of their presence. I can feel it in every step and breath and blink of the eye. It's as if, if I close my eyes and stand on the spongy earth, I can see through to the worlds beyond and hear them calling. They only wait for me to call back!

Here, we can touch the Old Ones. This is a pathway. An altar.

Sarah is still speaking in tongues. She thinks that the idiot languages of the ancients will be more easily understood by the Old Ones. This whole notion that primitive Man could have communed with them is ridiculous. Still, Sarah dances around in the sunlight, babbling, smiling, laughing, an idiot herself.

David Dunwoody

Sometimes I'm ashamed to be in her company. The sibling connection we used to share is gone. It's like . . . I'm not sure how to describe it. Once we thought that we'd been called as one to pay tribute to them, to sing their songs and do their bidding . . . but her spirit's drifted apart from mine.

Now, I wonder . . . perhaps this is meant to be a new stage, when one twin absorbs the other, and the true potential of our bond is realized. Fully concentrating our spiritual energies to serve the Old Ones?

She's rolling around in the dirt like a mongrel. She's regressing . . . submitting.

I'll just close my eyes and listen a bit to the songs in the air, and figure out what I'm to do.

September 14, 2086

I killed my sister. I drove a spade through her mouth into the dirt, drank blood from her throat and watched the light fade from her eyes as I severed her life completely. Sarah, we're one now, as we were always meant to be—the purpose of our separate vessels is ended, and now we are together in body and spirit.

I chopped her up before the energy in the earth could saturate her limbs. These undead, stumbling about like broken robots, barely subsisting on the Old Ones' energy—this is not what *they* want from us. No, no, no!

My builders will be here next week. I'll want to take another look at the house plans now that Sarah won't be needing her own wing. The astrological seals to be set in the foundations will need to be re-configured, I think.

October 10, 2090

Among the crude theories of my predecessors is a notion that this energy lying dormant in the earth is not a gift from the Old Ones, but mere leavings—as if a writhing cluster of idiot-gods simply shat chaos into our universe and forgot all about it. If so, is that why I have volume upon volume of translated dreams in which the Old Ones have prodded us to wake up?

I'm not the only one to have heard them calling! When it was Sarah and me, we weren't the only ones!

These undead may appear to be a random, chaotic phenomenon, but that is only because they are a gross misrepresentation of the power bestowed upon us by our benefactors. I'll figure this out yet.

October 31, 2090

It's cold and empty and quiet here. There's nothing here.

May 3, 2103

I understand now.

They want living bodies.

This rotting tissue is a paltry offering. These dead bodies are substandard vessels for the Old Ones. They require fresh, living tissue threaded with spiritual energy. That is what they want! Only then will they themselves cross over so that we may honor them.

The question becomes how to procure living, breathing, willing vessels?

The others who've spread their wealth about Jefferson Harbor, trying to maintain the city and build up its defenses as the undead grow in number—they have children, don't they? So many little children who are at great risk and at the same time are a great burden.

What if I were to take them all into my custody?

Children! Pliant young souls!

I am a doctor, after all, standing among the dead and grimly watching this plague unfold—my sworn duty is to preserve the precious youth of our most privileged neighbors, so that they may give rise to stronger future generations.

David Dunwoody

Yes yes yes, I will compose a letter here, then copy it and send it out to the others tomorrow:

May 4, 2103
Dearest,
Your family is humanity's hope for a future. Your children, young and strong, are my hope for a cure.

I am pursuing an end to this plague that has brought down our community and threatened our existence. I mean not only to protect your children from the undead that beat on our city walls, but to ensure that your children live in a world free of this nightmare.

In studying the blood-borne plague I have erected a secure compound in the west end of Jefferson Harbor that houses a medical research laboratory that rivals the city center's hospital complex. Here I conduct private research with the goal of eradicating the plague entirely, not merely treating its after-effects and watching chaos unfold regardless.

Infection is damnation. This is a fact which must be undone. We must shift the paradigm so that the infection can be reversed. We must do this using the strongest, newest members of our species. Our Adams and Eves, if you will.

I don't mean to sound cold. That is not my intention. Rather, I am appealing to you to provide me with your children so that we all may benefit from that which is most pure and untouched. From your healthy young, I can glean the answers that are not offered up by the bodies of the infected and dead! The solution to this plague lies in the living, those who carry on in answering Nature's call and propagating the species. The plague is one of undeath, of a phase after death; the enduring young of our species stand in opposition to this and hold the seeds of our continuation.

I am offering your children full protection from infection, the elements, rogue outsiders and all the other calamities that may befall us while we toil against this apocalyptic menace.

Physical, medical, and emotional health care. Guaranteed security against any "rotters" or criminals who come within earshot of the property. It is a fortress against the undead and I will make it a war machine against the virus!

For you—escape. Leave Jefferson Harbor and its trappings and live while you can, while I forge a real life for your children and their children. Secure your holdings, see your families, see the surviving world—and know your children are safe. Know your children are part of the fight and part of the future.

Bring him/her/them to the Addison Estate and they will be registered and secured. I have sent this letter to all of you, the Harbor elite, and I am prepared to welcome of your children into the compound for as long as it takes.

This is not abandonment. This is an investment in your life and theirs. We will be doing what is best for ourselves, our families, our existence. I hope each of you understand that.

This is a plea to save humanity. Let me and your child defeat this horrid plague and give rise to a new age, a new dawn of Man, one where we'll have torn ourselves away from the clutches of extinction and laid claim to this world by our own hand. If we can overcome this virus, I believe we shall see a rebirth of society and understanding. Indeed, you and your child may be reunited in a new world.

(Please find enclosed a check for $500,000.00 USD)

Sincerely, on this Eve of Mankind,
Steven Addison

July 6, 2104

Baron Tetch continues to be a thorn in my side. He's an insolent boy with a sick fixation on the rotters outside the manor. He's the only one that doesn't seem to be afraid of them, he likes poking them and egging them on through the gates. It'll be another sojourn in Hell for him.

He'd never understand the Old Ones, but that's just as well, as I don't think they'd have much use for him either other than his living flesh. He's not one who understands order and reverence. The dog hates him too.

Young Lilith gave me an odd look today. I think there's something special about her. She reminds me of Sarah, in certain ways; there are just little nuances that make me think of my sister and her love for all that fairytale nonsense. She was never able to separate fact from fiction when we researched the Old Ones. Too often she got caught up in the rubbish about dances and spells. I guess all little girls want to be witches.

Strange dream last night. I dreamed it was pitch black, and I was riding atop a dog, a huge dog, and then I sank into its flesh, limbs first! My hands and feet melted right through its coat and suddenly it was as if our bones had joined; when my head passed into the dog's skull, I saw what it saw, us tearing down this cold black tunnel. Faster and faster we flew, through nothing, great whistling black winds! The skin was stripped from our bones and we were just a skeleton hurtling through an absolute vacuum and it was exhilarating and terrifying all at once!

Then I had a sensation of something settling over us, or me, like a blanket or a cloak, made of night; enveloping blackness all around me, and the tunnel narrowing as I screamed along at ever-increasing speeds. The walls were closing in around me, and the night was hugging me, seeping into my bones and chilling me through my soul. And the speed! Faster, faster, faster! I was being borne down into some sort of infinitesimal, blacker-than-black pit. My being whittled away until I was one with the night itself, flying along a straight line, to the end of it all, to . . .

Cold, unyielding, chaos.

A concentrated pit of boundless lunacy, without entrance, exit or explanation! To think that at the beginning and end of all things there would just be a senseless, colorless chaos! And that it would laugh and scream and turn in its never-ending spasms, and then somehow stop, and sink an icy, razor-sharp talon into my subconscious and twist my head around so that I stared into the eye of madness.

And pull me in, and press its eye against mine so that for one perfect, horrifying moment we would see the exact same thing. And it would be me, and I it, and it would tell me in its lilting, drunken voice that *THERE ARE NO OLD ONES*.

ABOUT THE AUTHOR

David Dunwoody is the author of the collections *Dark Entities,* from Dark Regions Press, and *Unbound & Other Tales,* from Library of Horror Press. Upcoming novels include the sequel to *Empire* and the apocalyptic novel *The Harvest Cycle,* both from Permuted Press. Dave is in a room in Utah and can be visited on the web at www.daviddunwoody.com.